ALONE & LONELY

Missing Persons #4

Adrian J. Smith

Supposed Crimes LLC • Matthews, North Carolina

Published in the United States.

ISBN: 978-1-952150-37-1

www.supposedcrimes.com

This book is typeset in Goudy Old Style.

ALONE & LONELY

GROWING UP

GRACE STEPPED on the gas as the light turned green. Kit sat in the passenger seat of Amya's newest SUV, completely silent, but her leg bounced up and down, her jaw was clenched tight, and she was undoubtedly nervous as fuck. Amya was supposed to take her, but the emergency call had come in, and the task had fallen to Grace.

Even Peter would have been a better option. Grace was not known for her patience or for being a friendly face in the world of any big emotion.

"You'll do fine," Grace muttered, trying her best to calm the seventeen-year-old girl.

"I know," Kit answered, rolling her eyes and giving Grace a large heave of breath.

And that was why Grace rarely tried to console Kit. She was always looking for attention and love, but the kid made it so hard to love her some moments. She was just a normal teenager who had more than her fair share of struggles. Most people saw her as a troubled teen who had no chance of real success. Grace and Amya had worked their asses off to try and change that outcome for Kit, and to help her see something else in herself.

"Do you want any last minute pointers?"

"No." Kit nearly growled.

Grace gripped the steering wheel tighter as she took the next turn at the light. Kit would need to get her own driver's license soon but that had been waylaid because of all the issues with guardianship. The month before, Kit's case had finally gone before a judge and he had awarded Grace and Amya temporary custody. Essentially, the goal was to keep Kit in one home until she turned eighteen at which point the courts and child services wouldn't give a crap—not that they did now.

It'd been a long year of having her in and out of the house, but the last few months of her staying there had been exactly what everyone needed—mostly what Kit needed. Although, Grace wouldn't lie, having her under their roof definitely made the house feel more like a home than it had in the past. Having Peter there for the last year was also an added bonus.

Grace pulled up outside the grocery store and parked near the front of the building. When Kit reached for the doorhandles, Grace gripped her hand to stop her and get her attention. "You'll do great. I'm serious. You always nailed the practice interviews we did at group."

Kit rolled her eyes. "That's not what you told me at group."

Grace snorted. "I was trying to tame your attitude. Keep that in check, and you'll definitely get a job today."

"Can I go now?"

"I'll be here when you're done."

"Right."

Kit opened the door to the SUV and stopped as soon as she was out of it, staring into Grace's brown eyes. "Thanks, G."

She slammed the door and took off, the new black slacks they'd bought her just for the interview clean and pressed, although Grace did spy some dog hair on them from Roslin. Giving up on pushing it any further, Grace grabbed her cell phone and called her best friend, Crystal.

"What's happening, Detective?"

Grace smiled. "Just dropped Kit off for her interview. I'm waiting for her to be done and come back out."

"Oh, at the grocery store?"

"Yup! She wants to be a bag lady." Grace couldn't stop the chuckle that left her lips.

Crystal echoed the laugh. "She'll do great."

"She will. She needs this job I think. It'll help keep her out of trouble."

"Oh?"

"Ugh, yeah. She's starting to hang out with a not so great crowd at school. She's got one more year, and then she has to figure out what it is she wants to do with her life."

"She still doesn't want to go to college?"

"No. And that's fine by me. But kid needs a job to pay for life."

"That's true," Crystal murmured.

Grace stared out the front windshield and people walked into the store and came out, some with shopping carts completely filled to the brim. She didn't envy working at a grocery store during the holiday season. It'd be the worst time to start if anyone asked her, but Kit really wanted a job, and retail was always hiring during the holidays.

"What are you doing for Thanksgiving?" Grace asked, seemingly out of nowhere, she was sure for Crystal, but she'd seen three carts roll by with turkeys in them.

"Oh...um...I'm going to my parents."

Grace sighed. She had worked Thanksgiving for years to give those who had families the day off, so she'd never built up a backup plan. But now that she was a detective, those days were typically off unless she was the one on-call, and this Thanksgiving, like all others, she was scheduled to work. Peter had to work his job, Amya was on-call as well, and who knew about Kit. She'd probably be working, too, if she got this job. They'd likely have to celebrate on a completely different day just so they could all be there.

"That'll be fun. Is your mom making that cheesecake again?"

"She always does," Crystal murmured.

"What's wrong? I thought you liked going to your parents."

"I do." Crystal sighed. "My dad isn't doing so well."

"His health you mean?"

"Yeah."

Grace clenched her jaw as she glanced at the clock. Ten minutes. Another twenty and she'd think she could be leaving with Kit in hand, hopefully newly employed. "Did he have another heart attack?"

"No, but the stents aren't working well, and he may need to get some new ones."

"I'm so sorry, Crystal." Grace's heart broke. In some ways, she knew exactly what Crystal was going through. She'd seen it first hand with her own mother as she'd wasted away from chemotherapy twenty years before. It was hard to imagine her mother had now missed more than half her life, had never met Amya, never saw her get her GED or be pinned after the academy.

"Yeah, so I want to spend as much time at home as I can."

"Makes sense." Grace glanced toward the door of the store in time to see Kit coming toward her. "Oh! Kit's coming back. I'll text you what happened."

"Please do!"

"Love you, Crystal."

"You too, Grace. And don't be a stranger, come visit again."

"For sure." Hanging up just as Kit slid into the passenger seat, Grace raised an eyebrow in her direction.

"Are we going home yet?"

Grace bit her tongue to try and keep the retort from flying. "What happened? How did it go?"

"They need parental signature."

Grace's stomach flopped as she waited for Kit's reaction and to figure out what the problem was exactly. Kit crossed her arms over her chest, melting into the seat with a pout on her lips. Her crystalline eyes had dark makeup around them, making them look large and unwelcoming as fear was written all in them.

"So what's the problem? They didn't give you the job?"

"I got it, if I can get parental signature. They won't give it to me."

"Kit." Grace waited until Kit turned to look at her fully. "You're a ward of the state. When they say parental signature, they mean your guardian. That's me and Amya, not your parents."

"I..." Kit shook her head. "I didn't even think about that."

"No shit." Grace grinned. "You wanted a job and you got one, kid. Congratulations!"

Kit's grin bloomed. "I got a job."

"You did. I'm proud of you."

Grace's own chest was full of joy as she pulled out of the parking spot and headed for home. Hopefully Amya would be home soon and they could all celebrate. This was a huge feat for Kit, something moving her toward normalcy and independence, which the girl was vying for at every turn.

When Grace pulled into the driveway, she turned to Kit. "I really am proud of you, Kit. I hope you know that."

"I do. I can't wait to tell Annabelle."

"She'll be excited, too, although, she'll be sad to miss more time with you I'm sure."

"She's been working on trying to get a job, too."

"Oh?" Grace's eyebrow shot upward. Annabelle could probably handle a job much easier than Kit, but Kit needed one more than Annabelle. "Where?"

"Some place at the mall. She's put in a few applications, but no one is calling her back."

"Interesting." Grace put the car in park and pulled out the keys. "What do you want to do to celebrate?"

"Indian?"

"My kind of kid!" Grace grinned. Amya hated Indian food, but ever since Grace had introduced Kit to it, they'd often overruled Amya so they could get some. "We'll order soon and surprise Amya."

"She's going to hate that." Kit got out of the car and slammed the door.

Grace followed her. "You're probably right, but who cares, this is your celebration, and you get what you want."

Kit grinned. "I'm going to go tell Peter."

Kit raced inside the house, and Grace moved far more slowly. Her leg ached from the cold air outside. It had done that ever since she'd had her accident at work, the one that nearly ended her career, but her body had healed well enough. Moving into being a detective made it easier for sure. Shutting the front door, Grace dropped her keys and wallet into the bowl on the shelf and ditched her jacket.

Roslin and Izzy came to greet her at the door, their tails wagging. Roslin's old and weary body moved slowly as Grace took them to the back to let them into the back yard. She returned to the kitchen, grabbed the menu she'd kept stashed in her favorite drawer for years and figured out what she was going to order. Peter and Amya always ordered the same thing, but she and Kit usually mixed it up.

Seeing as Kit wasn't emerging from Peter's room, Grace picked a variety of items and then called in the order. It'd be an hour before it was delivered. Grace set her cell phone down on the counter and strode to the living room, flopping on the couch. Her bones were weary and ached, but it wasn't her age. It was her work. Thirteen years working for the Sheriff's Department might finally be catching up with her, or it was the fact that her new temporary boss made her work random and odd hours. Closing her eyes, Grace relaxed. She listened to the music from Peter's room, to Kit's and Peter's voices as they chatted, to the wind as it ran into the house. Before she knew it, she was asleep.

Amya slipped into the house after finishing up her call at the Sheriff's Department for a death notification. She was always called to those, especially when it involved some nefarious crime. Grace sat on the couch, her head tilted back against the cushion, her eyes closed, and her jaw wide open as she snored lightly.

A smile lit on Amya's face as she quietly put her keys in the bowl, shucked her jacket, and toed off her shoes. Grace didn't budge. The music from Peter's room was loud enough that she could make out all the words, but quiet enough it wasn't obnoxious. Amya walked to sit next to Grace on the couch, pressing a hand into her thigh. Grace jerked with a start, her head coming up, her arm flailing around. Amya gripped her thigh tightly. "It's only me."

"Scared the shit out of me," Grace muttered before rubbing her hands over her face and down to her legs. "What time is it?"

"Just past six."

"Dinner should be here soon." Grace paled when Amya rolled her eyes. "What?"

"We said we weren't going to order out anymore."

"It's a special occasion."

Amya gazed into Grace's eyes, trying to read her. Sometimes Grace was the easiest person on the planet to read, and other times, no one could figure out what was going through that mind of hers. Leaning in, Amya pressed their mouths together in a gentle kiss.

"I take it Kit got the job."

"Yeah, and then promptly thought she lost it when they told her she needed parental signature."

"What?"

"She—for whatever reason—didn't make the connection that we're now the ones that sign those forms, not her parents."

"Oh."

Grace's jaw hardened. "Yeah, so once I explained that, she was much happier."

"I thought she knew all that. She was at the hearing."

"I think she's so used to finding barriers in life that she just thought this was going to be another one."

Amya raised an eyebrow.

"What?"

"You sounded like me just now."

"Shut up." Grace flushed. "I do not."

"Admit it, you like having a house full of kids."

"What I'd like is for the kids to leave when they're adults, not come back to stay for who knows how long."

Amya sighed. She turned to glance at the doors down the hallway to make sure it was shut and the kids couldn't hear her. "You know why Peter came back."

"Yes, and on one hand, I'm glad he did. He needed to sober up and get his life straight. On the other hand, I didn't think I'd be playing parent to a twenty-two-year-old grad school drop out."

"Grace."

"What?" Grace pushed off the couch. "He needed a place to crash. We gave him that."

"He's been working on it."

"I know." Grace walked into the kitchen and started pulling out plates and silverware for dinner. "But when's he going to leave?"

"When he feels ready to leave."

Grace gave Amya a flat look. "We pay ninety-percent of his bills. You think he's just going to up and leave that?"

Amya shook her head as she followed Grace into the kitchen. "I don't think that's why he stays here, and I don't think that's why you think he stays here either. So why are you complaining about the financial cost of having him under our roof when you could be working with him on becoming an adult."

Grace pouted, and Amya knew she'd caught her in whatever circle she was trying to spin. "He could just stay in town."

"He wants to go to seminary."

"And we saw how well that went last time."

"Grace..."

"Amya." Grace countered. "He doesn't need to go back down that rabbit hole."

"He doesn't. That's the entire point of getting him on his feet now, so he doesn't do it again."

"I know," Grace muttered and stopped talking as she nodded her head toward the hallway.

Amya stayed still as she listened, hearing footsteps on the hardwood. Peter and Kit rounded the corner. Peter's dark shaggy hair never looked like it'd been washed, but the bright look in his eyes lifted Amya's soul. He was definitely doing better than when he'd come home the year before, struggling with alcohol again. He'd been sober for nearly eight months now, and he was determined to keep it that way.

"Is dinner here?" Kit asked.

"Not yet," Grace muttered.

"Did you tell her?" Kit looked pointedly at Amya.

Amya glanced from Kit to Grace. "Tell me what?"

"We ordered Indian!"

Amya groaned. "You didn't."

"We did." Grace gave her a pointed look. "We're celebrating

Kit's new job, so she got to choose."

"Sure, put all the blame on me." Kit snickered.

Amya smiled. This was what she'd always hoped for Kit when Grace had first brought her home last Christmas. She wanted a place where Kit felt comfortable to be herself, to grow, where she didn't have to worry about the adult things in life like rent and buying food but could simply just be herself.

"I plan to." Grace handed the plates over. "Set the table so we can eat when it gets here, will you?"

Kit grumbled but did as she was told. Peter leaned over the kitchen counter, staring at it. Amya knew he had something to talk to them about. He always got quiet like this when he had a bit revelation or question to ask them. He played his fingers against the counter while Amya and Grace stared at him, waiting for the dam to break like it always did.

Grace was the first to give in, as she typically was. "What's on your mind, Peter?"

His gaze flicked up to meet Grace then Amya then back down to the counter. "I was just thinking."

"Oh, here we go," Grace muttered.

Amya elbowed her in the side. "Thinking about what?"

"Going back to school in the spring."

It was as if the air was sucked out of the room. Amya faced Grace, gaging her reaction, but it was the same as Amya's. As much as Grace had been complaining about having him at the house only moments before, they were both unsure about him returning to school so soon after sobering up again. There hadn't been a lot of time for him to find his feet or test some of the waters of the stresses of life without them there.

"Why?" Grace finally asked, her tone so sharp Amya worried Peter might take it a different way than Grace meant it.

Peter sighed, straightening his shoulders. "I want to get my degree. I want to help people."

"You can volunteer here, like you were doing before grad school." Grace, always blunt, gave him her opinion. She didn't think he was ready to leave the nest yet.

"I can," Peter answered. He'd clearly thought of this rebuttal, and Amya stayed quiet to see what he had to say. The call to ministry was a strong one, and resisting it was hard, even if he needed to resist it for his own well-being, at least for a short time. "But I want to do more than that. I want to lead people to Christ."

Grace scoffed. Amya put a hand on her arm to stop her. It had been one of their constant debates in their relationship, but to so outwardly dismiss Peter's faith and desires because Grace herself didn't believe was only going to put more distance between them. Grace reined it in with the reminder from Amya.

"You're an adult, Peter. If you want to go back to school, we can't stop you from doing that." Amya pressed her lips tightly together. "However, I want you to come up with a plan this time to make your experience different than last time."

"Already working on it." Peter's eyes lit up, his lips curving upward. "My sponsor is helping me too. He knows some people out there and says he can get me a new sponsor once I go back."

The wind knocked out of Amya's chest. She nodded at him, not quite sure what to say, but leave it to Peter to do all of the thinking before he actually brought it up to them. Kit came back and grabbed the silverware that hadn't been touched on the counter yet. Amya couldn't take her eyes from Peter. He did look extremely happy about his decision.

"I think you should come home for all of your breaks," Amya suggested. "Give yourself a bit of a respite."

"And keep me out of trouble?" Peter asked.

"I wasn't going to say that."

"Like you'd ever say that," Kit mumbled loud enough or all of them to hear, whether she meant to or not.

Grace shot her a look and then shrugged. Kit was right. They all knew it. Grace's voice was firm when she spoke. "Come up with a plan, Peter. We'll talk about it."

"Really?"

"Yes, kid. Now go help Kit so she's not the only one working around her."

He grabbed the paper towels and started to help Kit. Grace turned to Amya where the kids couldn't see her and widened her eyes, letting out a breath from her pursed lips. Amya felt the same way, even if she couldn't show it in that moment.

At the knock on the door, Kit skittered toward it with a whoop loud enough to get the dogs attention outside. They scratched at the door. Grace sighed, letting them in. Amya helped finish the set up at the table, putting all of the food around it. She took her normal spot and waited for Grace to come back while the dogs settled in after telling her hello.

If Peter did go back to school in the spring, and Kit graduated in June, their house was going to be empty faster than either one of them thought. Even if Peter waited until the fall, they had less than a year left with Kit and Peter at home. It was going to be odd to come home and find no one in the house, to not have the chaos of schedules going here and there and racing to keep up with life.

Amya took a sip of whatever drink Grace had put in front of her. She glanced from Kit to Peter and back again. They were both ready for it. She knew that as much as Grace did, but the resistance to still keep them both home and safe was strong. But it was time they grew up, and it was time for Grace and Amya to have some serious conversations about the future.

THE CASE

GRACE'S MORNING came earlier than she'd anticipated. At one point, she had enjoyed going into the office. Lately, it'd been a chore to get herself ready in the mornings and to leave. She'd been late on more than one occasion—actually, quite often—which was completely outside of her norm. This morning was no different.

Grace took her time showering, getting some coffee, sipping it at the counter. She didn't even bother checking her watch. She knew she was going to be late. Kit ran into the kitchen, made herself her own cup of coffee, and gave Grace an odd look. Grace raised an eyebrow back at her.

"Yes?"

"You're going to be late."

"So are you," she pointed out. "I have to take you to school, remember?"

"Uh...yeah."

"So get moving."

Kit raced back to her room, coming into the kitchen for a second time with her backpack slung over one shoulder. "Ready."

Grace inwardly cursed. Leave it to Kit to be punctual for once. Sighing, Grace took her travel mug and walked toward the door. She had her keys in her hand and her wallet in her pocket when Amya stepped out of the bedroom dressed to the nines in a sleek dark gray pencil skirt, white blouse, and a suit jacket to match. She must have a meeting with someone high up today for her to be dressed that well.

Melting, Grace stared at her girlfriend of four years, her jaw dropping as Amya walked closer with a satisfied smirk on her lips. As soon as she stood in front of Grace, she used one finger to close her mouth. "Glad to see I can still do that."

"Shove it," Grace mumbled. "Of course you can still do that."

Amya chuckled lightly and pulled Grace in for a long kiss, their tongues touching for a brief moment before Kit cleared her throat. Amya pecked Grace's lips three more times before she stepped away.

"Is there coffee left or have the two of you drank it all?"

"There's enough for one cup."

"Good. I have to go in early today."

"Meeting?" Grace asked, still stalling. If Kit was late, whatever. She could write her a note. She really just didn't want to go into the office. Amya sashayed to the kitchen to grab the coffee pot.

"Yeah, with the chief."

"Really? What for?"

"Because of the notification yesterday. I told you about that."

Had she? Grace wracked her brain for the information Amya swore she told her, but she came up empty. Shaking her head, she went to walk toward the kitchen, but Kit stopped her with a hand on her arm.

"I'm going to be late."

"Yeah, we'll leave in a minute. Amya, you didn't tell me anything other than you had a notification."

Amya's gaze flicked to Kit and back to Grace. "I'll text it."

"I'm not stupid. I know what you do, and I'm not a kid. You can say it in front of me."

Amya set her coffee mug down that she'd just filled. She moved her gaze from Kit to Grace, studying her as she spoke. "There was an officer killed in a vehicular accident last night. Traffic stop and another driver didn't see them when they were outside their vehicle."

Grace clenched her jaw, every muscle in her body tightening. She hated it when officers were killed in the line of duty, and the rash of them four years ago was what prompted her to move up in rank to avoid being on the street so much.

"Grace?" Amya asked.

"I'm fine. Let's go, Kit." Turning sharply, Grace opened the door. Kit ran out to get in her cruiser. Grace sent a look over her shoulder to confirm to Amya she really was fine even though they both knew she wasn't.

It didn't take her long to drop Kit off and get to the station. The unit was buzzing with energy and a murmur of conversation. Grace looked from one detective to another, finally catching sight of Kline in the corner. She waved at her before setting her bag at her desk.

"Halling!" Paige's voice rang through the room, and silence echoed a response.

Grace cringed. Paige was the reason she didn't want to be at work. Everything since last spring had been awkward, and it hadn't gotten any better. No matter how hard Grace tried to set boundaries, Paige pushed them. It was exhausting.

Turning on her toes, Grace found Paige standing in the captain's office with her hands on her hips. She was just about to be caught coming in late—again. Though the last dozen times Paige hadn't said anything except to tell her not to do it again. No punishment, nothing. Paige didn't look happy this morning, though.

Fearing for the worst, Grace made her way to Paige's temporary office. She honestly couldn't wait until they hired a new captain. Paige with the added power of the position was making her life miserable. Paige shut the door behind her, and Grace tensed, ready for the onslaught and the yelling.

"What's going on?" Grace asked, already defensive.

"We'll talk about you being late another day."

Grace swallowed hard. "Then why call me in here."

"Case."

"Great." Grace had just finished her last case two days before, and she hadn't thought she'd land herself a new one just yet. Although, she probably should have figured that out because Paige seemed to always give her a case, no matter what, and it was always the high profile ones, the hard ones, the ones that would in theory give her the most credit so she could move up. And while Grace appreciated that on the one hand, on the other she really wanted the break for a week or more.

Paige narrowed her gaze, her green eyes piercing Grace. "You'll be working with homicide on this one?"

"Is the person missing dead?"

"No, Halling. There's a missing baby. The mother's dead."

"Oh." Grace crossed her arms. "Who do I get to work with?"

"Sergeant Link Abrams. You'll be working alongside him, but

still under me."

Great, Grace thought. That had been her one opportunity to get out. She waited for the rest of the description of what was happening, but Paige was less than forthcoming. Instead, she crossed her arms and leaned against the desk.

"Abrams is good, but he's got an attitude problem, so watch your tongue with him. If you tick him off, that'll be the end of it. You can't afford to get on his bad side."

"Okay," Grace responded, though she wasn't someone who usually got on others bad sides. That would be Paige.

"I wish I could go with you and work this case, but I'm stuck here. Since I used to work homicide, I'm sure the two of us could work it without any problems."

Grace clenched her jaw. "Is there a file?"

"Not yet. Abrams is waiting for you at the crime scene."

"Address?"

Paige handed over a sticky note.

Grace glanced at it and then Paige. "I'll head on over."

"Update me every hour. This is a high profile case, Halling. We can't afford to screw it up."

As she left the office, Grace rolled her eyes. High profile her ass. That wasn't why Paige wanted hourly updates, but either way, she'd have to play along or risk getting written up for insubordination. That would not look good on her record if she ever wanted to transfer to another unit.

Leaving her bag where it was, Grace took her keys and her wallet and walked back to her cruiser. She thought about stopping by Amya's offices to fill her in. No doubt Amya would be involved in the case somehow. Missing babies were a touchy subject, and not only would the media be all over it, but so would the family. Grace would need her help navigating the family dynamics for sure.

Bypassing Amya's offices, Grace left the building and walked into the chill fall air. Kit had a full week of school left before she would off for the holiday. It used to be Grace's favorite time of the year, but lately, nothing was making her happy.

Grace slid into the front seat of the cruiser and looked at the address again. It was in her old haunt, so she knew exactly where she needed to go.

The apartment was filled with uniforms and with two detectives. Grace pressed her lips firmly together in a line as she showed her badge and walked toward the detective she thought might be in charge, the older looking one. Stepping right up, she looked them over. The one on the left had bright blue eyes that reminded her of a blue jay, salt-and-pepper hair cut military style. The other one was taller, but younger, his hair brown in a crew cut and hazel eyes.

"I'm Detective Grace Halling from Missing Persons. Lieutenant Delwin sent me."

"Took you long enough," the younger one growled.

Grace sincerely hoped he was not the sergeant she was supposed to work with. He seemed cocky with an attitude to boot. "I was just handed this case...Detective...?"

"Detective Honeywell," the older one answered. "And excuse him because he's bitter he doesn't get to work this case."

Grace clenched her jaw. She'd be bitter too, if she were honest, but it wasn't her problem to deal with.

"I'm Sergeant Abrams. Delwin said you were coming."

"Care to fill me in? Delwin was skimpy on details."

"Was she? That doesn't sound like her."

Grace didn't comment because she was pretty sure most officers had a very different experience of Paige Delwin than she did, but how could she tell anyone that without jeopardizing her current position? She couldn't. Not even Alonzo Esparza in IAB could help her with this one.

Abrams moved his hand out in front of him, telling Grace to move on ahead. They walked quietly, although the apartment was anything but. It was small, one bedroom, the kitchen and living room basically joined together and no larger than Peter's room, which was the smallest bedroom in her house.

"The mother we found dead in the kitchen."

They stopped at the edge of the very cheap linoleum. There was a blood stain on the floor, but no body. Grace figured they must have already taken it down to the morgue since she was so late.

"She was stabbed at least four or five times from what we could see, but I'm thinking it might be more based on how much blood there is."

Grace skimmed the room. There was blood everywhere, not just on the floor but on the lower cabinets to the kitchen, the counter, the upper cabinets on the exterior wall, and even some on the ceiling. She would get pictures of that later, though it was less for her case than it was for homicide's.

"Paige said there was a baby."

"Yeah, few weeks old."

"Weeks?" Surprise registered in her chest. Grace turned on him, her gaze locking on his.

He nodded. "Found the hospital band on the dresser. Here."

Abrams led the way into the small one bedroom. A crib sat in the corner of the room, pressed against the wall just under the window. The dresser was across from it with personal items scattered all over the top. Grace pulled a glove out of the pocket on her suit jacket and shoved it onto her left hand. She picked up the hospital band.

Andrew Erickson.

His date of birth was exactly three weeks ago. She had the doctors name who delivered him, and Grace knew she'd be paying the hospital a visit to try and get some information from the staff. She couldn't imagine having a three week old baby and then having them go missing. The father's name on the tag was blank. That would take some digging.

"How long ago was the mother found?"

"Three hours."

"Know how long she was dead yet?"

"Not yet. Best guess is a couple days."

"Days?" Grace spun on him. "No one knew she was dead for days?"

Abrams shrugged. "We come when we're called. We don't go searching for dead bodies."

"Yeah, but still. Any pictures?"

"Best guess is she has some on her phone." Abrams handed the device over. It was shoved in a plastic evidence bag. Grace looked down at it.

"It's locked, isn't it?"

"Took the words right out of my mouth, Halling."

"I'll take it back for the tech team to work on it. Hard to put out an Amber Alert without a good description."

"Call the hospital. They take all that shit down for their records."

Grace hummed. "I'll do that."

She turned to look around the room even more. It was cluttered but in order. There were diapers on the bed, the curtains were drawn.

"Is the diaper bag here?"

"Don't know."

Grace stepped forward, looking for whatever Andrew's mother had used for a diaper bag. She had no idea who would want to kidnap an infant, to the point of killing the mother. Grace opened the closet door, peeking inside. It was a mess. Clothes on the floor in a pile, stuff hung up but also stuff just hanging out anywhere it would fit. Rummaging around a bit, Grace stepped back. If there was a diaper bag in there, it would be on top of everything since Andrew's mom would need it.

"Is there one out there?"

"Not that we've seen."

"So it was likely taken with the baby unless it's in the car."

"She didn't have a car registered under her name."

"How did she get places? There's no public transportation nearby here."

"How do you know that?" he asked.

Grace shrugged. "Used to be my old beat. Public transportation in this city isn't awful, but it's not great on this side of town, especially in the poorer areas like this one."

Abrams raised his eyebrows at her. "The crime scene guys are going to finish up here, and Honeywell can stay until they're done. Did you want to go down to the morgue?"

"Yeah." Grace grimaced. "Probably a good thing to do that."

"We can get the preliminary report and go from there."

They took separate vehicles, Grace following Abrams. The city morgue was located in its own building, and Grace had rarely been there in her tenure at the Sheriff's Department. That had been the advantage to being in missing persons, unless they ended up dead, she didn't need to go there.

She'd called the hospital on the way over, and they were going to send Andrew's birth records so she could at least have a description of him for the Amber Alert and to notify the FBI. She should make Amya do that, since her sister worked there.

Grace got out of her cruiser and walked next to Abrams as they went into the building. The morgue was cold, the chill in the air always going straight to her bones. She wasn't the hugest fan of the morgue, but she couldn't honestly think of a detective who liked it. If they did, they most often went back to school to get a job there instead of continuing in the Sheriff's Department.

They were led down a hallway into a large open room. The body of the mother was still on the stretcher it had come in on. Grace bit her cheek as she stared at it, the body bag open so they could see her face. The medical examiner opened it the rest of the way, staring first at Grace and then at Abrams.

"She new?" he asked.

"No," Abrams answered, but he didn't elaborate, which Grace was thankful for. She wasn't sure how much Abrams knew anyway.

Grace waited patiently and quietly for the medical examiner to tell them what had happened—at least, what he knew of what had happened so far. She figured that would change as soon as he was able to really look at the body.

"She was stabbed to death."

"Guessed that one," Abrams said with a smirk. "Tell me something I don't know."

"She's been dead about thirty-six hours."

"Damn it," Grace muttered.

Abrams shot her a dirty look, so she ground her molars to keep from saying anything else stupid. But Abrams must have had other plans. He put a fist on his hip and stared at her directly. "Did you have something to add?"

"Thirty-six hours is a bit late to get started on a critical missing case." She sent him a serious look, daring him to challenge her. When he didn't, Grace turned back to the medical examiner.

"Critical missing?" he asked.

"She had a baby three weeks ago," Grace supplied when Abrams didn't speak for her. She wasn't used to men in charge not railroading her. "Baby is missing. I work with missing persons, paired with Abrams for the deceased."

The shocked expression on the medical examiner's face was near priceless. Grace supposed he hadn't really looked at the body yet otherwise he probably would have been able to figure out she'd given birth recently. She wondered if he'd even have any more information for them or if they were going in blind for the next few days of their investigation while they waited for his first report.

"Any idea what she was stabbed with?" Abrams asked.

"Knife."

Abrams rolled his eyes. "I could have sworn it was with a spoon."

Grace snorted. If this was Abrams' norm, then she was fast going to like him. He was snarky like her, but gave her the responsibility of her rank without trying to take it away. Whatever Paige had meant by him, she had been wrong.

"Serrated knife I think, but I won't know more until I can really look at it."

Tapping her toe on the cement floor, Grace couldn't figure out why they were there if they had no new information to gain. She had better things she could be doing. A look to Abrams told her he was thinking the same. They made quick chit chat with the medical examiner, told him they'd be back, and left.

Outside, Grace opened the door to the cruiser, but Abrams stopped her by calling her rank and name. Freezing on the spot, Grace turned to him. "Yes?"

"What are you thinking?"

"That I have a list of phone calls to make." She knew there was too much snark in her tone, but she couldn't help it. They hadn't exactly discussed the parameters of what they were doing or how they were going to investigate together and separately, but with the morning she'd had, she just wanted to dive in as deep as she could to the case.

"Like where?"

Grace sighed. "Have you worked a missing persons case before?"

Abrams shook his head. "Nope. Been in homicide since I transferred from warrants ten years ago."

"Right. This is a critical missing case. I have to call the FBI, put out the Amber Alert, call hospitals in this county and every neighboring county, put out notices in neighboring counties to look for a kid that I don't have a picture of."

"Didn't realize you had to talk to the FBI."

Grace shrugged. "Did you work with Delwin often?"

"Yeah." He grunted, but again, didn't elaborate.

She wanted to ask him more questions, but after only knowing him for a few short hours, Grace didn't think it wise to open that can of worms just yet. With her hand on the door to the cruiser, she moved to get in it, once again, stopped by his voice.

"We're working this together, Halling."

"I know," she answered. "Did you have more to the plan than that?"

"You're a tough cookie, aren't you?"

"Some days," Grace mumbled. "Did you want to meet up this afternoon and go over notes or something?"

"Or something. Tomorrow. Doc Mendez should have more information by then."

"I should hope."

"Notification?"

Grace's stomach clenched. "I thought you did it already."

"Waited on you, since you have a notification to do too."

"Wonderful. Where we going first?"

"Mom's."

"I'll follow you. Figure out who baby daddy is?"

"Not yet."

"We'll have to ask that."

Grace did get behind the wheel then. Abrams handed her a card through the open door before stepping away and walking to his cruiser. It had his number on it. She would have to be the one to call him tomorrow to set up the time. Groaning, Grace followed Abrams. It was going to be a long day.

The first notification went as well as expected. Felicia's mom had no information for them except a name for the baby daddy, which was a bonus. Though apparently he was only the suspected baby daddy. Grace filed that information away in the back of her mind while she followed Abrams to the next house. They had three more notifications to do before they could go to the station and sit down with all the information they had and dissect it.

As much as Grace wanted to do that, the idea of going back to the station was not something that appealed to her. Abrams and she seemed to get along well enough, but Grace had avoided updating Paige all morning, and Paige had left numerous messages on her phone and texts, ordering her to call and give an update.

Abrams caught Grace ignoring Paige's calls on more than one occasion, but he hadn't commented on it, thankfully. As Grace got into her cruiser after the last notification, she pulled out her phone and flipped through the messages. Three more from Paige and one from Amya—who was apparently mad they hadn't asked for her assistance on the notifications since it was a sensitive case. Grace cringed. They probably should have called in the Chaplain, but it had been easier and less time consuming not to. And so far, the family had handled it well enough. They could have always called Amya in after the fact if need be.

At the station, Grace got out of her cruiser and dragged her feet inside. Her first call would be to start the Amber Alert—assuming the hospital had sent the necessary information over and Paige hadn't started it already. Her second call would be to the FBI, which would start the time limit on her case. She'd only have so much time to find Andrew before the FBI would step in to help out and even then only so much time before they took over the investigation completely. With the added pressure, Grace couldn't afford to let anything slip this time.

COLLABORATION

GRACE'S HEAD ached already. Walking into her unit, she knew that it was going to be a trial just to be there for the rest of the day, and she had to talk to Paige because Paige still tried to play the role of her partner even though she was also running the unit and didn't really have the time for both.

Plopping down at her desk, Grace turned on her computer and pulled out her notebook that was littered with scribbles from everything she had done that day. She'd be at the office late for sure trying to type it all up and get everything straight. At least Amya was aware of what was going on. She got up while her computer booted on and poured herself another coffee. It had been her lifeline lately, and she was drinking as much of it as Amya normally would if not more. It was a sure sign that something was not going quite right.

Back in her seat, Detective Kline came over, sitting go the edge of the desk. "She talk to you yet?"

"No. I'm hoping she hasn't noticed I'm back."

"She's mad."

"I'm sure. I've avoided my hourly check-ins with her. I bet she's wanting a full update on the case."

"Hourly?"

"Yeah." Grace stared up into Kline's open face. They had become better friends over the past summer and fall, but they weren't best friends yet. Grace had held back on it seeing as the last person she'd made friends with in her unit struggled to keep boundaries in check. Grace didn't want to have to deal with more than one person who wanted a piece of her in some form or fashion.

Kline scoffed. "That's absolutely ridiculous."

"Well, we know from experience that she likes to keep close tabs on me."

"Yeah, but you're a seasoned detective at this point. You know what you're doing."

Grace didn't respond because she knew it wasn't because of her experience that Paige was insisting on keeping an eye on her. The motive behind it was entirely different. What Grace didn't know was how to handle it without running from it, and the thought had occurred to her more than once. She had never hated coming in to work as much as she did now that Paige was in charge of the unit. She just kept holding out hope that they would hire someone else to fill the empty permanent captain's position and that everything would go back to the way it was before, which wasn't great, but it was at least tolerable.

"I've got to call the FBI."

"Critical missing?"

"Mom dead, stabbed. Baby missing three days."

"You're kidding."

"Well, the mom's been dead three days, so that's our best guess."

"Any clues where the baby is at."

"Nope. Baby daddy didn't have him at all, and in fact, I'm not sure he's ever met the baby."

"Sad. How old is the kid?"

"Three weeks."

"Damn."

Grace tightened her jaw as she opened a new file to begin her reporting. Kline remained next to her, leaning against her desk, which had become somewhat normal since Paige had moved into the big office, and Grace didn't mind it. Kline was older, a parent to grown adults, but she was sweet and definitely able to connect with Grace on a basic level. They had common interests and shared a job together. Beyond that, they likely wouldn't become best friends or fast friends, but they could at least be work friends.

"Halling!" Paige's voice boomed through the room, and once again, everyone stilled in response.

Grace hated it when Paige did that. Bolstering herself, Grace turned in her chair to look over at Paige standing just outside the door to her office. "Yeah?"

"My office. Now." The angry tone in Paige's voice wasn't missed by anyone. Paige spun around and walked into her office out of sight from most everyone else.

Grace shot Kline a look and shuffled her feet as she stood up and made her way to Paige. Tensing as she entered the office, Grace moved in.

"Shut the door."

Fuck, Grace thought as she closed the door behind her. She hated closed doors where it involved Paige. "What do you need?"

"I needed an update, on the hour."

Sitting in the chair on the opposite side of Paige's desk while Paige leaned against the front of it, towering over her, Grace stared at her shoes. "Not much to update."

"What were you doing for hours then?"

"Went to the apartment, the morgue, did three notifications, talked to Abrams to figure out how we're going to be doing this exchange of information and joint investigation."

"He behave?"

"Yup." Grace pressed her lips together tightly. There had been no signs that Sergeant Link Abrams was going to misbehave, then again, there'd been no sign Paige was going to go down that road until last year either. Holding her own, Grace waited for the next question and answer game they were going to play.

"How long?"

"Felicia Erikson was killed about three days ago. From what we can tell, the baby has been missing that long. No one even knew she was gone. We were able to get a photo from the maternal grandmother, so I will alert the news media in a minute so they can run a special on it tonight."

"You think that's wise?"

"Yes." Grace shifted her gaze to Paige's green eyes. "We're already three days out on this case. We need all the help we can get to find Andrew."

"Makes sense. I did put out the Amber Alert when the medical file came in." Paige reached to her desk and pulled out a small stack of papers, handing it over to Grace.

Skimming the file, Grace noted everything she already knew, but also found out something she didn't. Andrew had a birthmark on his chest on the bottom side of his left chest. That would definitely be helping in identifying him when she found him, although, it wouldn't readily be seen without him being naked, which wasn't too much of a help unless she knew where to look.

"Thanks," Grace muttered. "I'll contact the FBI here in a minute."

"I can do that."

Shaking her head, Grace tensed. "I don't mind."

"Oh, I forget you have a connection there."

"Yeah." Grace swallowed. She'd never met her sister-in-law, and they'd only spoken once or twice on the phone, but between Amya and her mother-in-law, Patti, she knew a lot about Special Agent to the FBI Morgan Stone. "She probably won't handle the case, but I can also ask her for a profile, too."

"Good thinking." Paige eyed Grace. "We need to get ahead on this case. We're already days behind where we should be."

"Not of our own fault," Grace muttered.

"Still. Three days missing already means we're outside the first three windows."

"I'm well aware, Paige. I've been in Missing Persons for three years at this point. I know how to run an investigation." Grace hadn't meant to be so forward, but she was tired of holding back. Paige had gone from walking to her like an equal in the beginning to babying every move she made. Most detectives transferred units every three to five years, so she was already one of the more senior officers with all her current experience. Technically, she'd been in missing persons longer than Paige, but she didn't have the ranking to fill in as Captain since she hadn't been on the force as long.

"I'm going to approve any over time you need."

And there it was. Grace's stomach clenched. Paige was going to expect her to work night and day to solve this case, which she would have already wanted to do anyway, but the expectation of it made it worse, especially because Paige insisted on being in the unit any time Grace stayed late, so they'd have a bunch of interactions Grace would have to navigate instead of putting all her focus on Andrew like she should.

"Great. I've got some calls to make, reports to enter, and investigation to line up for tomorrow." Grace moved her thumb over her shoulder, indicating she wanted to leave the office.

Paige stepped forward, standing right next to Grace's shoulder and touched her softly. Grace shivered at the contact, but it wasn't a good shiver. Paige smiled down at her, those green eyes unwavering in their desire, and Grace tried her best to ignore it. Paige's voice was clear but quiet when she spoke. "Let me know if you need help on anything, Grace. I'm always here for you. You know that."

"Uh...thanks." Awkwardly standing, Grace made sure Paige had to move her hand as she stepped away and on the other side of the chair to separate them. Grace eyed Paige carefully, trying to show her dislike of everything going on in that room, but she wasn't sure Paige even picked up on it. They had gone from working so well together to barely being able to communicate the necessities. It was probably a good thing Paige wasn't really working cases with her anymore.

"I mean it, Grace."

"I hear you." Grace walked to the door and let herself out. Paige's gaze followed her to her desk only ten feet away, her eyes burning a hole in Grace's back. She wondered what people thought of Paige babying all of Grace's cases but also always giving her the big cases. It definitely could be seen as favoritism, but it wasn't like Paige hid the fact she was a lesbian, and since Grace was in a relationship with the Police Chaplain, everyone knew which way she swung.

Cursing under her breath, Grace hunched over her desk as she focused on the work in front of her. People probably thought she and Paige was doing the nasty in the interview rooms when no one was looking or something. There was no way to escape the chaos Paige had rained down on her.

Grace got to work on time the next morning. She managed to avoid Paige, somehow, she wasn't quite sure how. With her notebook in hand and some of her research from the night before, she trekked down the hall toward homicide. Their unit was much larger than hers, at least double the size.

It took her a moment to spy Abrams at his desk on the far wall by one of the three windows in the room. He caught sight of her and waved her over. Grace stepped into the large room, glancing every which way as people moved and worked. She'd been in homicide's room before but never as a visiting detective and never because she had a case she needed to still work.

Abrams was on the phone, so Grace stood by his desk and waited for him to finish. He glanced up at her as he hung up and gave her a wan smile. "I figure we can work in one of the interview rooms for now."

"Sounds good." Grace bit the inside of her cheek.

After her conversation with Paige the day before, her defenses were up where it involved Abrams. She couldn't figure out why she let Paige affect her so much. At one point they had been good partners, and then everything had gone to absolute shit.

Grace walked slowly behind Abrams after he gathered up his papers. They went into an interview room, the door left open, which made Grace feel safer, and she was glad he did that. Not that anything Abrams had done made her feel unsafe, but having the added layer of protection was always welcome, especially considering her issues with Paige.

"Were you able to get hold of the FBI?" Abrams asked.

"I was. They were not super helpful, but they usually aren't in general."

"And you don't want them to take your case."

Grace smirked. "Who would?"

Abrams chuckled. "I hear you there. So, what have you found so far?"

Laying her notebook on top of the desk, Grace spoke from memory. "I've started to map out familial connections, starting with the baby daddy because he would be our number one suspect."

"Agreed."

"He definitely didn't have the kid with him yesterday, but that doesn't mean he hasn't stashed him anywhere."

"Also true." Abrams looked directly into Grace's eyes as she spoke, letting her ramble on about what she knew and didn't know.

"I want to pull in the paternal grandparents at some time. Bring them down here for an interview and do it separately if I can to see if I can get any more information from them. They were definitely holding back yesterday, but I didn't want to push it."

"I got that sense too." Abrams flipped his pen back and forth between his pointer finger and his thumb. "I thought the grandfather was going to say something, but one look from the wife, and he shut right up."

"Glad you caught that, too. I don't want to wait too long to do that."

"Agreed." Abrams wrote something down on his large legal pad.

"I think we also need to interview more of Felicia's family. Get a sense of who she was and what she might be doing so soon after giving birth. I mean, was she really excited about having a baby or was it stressing her out. Did she do drugs?"

"We didn't find any in the apartment."

Grace cocked her head to the side. "Doesn't mean she hasn't

done them in the past. The hospital records were clear that she wasn't on drugs any time during her pregnancy, but a lot of people stop when they're pregnant and start up again."

"I think she loved that baby." Abrams' face hardened.

Grace's lips parted, and she tried to back track. Perhaps she had been too forward with her thoughts. "I wasn't saying otherwise."

Abrams sighed and rubbed his temple. "There was a crib. Clothes not just for the baby now but also for the future, including diapers in larger sizes."

"All of which she could have gotten if she'd had a shower of some sort. Doesn't mean she purchased them."

"I'm looking into her financials."

"That'll help I'm sure." Grace shut her mouth, really not wanting to push him just in case Paige had been right. If Abrams had a temper, she needed to stay on his good side.

He cast her an odd look before setting his pen on the top of the table. "Shall we make a map of the family connections you have and the ones I have?"

"Sure."

They spent the next thirty minutes writing them all out, including a few friends that they knew of from talking with Felicia's parents and ex. Grace leaned into the hard chair and stretched her back, popping it in certain places. Abrams glanced up at her with a curious look in his eye, but Grace decided not to comment on it.

"We can split up to talk to them, if you'd like."

"We could," Abrams answered. "Or we could go together."

"That will take considerably more time." Grace stared into his bright blue eyes, wondering what that would even accomplish. They could just as easily work separately and meet up to discuss what they'd learned. Having a second person there was helpful, but with the vast list of people they needed to interview, separate would be better.

Abrams crossed his arms and one ankle over his leg. "Are you avoiding me?"

"No, sir." Grace added the salutation at the last minute, remembering that Abrams definitely outranked her. "Just trying to get the work done efficiently."

He pursed his lips as he stared at her. Grace felt completely exposed under his gaze, like he could see why she was really hesitating, and it had nothing to do with him and everything to do with Paige.

"I know you haven't worked Homicide before, but here, we do everything in pairs."

Grace paused. Typically they did things in pairs in Missing Persons too, but not always, especially when they had an influx of cases and couldn't keep up with their small staff. She wasn't quite sure what to say to him, so Grace remained silent.

"Is there something going on I don't know about?"

"No, sir," Grace answered, her defenses kicking into high gear. "I'm here to solve this case as quickly and efficiently as possible. If that makes going our separate ways for a bit and reconvening useful then we can do it. If you prefer to work together, then we'll do that. You are the ranking deputy on the case."

"I am." He still eyed her.

Grace grew uneasy under his gaze.

"You're dating Chaplain Stone, right?"

Grace tensed. "Yes."

"Amya and I have quite a history of discussions. I'm sure she's mentioned me."

Shaking her head, Grace's stomach twisted. Amya had not mentioned Abrams at all, not that she would, but to hear him refer to Amya by her first name set a different tone to their relationships. "She doesn't talk about work often. Well, she does, but not in specific details, much like I don't also talk in specific details about my work to her."

"Interesting." His gaze narrowed. "She teaches at the church I attend sometimes."

"St. Anthony's?"

"Yeah."

Grace drew in a breath, not quite sure where this conversation was going and really wanting to get out of it. She opened her notebook and skimmed the notes she'd taken during their interviews yesterday. "When do you want to bring the baby daddy in?"

"Not today."

"When?"

"I want to see what he does first, track him before we interview him."

"Okay. So what are we doing today?"

"Canvassing."

"Great," Grace mumbled. Spending the day going door-to-door was not her idea of pleasant or productive. She preferred to figure out who she wanted to talk to and go straight to the source, but

Abrams was her superior, so she had to follow what he told her.

"The preliminary medical examiners report came in yesterday afternoon about Felicia."

"Oh?"

Abrams reached into his file and slipped it across the table. Grace skimmed over it in silence before glancing up at him. "This doesn't tell us anything that we didn't already know."

"We didn't really expect it to."

"When is the autopsy scheduled?"

"Few days from now, and it'll take a few weeks for the drug analysis to come back."

"Wonderful." Grace licked her lips. "Out of curiosity, which case is taking priority?"

"Yours," Abrams answered. "You have the living victim."

"Presumed living," Grace corrected.

Abrams put his hands out in a show of acquiescence. "I imagine the same person who took the baby has the baby."

Grace nodded. "My research into kidnappings of infants from the home is that the person who takes the baby usually is a close friend or family member, someone who knows the victim personally. They may or may not kill in order to get what they want, but the baby is usually decently cared for once taken."

"Decently?"

Lifting one shoulder, she let it drop. "It's a kidnapping. How decent can it be when you're ripped from everything you know and from the one person the infant has known since before birth."

"I'll give you that one."

"Secondly, this person who committed the murder and kidnapping is clearly not mentally stable. Something pushed them to do this, and that same thing can push them to do something else. I believe there is a window in order to find and rescue Andrew in which he has the least likelihood of harm coming to him, but the longer he is with his kidnapper the more likely harm will happen."

"Agreed. Logically that makes sense."

"It's also why I want to focus on family and friends and not on strangers. Media is all about stranger danger." Grace widened her eyes. "But pathology of those convicted and guilty shows that in cases like these it's most often someone close to the family."

"Will you write up a basic profile for me?"

Grace's lips parted. "Sure, if that's what you want."

"It is. I'm not used to working Missing Persons. I think it'll be helpful as we work this case together."

"Okay." Grace locked her gaze with him. Everything Paige had implied so far had been completely off base, and Grace needed to figure out why Paige had tried to spin her perception of Abrams so early on. "Canvassing?"

"Yes," Abrams started, pulling the paper they had mapped out connections on in front of him. "Where would you like to start?"

Grace glanced at the paper, but she already knew the answer. If Abrams wanted to hold off on the baby-daddy, then she wanted to start with his family. "Paternal family. His sister."

"Sounds like a plan." Abrams gathered up all of his paperwork and shoved it into the file he'd brought into the room. "Take one car or two?"

"One makes more sense."

"It does, but it's your choice."

"We can take one." Grace eased out of the chair. Abrams was a completely different person from what Paige had implied. "Can we grab coffee first? I was up late."

"Were you?"

Grace shrugged. "Had research to get done."

"How late did you stay?" Abrams asked as he walked out of the interview room and started down the hall.

"Midnight," Grace mumbled, half-hoping Abrams didn't hear her.

"What the hell? Why did you stay so late?"

Her eyes widened. She'd stayed that late because Paige had insisted she finish a bunch of reports before she left, not just the reports from her own case and her own research, but finalizing and making sure everyone else had their reports in so Paige could officially sign off on them. But Grace wasn't about to out that to a sergeant she barely knew. "Long story."

"Don't work so late tonight. You won't be thinking straight tomorrow when we have more work to do."

Grace didn't answer him, because no matter what he said, she wasn't particularly sure she was going to have a choice in the matter. She either stayed late when Paige told her to or she had hell to pay for it for the next day. It was one of the big reasons why she'd begun to hate her job, and she had to keep reminding herself that she was only seven years away from her full pension and she had kids to feed and now she had graduate school to help pay for. There was never a good reason to up a quit anything.

OVERTIME

THE AFTERNOON rolled around, finally nearing the end of her shift. Abrams and she had managed to catch only twenty percent of their list to interview, and it was very likely Grace would end up working the entire weekend to try and make that up and get hold of people when they were home. Amya would not be happy about that. Neither was Grace, frankly, but that was part of her job and she'd accepted it when she'd decided to apply for a detective position and promotion.

Rubbing the back of her head, Grace leaned over her desk. She combed through the phone records she'd finally gotten in. Abrams had gotten the same records, and they were texting back and forth any time something popped up. She stopped sharply when she felt someone watching her.

Grace stretched her neck and sat up straight, glancing around the room. A lot of people were at their desks working, no doubt trying to finish up reports before the weekend began. Fridays she always left early to go to the after school program she'd started at Hamilton High School for students who needed some extra help in life. The ones who were forgotten, like Kit. It'd been where they'd done a good chunk of their bonding.

Finding no one staring at her, Grace turned back to her computer and the records. Felicia was popular. The number of calls in and out were massive, at least thirty a day, and her texts. It was going to give Grace a headache just trying to follow them, and she swore half of them were in code. She'd need to ask Peter about some of the phrases because she was at a loss for how to decipher what was said.

"Grace." Paige's voice was soft but firm.

Spinning in her chair, Grace came face-to-face with Paige who was bent over Grace's desk. "Jesus, scare the shit out of me why don't you."

"I thought you knew I was standing here."

"I didn't. What do you need?"

"How's the case coming?"

Grace scoffed. "Slow as molasses."

"Any leads?"

"None. It's like the kid just vanished. It's hard enough to find anyone in the family. They're never at home, never at work. I have no idea where they go."

"Abrams making any headway?"

Grace shook her head. She wasn't going to elaborate that they'd spent most of the day together because she had a feeling it was only going to tick Paige off. Her current goal was to exist under Paige's radar at all times and all places possible.

"You've got to find something."

"I know. I'm working on it."

"I'm going to need you to stay late again."

Grace's eye widened. "What for?"

"To work this case, Halling. You know the rules. If it's critical missing, it needs to be worked."

"Let me leave for two and a half hours. That's it. I'll come back here and work all night, but you know I go to the school on Fridays."

"Not today, Grace." To her credit, Paige did seem slightly sympathetic, although Grace knew she'd never understood it. Ever since the school year had started up again in the fall, Paige had tried to find reasons to keep Grace at the office and away from the school. Before she'd had that power she'd made comments about not understanding why Grace would spend her free time with a bunch of high school kids.

"Paige."

"Not today," Paige reiterated.

"I can't find a sub with this short of notice."

"Not my problem." Without another word, she stood up and

walked away.

"Fuck this," Grace muttered. She got up from her desk, pushing her chair out and stalking out of the room. It didn't take her long to make it to the chaplain's offices. As soon as she walked in, Khloe waved hello at her. "She in a meeting?"

"She's about done."

Crossing her arms, Grace tapped her foot on the ground unable to hide her anger and frustration. Khloe shot her a few glances but thankfully didn't comment on it. As whoever was in Amya's office left, Grace looked up, catching Amya's gaze. Amya's lips parted in surprise, and she cocked her head to the side nodding toward the office.

Grace didn't hesitate. She barreled right through the door. Amya shut it and locked it. Grace spun, her hands flailing out to her sides as she shook her head, tears pricking her eyes. She had no idea why she wanted to cry, but she wouldn't let herself do it.

"What's wrong? Did something happen with Kit? Peter?"

Grace shook her head. "No, nothing with them. They're fine."

"Okay, good. What's wrong?"

Every muscle in Grace's body was jittery from the tension she was attempting to hold in. She didn't want to unleash it all on Amya right then and there in her office, but if Amya pushed her to talk, she might just explode. "I can't go this afternoon. Can you?"

"I...I think I have the time to take. Why can't you go?"

Grace glared, drew in a long breath and let it out slowly. "I'll give you one guess."

Amya sighed. She gripped Grace's hand and tugged her toward the small couch on the far wall of her office. They sat down together, Amya's hands wrapping around Grace's clenched fists. "You're going to have to do something about it."

"What can I do? She's currently my supervisor. I can't fault her. I'm working a critical missing. I'm barely over twenty-four hours into it, and I have shit for leads. I really can't blame her for making me stay and work."

"How late will you be here?"

Grace's eyes teared up again, the salty drops stinging the backs of her eyes. "I don't know."

"This is the fourth week in a row you've had to cancel. Those kids want you there. They need you there. Not me or Crystal. It's you who they connect with. You're the one who started this program."

"I know. I know." Grace pressed her thumb and forefinger to

the bridge of her nose. "I can't win this one."

"You have to figure out something because I'm not always going to be able to cover for you."

Turning her gaze to Amya's crystalline eyes, Grace swallowed. Amya was right. At some point the program would fail if she didn't show up for it. They'd lose funding. They'd lost trust with Hamilton High School and the principal. She wouldn't be able to fulfill her commitments and those kids would be the ones to lose out. Sure, she'd miss it, but this program literally saved their lives.

"I'm well aware. But I can't deal with that right now, Amya. I've got a missing baby, a boss with a vendetta, and a case to solve."

"You also have a family."

Grace stilled, staring directly into Amya's eyes. She couldn't read her, couldn't see if she was angry, annoyed, lost, sympathetic. "What do you mean?"

"Kit counts on you to be there, to pick her up after school. You told her you'd take her down to the grocery store today to fill out paperwork since you didn't yesterday."

"Damn it." She'd completely forgotten.

Amya drew in a deep breath. "For kids like Kit it matters if you show up."

"I know. I took the same damn classes you did."

"Well, then think about it. We made a commitment to her, and we need to honor that."

"I hate when you talk to me like I'm two."

"I'm not... Listen, Grace, I don't want to go to the school every week. I might as well run the program if that's how it's going to be, and I don't want it. It's not in my talent wheel. You're the one who connects with those kids. They see me, and they see danger. I'm far too close to a social worker for them."

"You've earned their respect."

"Respect, yes. Trust, no. Trust is what *you* have."

"What do you want me to do?"

"I want you to consider Alonzo's offer."

"To transfer to IAB? Fuck that. Absolutely not."

"Grace...you know what? Never mind. I need to get going to the school. We can talk about this some other time." Amya stood up from the couch, now clearly annoyed and angry.

Grace didn't want to leave it on that note, but she wasn't sure how else to change the conversation, to repair it. Standing herself, she gripped Amya's fingers and pulled her forward for a gentle kiss. "I'm so sorry."

"Tell that to the kids you're walking out on."

"Don't do this," Grace fired back.

"Do I have a choice?"

"Amya—"

"Come on, out. I've got to figure out what we're talking about today."

Grace sighed. "Taxes."

"You're kidding me." Amya's eyes widened.

"Nope. They need to know these things."

Amya rubbed her temple. "Could you have picked a topic I know more about?"

"You can always talk to them about God."

Amya shot Grace a sharp look. "For a public school program? That'll go over real great."

"I was going to talk about safe sex next week."

"Jesus, Grace."

"What?" Grace's eyes widened. "These are things they need to know!"

"I know, it's just... why can't I do mock interviews or something less touchy as sex and money."

Grace shrugged. "There's a whole lot about sex and money in the Bible. You should be used to it."

Amya's jaw dropped, and Grace smirked.

"What? I do pay attention." Sighing, Grace pressed her lips gently to Amya's. "Thanks. I don't know what I'd do without you."

"Go to the school is what you'd do."

"I wish. I'll see you at home tonight."

"Hmm...try not to wake me when you come in this time."

"I'll try." Their lips brushed again, and Grace left Amya's office with a wave to Khloe.

She was definitely calmer than when she'd first walked in, but the sense of unease and doom hadn't left the center of her chest. Amya's suggestion was off the table, but she would have to figure out how to deal with Paige sooner rather than later.

It was getting to be too much for the family, which had been Amya's real point in her suggestion. IAB? Grace couldn't imagine it. She'd never work in Internal Affairs.

The family was closed lipped. Grace had managed to get the

sister on the phone, but she had no information that was useful and half the time she'd spent blubbering. Hanging up, Grace wrote down all the notes she needed to file in the report and moved on to the next call. Maybe she could finish enough of them that she could leave the office at a reasonable hour the next day instead of pulling a ten or twelve hour shift.

She texted Abrams, who promptly told her to go home and stop working. Grace glanced at the clock, realizing it was nearing ten at night, and she'd have to stop calling family members to talk to them. Typing up all her notes, she emailed them to Abrams so he would have record.

The cup that slid in front of her surprised her. Paige sat on the corner of her desk, a smile on her lips as she stared down at it. "Thought you could use a pick-me-up."

"Uh...thanks." Grace took the orange juice and sipped at it. Finally looking around the room, she realized she and Paige were the only ones left, which had been something she'd sought to avoid as much as she possibly could. "Didn't think you'd still be here."

Paige cocked her head. "Figured I could stay to help you out a bit."

"I don't need help, Paige. Abrams has been quite helpful already."

"I'm sure he has, but he's never worked Missing Persons before."

Grace curled her toes in her boots. "True. Still, we seem to be working well together."

Paige gave a small hum as she pointed at the computer. "What have you found out so far?"

"Not a whole lot. No one has seen the baby in over a week. Felicia, it seems, didn't actually interact much with her family."

"Who did she talk to then?"

"I haven't quite figured that one out. She's got a lot of incoming and outgoing calls, and a bunch of text messages. I've started the process to get records of who the numbers are registered to, but that takes some time and we just hit a weekend."

Paige nodded. "I can help you with that paperwork."

"It's already filed."

"Oh." Disappointment echoed through Paige's tone. "What else do you have?"

"Baby daddy, or Jonas Erikson is actually an ex-husband. Their divorce was finalized right around the time of conception."

"No shit."

"Yeah, but he wanted a paternity test. We're obliging him since Felicia never got the chance to get one done."

"I saw the request for that." Paige reached down, her hand covering Grace's arm.

A shiver ran through Grace at the touch. Amya loved to touch her there, to hold on to her arm, to loop their arms together as they walked some place, and she would rest her head on Grace's shoulder. She moved her gaze, following the line of Paige's arm to her shoulder to her lips to her eyes. The desire in Paige was unmistakable, but she'd yet to do anything so forward as to give Grace reason to file a complaint. Ever since the last time Grace had talked to her about it, Paige had been far more careful in her attempts to woo.

Grace wanted to move away, but there was very little excuse for her to get up and leave or to catch someone else's attention since there was no one else there. Her heart rate sped up, and she tried to find a way out of the conversation, a way to get away from Paige and back home to Amya. Never before had she been so uncomfortable in a job she'd had. Any time someone had tried something and she'd told them to back off, they had respected her. Paige just did not give up.

"What time will you be in tomorrow?" Paige asked.

Grace had hoped to avoid that one, because she'd really wanted to sleep in and arrive later, but since Paige was asking and she had to put an actual time to it, she knew it was going to be morning. "Seven or eight."

"Need a hand?"

"I think I've got it covered. Abrams will be joining." It was a lie. At least, she wasn't sure if it was a lie or not. They'd talked about meeting up to work on the case since it was so fresh, but they hadn't set a time or a place. But any buffer between her and Paige would be welcome.

"That's good. Do be careful with him, though. He tends to be nice upfront, but like I told you before, get on his bad side, and he'll stab you in the back."

Grace's chest tightened from the stress. She couldn't take too much more of this. Maybe Amya was right and a transfer to IAB was the only solution. Alonzo had pretty much guaranteed her a job there if she wanted, but Grace knew how these things worked. There wasn't always a job available to give.

"I think we need to do some more media releases."

"They've gone wild with it already." Paige's hand on Grace's arm tightened. "Are you sure?"

"Yes. The more chitchat we can get around Andrew the better, I think. What do we have to lose?"

"Setting off the kidnapper to the point that the kid is murdered isn't a concern of yours?"

Grace sighed. "They have to know we're looking for him. It's already been in the media, and an Amber Alert. They can't be stupid."

"Babies are easy to hide, Grace. They're small."

"They're noisy."

"They can easily be hidden under a guise of another gender, and they all look alike."

"They don't all look alike, Paige. That's a stupid assumption to make."

Paige turned her hand so she was gripping Grace's elbow and tugging the rolling chair closer. Grace tried to catch the corner of her desk with her foot to stop the chair, but she missed and instead rammed her knee into the corner of it. Cringing, she jerked her hands down to grab her injured knee.

"Jesus, Grace."

"I'm fine. I do it all the time."

Paige rolled her eyes. "Let me look."

"No, it's fine." The words came out rushed, but she was defensive. "I need to work on the case, anyway."

"Fine. Talk to me about your interviews."

Drawing in a deep breath, Grace licked her lips. "Felicia's mom seems the most concerned. Jonas seemed slightly concerned for Felicia but not for the baby."

"He might still be separating himself in case the kid isn't his."

"There's no reason to think he's not. No one has said Felicia has been with anyone except Jonas in the last few years."

"How long were they married?"

"Two years."

"Were they babies when they got married? Damn."

"Eighteen," Grace answered.

"All right. This baby—who would want him?"

"Anyone who has wanted a baby and couldn't have one, someone who wants the attention that comes with new parenthood. It's easy to fake being pregnant. It's not easy to fake when there is no baby at the end of a pregnancy."

Paige nodded. "Are there any records of anyone faking a pregnancy in our county? For whatever purposes?"

"What kind of records?" Grace furrowed her brow. "It's not like we keep track of all the lies criminals tell. That'd be a headache in and of itself."

Paige laughed, the trill of her voice echoing the room. "That's funny. No, if any of it did enter into the criminal sphere, like trying to adopt out the baby and then suddenly there being no baby. Or even just scour social media to see if someone has lied about it in the past."

"I mean, yes, that could help, but the research for that is immeasurable. It helps to have someone to focus on if we're going to do that."

Raising an eyebrow, Paige leaned down close to Grace, their face's only inches apart. "That's why you're the detective, Grace. Get too investigating."

"You want me to look at random social media posts about fake pregnancies? How far back should I go, to the dawn of the ages?"

"You make that call." Paige stood up from the desk. "But I'd like a report on it in the morning."

"Paige, this is ridiculous. I can't possibly do that amount of research in that short period of time."

Shooting a look over her shoulder, Paige smiled. "I have faith in you, Grace. You always get your work done on time and do it well to boot."

Paige slipped into her office, leaving the door open. Grace stared at her exit open mouthed until she turned back to her computer. Paige was chasing phantoms. Grace could focus on the family, but since Felicia didn't seem to have a close relationship with most of her family, she wasn't quite sure which one to begin with.

Scratching the back of her head, she glanced at the clock on the computer screen. She would not stay past eleven-thirty. Paige could go fuck a duck for all Grace cared. She was not going to work into tomorrow just to sleep for a few hours while on a wild goose chase. She needed her wits about her in order to properly do the investigation.

An hour. That was it. That was all the time she'd give to this stupid idea of Paige's. It took Grace the full hour to find out that Jonas' sister had been pregnant roughly around the same time as Felicia, but she'd announced her miscarriage two short days after she'd announced her pregnancy. That had been a dead end. She'd put it on her list of information that would be helpful to know, but unless they found baby Andrew at her house, she was reluctant to bring up bad memories and a sensitive topic.

Grace's head hurt. Paige had left fifteen minutes before, a soft caress to Grace's shoulders as she'd walked by, a wave at the door, and a wink as she stepped through it. Grace's stomach churned. Anger pooled within her, and after spending ten minutes glaring at her computer screen, she gave up.

Turning everything off, Grace grabbed her stuff and stalked out of the room. Once she was in her cruiser, she closed her eyes. She had no idea what to do. She could not keep working like this. She was going to mess up at some point from her exhaustion and her frustration, and it could be detrimental to a case, which she absolutely could not allow. She especially couldn't do that for baby Andrew's case. She had to find him.

Perhaps that was what she would do. Focus on Andrew and nothing else, get the case done, and then she'd deal with Paige. Dragging in a breath of fresh air and some relief, Grace put her cruiser in reverse and drove home. When she got to the house, every light was out except the front porch light. Amya's SUV was parked in the double driveway when Grace pulled up next to it.

Getting out of her car, she quietly moved into the house, dropping her keys and wallet and bag next to the front door. Izzy rustled from the couch, lifting her head to look over at Grace and whine. The cat lay curled up on the top of the couch arm, completely asleep. Even the animals were used to her coming home so late—which wasn't a good thing.

She settled on the far end of the couch and pulled off her shoes. Grace needed to figure out a way to make more time for the family. Amya was right. At the end of the day, they only had a couple short months left with Peter home if he really was going back for the spring semester, and only half a year with Kit before she graduated. And Kit was bound and determined to get out of the house as soon as she turned eighteen or as soon as she graduated. Grace was hoping it was the latter. There was no reason for her to leave at eighteen if she had a roof over her head and food to eat.

Grace waited until she got to their bedroom before she started stripping her clothes. She'd started that once in the hall and ran into Peter in the middle of the night and had never done it again. She was not used to having so many people in her house, but oddly, it felt good. Pulling on a loose pair of basketball shorts and a t-shirt, Grace slid onto the bed and under the covers.

Amya popped her head up, turning to look at Grace. Freezing, Grace waited to see if she was fully awake or still mostly asleep.

Amya narrowed her gaze and muttered, "What time is it?"

"About midnight."

"Jesus, Grace."

"I know," Grace whispered. "Go back to bed."

Amya sighed. "Come here."

Amya gripped Grace's hand and pulled her close to her back so Grace spooned her. Obliging, Grace pressed her front against Amya, wrapping her arm over her side so she could cup Amya's breast, her nose pressed into Amya's neck. She smelled so good.

"Grace?"

"Hmm."

"I want you home when I go to bed tomorrow."

"I'll try my best."

"No, Grace. I want you to hear me. Be home tomorrow when I go to bed."

"Okay." Grace closed her eyes, knowing she wouldn't have too much of a say about it, but she was planning on trying her damnedest to make that happen. "I love you, Amya."

"Love you, too, Grace."

"Night."

Amya's deep and even breathing told Grace she was already fast asleep again. It took Grace at least another hour before she was able to quiet her mind and fall asleep with Amya by her side.

TURDUCKEN

AMYA'S HEAD was full of to-do lists. Everyone was working on Thanksgiving. Since Kit got her final work schedule for the week when they filled out paperwork, Amya had balked. She'd known they needed to find another day to celebrate Thanksgiving, but the only day was Monday, which meant they had a whole meal to plan and cook in a few days. Luckily it was just the four of them and no one else, but still, it was rough.

Letting out a breath, Amya relaxed on the couch in the empty house. She'd just gotten back from the grocery store after dropping Kit off for her first official shift. Peter was at work, and Grace was...well, who knew where Grace was. It was Sunday afternoon, and while Amya had gone to church that morning, no one else had, and by the time she'd gotten back, Grace had been gone without a word as to when she'd return.

It was wearing on her. It was wearing on *them*. The amount of time they spent together was so small that Amya worried for their relationship and what the future might hold. Not only because Grace was working just about every waking hour there was but also because Paige was the one making her work.

And it was Paige who Amya had issues with. Ever since Grace had gotten her new partner two years before, Amya had been worried. Something about the way Paige treated Grace set Amya on edge every time she saw their interactions or Grace talked about her. It had taken Amya at least a year to fully realize just how jealous she was, and it wasn't because she thought Grace would do anything. No, she didn't trust Paige.

Since Paige had gotten the temporary promotion, it had made her home life a living hell. She saw Grace more at work than she did at home, and Kit and Peter felt the change too. Amya had tried to bring it up on multiple occasions but only one time did Grace truly admit what was happening, and that had been last winter. Since then, she'd done a spectacular job at avoiding. It was something Grace was fluent in—avoiding any strong emotions or big decisions as long as she possibly could.

Sighing, Amya stared out the front window of their house. It had begun lightly snowing about an hour before, and it was supposed to pick up through the night until the morning when they'd end up with at least three or four inches. They'd have to get up early to shovel so Grace and Kit weren't late, which they had been more often than not lately. Kit needed the structure and the adult to tell her to show up on time, especially where it concerned work if she wanted to keep the job.

Picking up her phone, Amya scrolled through her contacts. She could call one of her sisters, Beth or Morgan or even Carrie. She had seven of them to choose from, but the only one she trusted to actually talk to and not share with anyone else was Morgan. She understand confidentiality and all the nuances that came with it. But Morgan was touchy whenever it came to cheating, and Amya was not going to go near that with a ten foot pole.

She needed someone to talk to, someone to vent to. She'd sorely neglected most of her friendships since Kit and Peter had come to live with them, almost right at the same time too. She'd had to get used to parenting a seventeen-year-old and a twenty-one-year-old in one go of it. They'd instantly become a family of four. Well, they'd instantly become a family. Grace cared and loved her, but they were never going to make anything official, that much was clear.

Her thumb hovered over Crystal's name in her contact list. Crystal always had great insight into Grace. They'd been friends almost as long as they'd been alive at this point, and Crystal could say things to Grace in a way that would make her understand just how dire the need was. And Grace needed to take off her blindfold and face facts. Paige had a crush on Grace, and she was willing to push boundaries to get what she wanted no matter what Grace said or did, and that scared Amya.

Pressing the phone to her ear, Amya listened as it rang and rang and rang. She was just about to give up with Crystal answered with a worried tone. "Amya, what's wrong?"

"Nothing." Her voice shook as she answered, and she knew Crystal was observant enough to hear through it.

"Amya, you don't usually just call for chit chat. What's going on?"

"You got time?"

"To talk or to come over?"

"Both?"

"Yeah. I'll be right there." Crystal hung up.

Amya rubbed the back of her neck, trying to ease the tension that seemed to take up permanent residence at the base of her skull. It ached. She wouldn't have much longer to wait, Crystal only lived a short five minute drive, something Amya was pretty sure Grace planned when she'd bought the house all those years ago.

The knock on the door was sharp, but Crystal didn't hesitate as she walked right in. Her gaze softened as she caught sight of Amya on the couch. "What happened? What'd she do? I'll beat her up for you."

Amya snorted. "It's not that."

Crystal ditched her shoes and jacket and folded herself in half on the couch with Amya.

"I hope I didn't catch you at a bad time."

"You didn't. Quit beating around the bush. What's going on?"

Amya opened her hands to the house and moved it around. "It's Sunday."

"Okay?" Crystal cocked her head to the side as she looked around. "So it's Sunday."

"No one is home. I mean, I expect Peter and Kit to work. They have entry level jobs. They work when they're told, but Grace? Detectives are only scheduled Monday through Friday unless they're on call. She's been 'on call' every weekend for months."

"I noticed that, too." Crystal looked down at her hands. "She keeps saying Paige is making her stay late."

"See! At least you get that out of her. I don't even get that. I just get silence or that she has to work and has no other option."

"I'm not sure she does," Crystal muttered.

"What do you mean?"

"If she causes too much of a fuss, it'll affect her job."

"She can't keep working hours like this. No one can, but

especially in a job where it takes such a mental toll on us. She can't keep working this way."

"I think we all know that." Crystal reached across and pressed a hand to Amya's thigh. "Are you mad she working or are you mad she's working and Paige is there?"

That was it. Leave it to Crystal to ask the hard question she didn't want to ask herself. No matter what Amya did, no matter how much time had passed, she was still jealous. She could stuff that emotion away inside her as much as she wanted, but it was still there at the center of it all. She could mask it with concern for Grace and Grace's well-being, but in the end, it was all because she was completely uncomfortable with Paige. She had no trust in Paige or in Grace when she was with Paige.

"That's what I thought," Crystal added. She pushed a hand up into her hair and rested her elbow on the back of the couch as she faced down Amya. "Remember when you were so flipped out by Paige and Grace that you literally abandoned ship and came to my house for the night?"

"Yeah."

"I talked to Grace about that. Not about anything you said, but about what she felt on it. She loves you, Amya. I have never seen her be so entranced by someone before. She sucks at showing it—trust me, she is not the friend you go to have these emotional conversations or talk about love—but she does love you. You're her world, and if you were to vanish from it, I'm pretty sure she would be completely lost without you."

Amya clenched her jaw, not sure what to say. Grace would never say something like that. She was getting better about sharing those things, but still it was slow to work them out of her. Sometimes Amya just needed the reminder.

"What do I do?" she asked.

Crystal sighed. "I don't know. When Grace gets backed into a corner, she shuts down and shuts the world out. She's such a people pleaser and tries to make everyone happy, and in this situation, she can't do that. She's going to have to figure out what's important to her."

"I'm not sure how much longer I can wait for her to do that."

"Just hold on. I promise you, she'll make the right decision when the time comes."

They lapsed into a silence. Amya had forgotten how helpful Crystal was and how in tune she was with Grace, even though they hadn't seen each other in weeks if not longer. Amya shifted and put her head on Crystal's shoulder. "Thanks for coming over."

"Any time. You're like my sister, you know that, right?"

Amya groaned. "I have too many sisters for that to always be a good statement, but I appreciate the sentiment."

Crystal chuckled. "So...what's for dinner?"

Laughing, Amya pushed herself up from the couch and moved toward the kitchen. "Food. Food is what's for dinner."

She rummaged around for some leftovers and made them each a plate. As they sat down again, Amya asked the one question that had been burning in the back of her mind. "What do you think it'll take for Grace to make a decision?"

"She's going to have to lose something she really loves. And I don't think it'll be you, Amya. Trust me on that. But she's going to be faced with her love for what the job gives her and Paige, and she's going to make a pretty swift decision after that. Grace doesn't balk once a decision is made."

Amya knew that. From them dating to her moving in, Grace had hedged at every opportunity, but as soon as the decision was made, that was it, and Grace was all in. She was loyal to the core, too, which was probably why she was stretched so thin. Crystal spent the next few hours with her until it was time for Amya to go get Kit from her first day at work. As they parted ways, Crystal gave Amya a big hug and whispered, "Hang in there." Amya only hoped she had the patience to withstand the storm.

Grace had managed to get home that night just before seven, which was perfect because dinner was planned for seven. She'd done enough work on Sunday that when Monday of Thanksgiving week rolled around she'd snuck out when Paige wasn't looking and headed home with her face tilted down. They could all have dinner together, and she could get up early in the morning and go back to work.

Abrams hadn't managed to find Jonas for an interview with him that day, and they were going on a hunt to find him in the morning. They needed to have a serious in depth conversation with him. Grace got out of the cruiser and headed inside, welcomed by the scent of Thanksgiving dinner all laid out on the table before her.

Amya was in the kitchen, bent over something. Kit and Peter were setting the table, and the dogs were laying on the couch, watching to see what was happening. Grace slipped into the bedroom and changed out of her suit and into something far more comfortable. Originally she'd wanted to help Amya cook, but after figuring out that it wasn't going to likely happen, she'd given up that idea and hadn't even suggested it to Amya.

Her phone buzzed on the dresser as she was walking toward the door to the bedroom. She cringed when she saw Paige's name and almost ignored the text, but Abrams had also texted. She opened it up and read it. He wanted an update on the subpoena to get the names from Felicia's phone records.

Grace texted back her response that they should have the records in the next couple of days if they managed to do it before the holiday. Then she made the mistake of checking Paige's text, which was a shot in the dark about why Grace had left the office early and some annoyance as to when she'd finish up all her work. She had half a mind to completely ignore her.

Texting back that she'd get to it in the morning, Grace pocketed her phone and walked into the hallway. Kit was talking about work and a cute girl that also started with her and sat through orientation together. They'd even gotten lunch together.

Grace listened in before stepping into the room because she knew as soon as they knew she was there, the conversations like that would stop. Kit had been clamming up around her a lot lately, and Grace had no one but herself to blame. Her phone buzzed again. Cursing, Grace picked it up. This time it was a phone call.

"What's up?"

"I needed those reports tonight."

Grace shot Amya an annoyed look. "Tomorrow."

"No. Tonight, Halling."

"Then write me up for insubordination, Paige. I'm spending the evening with my family." Grace hung up and shoved the phone back in her pocket. She knew she'd been loud, but when she glanced up, she was surprised to find all of them staring at her with mouths agape. "What?"

"Did you really just talk to Paige like that?" Amya asked.

"You've wanted me to do that for months, don't start now."

Amya put both her hands up in the air in defense. "I wasn't. Would you grab the turducken?"

"The what?" Grace looked disgusted as she stared at the counter top with what looked like a turkey sitting on it, but if what she'd just heard from Amya's mouth was actually what was on the counter, she was not going to enjoy dinner.

"The turducken."

"Why the hell would you buy that?"

Amya looked flustered. "I told you I was buying it."

"No, you didn't."

"Yes, I did. I even texted it to you."

Grace narrowed her gaze. "I think I would remember if you said you were buying that thing."

"I thought we would try something new this year."

"A turducken?" Grace was still unimpressed and quite shocked that this was the route Amya decided to go. "You could just pick a different pie? Like, I don't know, pecan or something."

"I have pecan pie." Amya pointed to a pie sitting on the corner of the counter.

Grace balked. She hated pecan pie, and she hated duck. She'd have to just eat around the nastiness in the center of the turkey. "Fine."

Moving to the counter, Grace went to grab the turducken and her phone buzzed in her pocket again. Ignoring it, she took the food to the table and sat down. When her phone didn't stop ringing, she finally rolled her eyes at Amya, showed her the phone and stepped out of the room.

Answering with a gruff, "What?" Grace sat on the edge of the bed.

"You don't hang up on me, Detective."

"I'll have the reports to you in the morning, Paige. I'm working all week and not taking a day off, again. I need time with my family."

"We need to find Andrew."

Grace ground her molars. "I'm fully aware of that. Abrams and I will be interviewing Jonas tomorrow morning, and we'll go from there. We're working on the phone records, but we can't do much until we get the order signed by the judge. I have given you all these updates already, Paige."

"You better be in on time tomorrow."

"Plan on it."

Sighing, Grace hung up and stalked back out to the dining room. They had all waited for her. As soon as she sat next to Amya, they all held hands. Grace shot Kit a look to see how she was feeling about the praying thing. They'd had one talk about it months before, but they only ever did it when they all sat down together for a meal, which had become increasingly rare.

Peter spoke first. "Gracious God, bless this food we are about to eat, the family we have made, the friends we will meet, and may our love for each other be conveyed. Amen."

Amya muttered her "Amen" and they all dug in. They had been seated and eating for only twenty minutes when Grace's phone buzzed again. She was going to kill whoever called her. She didn't even want to look and see who it was because then she might have to answer.

When her phone rang again, this time catching Amya's attention, Grace issued her an apology and glanced at the name. She sighed. It was Paige. Again. There couldn't possibly be something else that she was calling for that needed to be addressed right that minute.

"Who is it?" Kit asked, catching on to what Grace was trying to hide.

"Work," she muttered. "I'll just be a minute."

Once more, Grace traipsed to her bedroom and answered the call.

"What is it, Paige?"

"Did you try the sister?"

"Which sister?" Great, now she sounded like Amya. "We talked to Jonas' sister and to Felicia's sister. I really think we need to put out another media blast, and you need to approve it. The longer we wait, the worse it'll be."

"I'll consider it."

Grace rolled her eyes. Paige was going to make her grovel for everything. That's what she had done every moment of this case, and it only pushed Grace further behind than she already was. "Consider this, Paige, if you don't do this, you are the one who is preventing us from finding Andrew, not my lack of attention to detail or my inability to work twenty-four-seven."

"Grace." Paige's tone was soft and gentle.

She didn't want to hear it though. It was the round and round they seemed to always go lately. "I will interview Jonas in the morning with Abrams. After that, I will double check on the subpoena for the phone records."

"That's all I wanted to know," Paige answered.

Grace had already told her that a dozen times, so why Paige kept on calling was beyond her, except with the specific intent to interrupt the family dinner Paige knew they were having. Two minutes after the phone call ended, Grace got an email. Abrams was obviously still working tonight.

Not even bothering to read the email, Grace left her phone on the dresser and went back out into the main area of the house. She wanted a nice family dinner, a Thanksgiving even if it was with turducken, because she desperately needed to reconnect with her family. Felicia's body wasn't going anywhere, and they weren't going to make a breakthrough in the next twelve hours. If they did, Abrams knew how to get hold of her. This was her boundary line, and she was drawing it. Bending to kiss the top of Amya's head, Grace sat down at the table and found her plate still half full. Everyone else was working on dessert.

"Everything okay?" Amya asked.

Grace grunted. "It's nothing. I'm here now."

She spent the next few hours focusing as best as she could on Kit and Peter, giving them the attention she had neglected to give them in the past few months. It almost felt normal, except for the looming struggle in the back of Grace's mind. She just had to keep telling herself, one foot down and then the other. She could rebuild a work life that she enjoyed. All she had to do was set boundaries.

Hours later, with a full belly, Grace curled up against Amya in their bed, naked and satiated. She pressed a gentle kiss to Amya's temple and closed her eyes, ready to sleep for hours and get a good full nights rest. Sighing, she settled in for the night, but Amya would not stop wiggling against her. Growling, Grace tugged Amya in tight.

"Stop moving."

"Can't get comfortable."

Scoffing, Grace moved to lay on her back, her arm thrown over her eyes. She'd wanted a good evening, and she'd been the one to ruin it. She just had to answer the text and the phone call. At least she was putting down some boundaries. It was a start.

"You didn't eat a lot of dinner," Amya murmured.

"I don't like duck." Grace turned to look at Amya in the dim light.

"Since when?"

"Since I was nine."

Amya furrowed her brow. "Why?"

"We ate a lot of it for an entire year when we had no money. I've sworn on my mother's grave I will never eat another duck in my life."

"Oh." Amya's cheeks tinged red.

Grace turned back onto her side, skimming a hand over Amya's curves. "I thought I'd told you that."

"You don't ever talk about your mom, Grace."

Swallowing the lump in her throat, Grace nodded. "You're right. It's still hard."

"What was she like?"

Moving her gaze up to Amya's eyes, Grace let out a sigh. "She wasn't the most loving mother out there, but she had her fair share of shit to deal with, so I don't blame her."

"She looked exactly like you."

"Yeah. I prefer that over the alternative." Grace pecked Amya's lips. "As much as I'd love to tell you about my mother, I'd really like some sleep. Especially since I haven't been getting much lately."

"Okay." Amya didn't look okay though.

Grace wanted to pry, wanted to push a little and get some kind of response, but she was way too tired, and five in the morning was going to roll around faster than she could imagine. "Will you be able to take Kit to school tomorrow?"

"Yeah, I can do that."

"Good. I need to find a break in this case." Grace yawned, her eyes watering. "I want to get in early."

"That's a first."

"What?"

"I said that's a first. You haven't wanted to go in to work early since last March."

Grace paused. "You're right. I'm kind of enjoying working with Homicide on this one. It's fun to see how other departments work, and how other detectives think."

"Who are you working with?"

"Huh? Oh, Link Abrams. I think he said he knew you." Grace yawned again. "I'm sorry, Amya. I've really got to sleep."

"Go to bed, Grace. I'll be right here when you wake up."

Grace flipped onto her other side, and Amya curled around her back. She pulled a pillow to her chest and closed her eyes. She was fast asleep in seconds.

FALSE HOPES

JONAS WAS nervous. His brown hair curled against his face and at the line of his neck, either because he didn't wash his hair all that often or he used enough product to make him look like Orlando Bloom in *Pirates of the Caribbean*. Either way, he was definitely younger and not as cute.

Abrams sat across from him, Grace at the other end of the table so they in a way had him cornered. Jonas didn't even look up, his eyes glued to the table top as if there was something utterly fascinating happening with the faux wood grain. Grace tapped her nails against the top of the table to get his attention.

"You're not in trouble, Jonas, but we do need to talk about Felicia and Andrew."

His lips pulled tight. Grace shot a look to Abrams to see if he'd picked up on that, which he apparently did. Grace focused back on Jonas.

"Tell us about how you and Felicia met."

"In high school," he muttered, his voice so quiet Grace had to strain to hear him.

They were in an interview room in the back of Homicide, Grace opting to do it there instead of in Missing Persons, where Paige would be able to linger and watch. She wanted the freedom to interview without her boss hanging over her shoulder and picking apart everything in the moment.

"How old were you?"

"Fifteen."

"So you've known her a long time then. It must be hard to hear about what happened to her."

Jonas' gaze flickered up to Grace then back down to the table. "I guess."

"You guess? You were married to her."

Jonas snorted. "So we could have sex."

"Oh?" Grace left the question open ended, hoping Jonas would start talking a bit more if she wasn't as particular in guiding the interview. She'd still manage to get around to the questions she wanted to ask, but with him being so resistant, she didn't want to push too hard too fast.

The pause put tension in the air. One quick glance at Abrams and Grace knew she was taking the lead on this interview. Her case was more pressing, but the likelihood that the killer and the kidnapper were one in the same was high.

"That's why we were only married for a couple years. We weren't ready for marriage. We just wanted to have sex, and Felicia wouldn't have sex without being married first."

Grace leaned back in her chair, relaxing her stance to try and encourage Jonas to continue talking. "If that was really why you two got married, then why do you think Andrew isn't yours?"

Jonas shot Grace a glare. "I don't know if he's mine or not. He probably is. But I want her to prove it."

"Prove what?"

"That she didn't cheat!" Jonas' eyes widened, the vehemence in his tone strong.

Grace held the silence, waiting to see if he'd add anything to his comment or if he'd take it back and try to reword what he'd said. Jonas' entire body was tense, and this was the first time he had looked her full on since they'd picked him up at work that morning. When he didn't continue, Grace held his gaze. "Why would she need to prove that?"

"Look, she's the one who tossed me out. Then she comes groveling back three months after the divorce is final, saying she's pregnant and it's mine. What am I supposed to think?"

"I don't know, Jonas. What did you think?"

"That I wasn't ready to be a dad. That I didn't want a kid. That there was no way in hell she'd get rid of it like I told her to."

"So what now? Three weeks ago she gave birth, where does that leave you?"

"I don't know." Jonas crumbled. He brought his hands up to his face and hid himself.

Grace let him have the moment. Abrams scooted his notebook over so Grace could see what he'd written on it. One word lit up the white paper. *Andrew.*

She was getting there, but she had to work up to it, gain Jonas' trust before she could really start asking questions about where Andrew was. Grace nodded at Abrams then focused all her attention on Jonas. She didn't want to have to bring Jonas in again. He was either their suspect or he wasn't, but Grace was determined to figure that out today.

"Jonas, I need to ask you where you were a week ago, when Felicia was murdered and Andrew was taken. What were you doing?"

Jonas didn't move, his gaze once again glued to the table top as he sat stiffly in the chair. Grace waited for an answer, feeling Abrams calm and patience next to her. It was so different from when she interviewed with Paige. There was a gentleness to Abrams that Paige did not possess.

"I was out with friends."

"Which friends?"

Jonas glanced at Grace. "I don't want to tell you."

"Why?"

"Because we were drunk and getting high."

"All right." Grace paused for a moment before continuing. "You don't have to tell me if you want, but if I can't verify where you were and what you were doing, then you are number one on my suspect list, and that means a whole lot more prying into your life."

Jonas paled. "Fine. I was with Bryan and Nathan. We've known each other since elementary school."

"I'm going to need their phone numbers." Grace slide her notebook and a pen across to Jonas. He reluctantly pulled out his phone and wrote it down.

Every bit of information he gave, convinced Grace more and more that he had nothing to do with Felicia's murder and Andrew's disappearance. He just didn't really have it in him from what she could tell. The kid was lost. He'd made bad mistakes, but unless he'd taken Andrew to kill him so he really wasn't a dad with that responsibility, then she doubted he had anything to do with the situation. And there'd be no reason to take the baby away and kill him out of the house.

Grace shifted the notebook to Abrams. "Do you know where Andrew is?"

Jonas shook his head slowly.

"Do you know anyone who might have wanted to take him?"

Again, Jonas' head moved side to side as his answer.

Grace pressed her lips tightly together. "Who were Felicia's friends?"

"Don't know. We haven't talked much in the last year."

"Who were they before this past year?"

"Harmony Crestwater. Olivia Philemon. Those were the only two I know that she talked to regularly."

One glance told Grace Abrams had taken down the names. "Okay, thanks. That is actually very helpful. We're going to have a uniformed officer take you home, and if you give him permission, he's going to look around your apartment real quick, just to make sure Andrew isn't there."

"Okay," Jonas mumbled.

"Good." Grace nodded to Abrams, who stood up and walked to the door. As soon as Jonas was gone and on his way, they sat back down in the interview room across from each other. Grace looked into Abrams' eyes and sighed. "Well, I don't think he did it."

"Me either. Not even sure he knows anything."

Grace shrugged. "It'll be interesting to see what happens since if the paternity test comes back that he is the father, when we find Andrew, Jonas will end up with custody."

"That's a problem for another day."

"True." Grace raised her eyebrows at him. "Who are we going to talk to next?"

"I think we should talk to the rest of his family before he can get hold of them and warn them we're coming."

"Parents first, sister second?"

"Yup."

Grace smiled as she gathered her notebook. "You driving?"

"Only if you want me too."

"Sure."

The house where Jonas grew up was one Grace knew, and that was not a good thing. When Abrams pulled up outside the house, she sighed and tried to remember if the names of Jonas' parents connected with the reason she'd been called out to that house, but for the life of her, she couldn't remember.

"I've been here before," Grace muttered.

"Really?"

She turned to Abrams. "Few years ago when I was still in uniform."

"For the Eriksons?"

"Can't remember."

Abrams raised his eyebrow. "It's always unsettling to go back to the house you've been called to previously. Even if it is under entirely different circumstances."

"It is." Grace heaved another breath before pushing the door to the cruiser open. "I'll take the dad if you want to take the mom."

Abrams chuckled. "Taking the easy road, I see."

She shrugged. "Consider it even for me doing most of the interview this morning."

"Fair."

Grace got to the front door first. Making a fist, she pounded the side of her hand against it. They'd interviewed the parents briefly during their notification, and the mother had been way too emotional to get much out of her. The father was definitely hiding something.

Jonas' mom answered the door, cracking it open slightly to reveal Grace and Abrams, who stood a few steps back. "Mrs. Erikson, we're here to talk about Felicia. Do you have a minute?"

Grace wasn't going to really give her an option even if she did say no.

"Uh...yes." She looked over her shoulder. "We can talk outside."

"Is your husband home?" Grace held her ground.

"He is."

"I'd like to speak with him." Putting her hand on the door, Grace held it open.

Abrams stepped forward. "I'll speak with you outside, ma'am. I'm Detective Abrams, I'm not sure if you remember from the other day."

"Oh." She stepped out of the doorway. "I'm Theresa."

Abrams gave her a soft smile as he nodded his head toward the two chairs on the porch. As soon as they were settled, Grace stepped through the doorway and into the house. "Mr. Erikson?"

"Yeah?"

"I'm Detective Halling. Do you remember me from the other day?" She followed the sound of his voice and the television into the other room. "Your wife let me in."

He nodded at her but didn't make to move from his lazy boy.

"Do you mind if I sit? I had a few more questions about Felicia I was hoping you'd be able to help us out with."

George sighed. "Sure."

"How long have you known Felicia?"

"Since she was in high school. Jonas and she dated for quite a while before they got married."

Grace rested her elbows on her knees as she observed everything about him. He looked like Jonas plus about a hundred pounds easily. They had the same features, soft brown eyes, curly dark brown hair, tall and lanky. And they had the same tells when they were holding back, which Grace planned to use to her advantage.

"It must be six or seven years now."

"When did you find out about Andrew?"

"Not until after she had him and showed up here."

"She showed up?" Grace was definitely intrigued now. Jonas had left this out of his story completely.

George eyed Grace. "With the baby, claiming he's Jonas'."

"And you don't think he is."

Shrugging, George focused on the television. "Don't know."

Grace hated to ask him if he'd care, but she held her tongue, knowing that wouldn't get her the answers she needed.

"How long ago was it that Felicia showed up?"

"Right after she got out of the hospital." George eyed Grace. "Didn't even go home first. Came straight here."

"Why would she come here instead of going to Jonas' apartment?"

George shrugged. "Guess she figured we might do something about it."

"Jonas didn't want the baby?"

"No. I don't either."

Clenching her jaw, Grace kept her mouth shut on that one. They might not have a choice if the baby proved to be Jonas' biologically—although, she could imagine there were lots of other homes where a baby was wanted he could go if that was the decision Jonas made. "What about your wife?"

"What about Theresa?"

"Does she want the baby?"

George rolled his eyes and heaved a sigh. "What woman doesn't want a baby?"

Grace tensed. She didn't, but that was another story. "Has she visited Andrew and Felicia outside of when they showed up here three weeks ago?"

"Four weeks."

Grace narrowed her gaze. He was right, it had been four weeks, and her slip up afforded her something she hadn't expected. As much as George didn't seem interested in Andrew, he knew exactly how old the baby was and how long it had been since he'd seen him. Not saying anything, Grace continued. "Right, four weeks."

"She's been a couple times."

"When?"

"Couple weeks ago, I think. Might have been a day or two before...well, you know."

Felicia's murder making him uncomfortable was also a good sign. Grace filed that bit of information away in the back of her mind. "Do you know what day, exactly?"

"No."

"Okay. Has anyone else visited Felicia?"

"I think Kadence did."

"Your daughter?"

George nodded. "She wanted to see if the baby looked like Jonas."

"All right, do you know when she visited?"

"Nope. You'll have to ask her or Theresa."

"Will do." Grace wrote down some of the small pieces of information in her notebook before relaxing. They were definitely going to have to talk to the sister now, so it was lucky she was already on their list to try and get hold of today.

Grace didn't spend too much longer with George, finding he was not a wealth of information like she had hoped he would be. She handed over her card, told him to call if he thought of something or something came up, and she walked toward the front door.

Abrams was still outside with Theresa, who was bawling into her hands. Grace's eyes widened in surprise, very glad she'd gotten to interview George instead of Theresa. Abrams, however, seemed to be handling it like a champ. He caught Grace's attention and put a hand on Theresa's shoulder. He stood up and walked over.

His voice was hushed when he spoke. "She wanted the baby, was planning on filing for custody."

"We can talk about that in a bit. George had not a whole lot of information. You about done here?"

"Yeah."

"Meet you back at the cruiser." Grace turned on her toes and walked to the street. She slipped into the passenger side of the vehicle, where she could still see Abrams if she needed to assist him with something. She checked her phone, found a few texts from Amya about driving Kit to and from work that week and how they were going to have to divvy it up.

Adding another working person into the household was going to be rough for a while, at least until Kit got her license and they could get her a car. Still, with Kit's history, Grace preferred to be the taxi driver, and she was pretty sure Amya felt the same way.

Abrams got behind the wheel after another ten minutes with Theresa. Grace shot him a curious look, interested in what he had discovered. "So?"

"She wanted the baby, to raise him."

"I assume Felicia told her to fuck off." Grace's words came out harsh, and she realized she hadn't actually cussed in front of Abrams before. The expression on his face told her as much.

Abrams rested in his seat. "Are you a parent, Halling?"

She shrugged, not quite sure how to answer that question.

When Abrams didn't press for an answer, he continued. "I believe that even if Andrew was a surprise, Felicia would not have willingly given up custody. Considering how her apartment was set up, she wanted to raise Andrew, with or without Jonas."

"Agreed." Grace bit the inside of her cheek. She'd really have to watch her mouth with him. He wasn't only a detective like her, he had massive seniority and ranking on her. "Did Theresa say why she wanted custody?"

"According to her, Felicia was into drugs."

"Nothing in her medical records indicate that, and they do drug testing on new mothers."

Abrams raised an eyebrow. "She may have stopped before then."

"Maybe, but I'm not sold."

"She was earning money somehow. There are deposits into her accounts, cash, but nothing in the last month and a half."

"No, she would have been preparing for the baby, and if she was doing anything illegal, then she probably would have wanted to back off on that a bit, especially if she was of sound mind and sober."

"We'll see when the autopsy reports all come back."

"Yeah, sure. Whatever." Grace crossed her arms and stared out the front windshield. "The sister went to visit her a few weeks ago. We going there next?"

"Yes." Abrams put the car in drive.

Kadence was at her apartment, thankfully. Grace entered first, Abrams following. He seemed to do that, and she wondered if it was because as a woman Grace came off less threatening, but she couldn't tell. It also could just be because it was her primary case they were trying to solve for now.

Grace gave Kadence a wan smile. "We had a few follow up questions we wanted to ask you."

"About Felicia? Andrew? Did you find him?"

Shaking her head, Grace looked into Kadence's brown eyes. "When was the last time you saw them?"

"The other week." Kadence pushed her fingers through her hair as she sat on her couch, Grace next to her. "I went to bring a gift for Andrew. Felicia let me hold him. I wasn't there very long, since I had to go to work."

"Did everything seem normal?"

"Yeah. Felicia didn't seem worried or anything."

"Was anyone else there?"

"No." Kadence flicked her gaze too Abrams. "Have you found something?"

"Nothing we can share at this time," Abrams interjected.

Grace reset herself. "We've been trying to connect with some of Felicia's friends, the people she would have talked to last. You two went to high school together, right?"

Kadence nodded. "For a couple years. She and Jonas are...were...in the same class together. I'm a couple years older, so we were only at school together for one year."

"But you were around her because of Jonas." Grace phrased it like a statement, but she really meant it to be a question.

"I guess? I don't know who her friends are. They kind of kept to themselves for the few years they were married and that was it. I didn't pay attention in high school because who cares about their little brother and his girlfriend, you know?"

Grace didn't know, since she didn't have siblings—or at least hadn't grown up with them—but from what she'd seen of Amya's family that was vastly untrue as a generic statement. "Do you know anyone who might have wanted to hurt Felicia or who might have wanted to take Andrew?"

"No. No one. My cousin just had a baby, too. They were so excited to have them grow up together."

"All right. I do have to ask, where were you the night Felicia was murdered?"

Kadence paled, her eyes watering. Grace feared she was going to cry like Theresa had, and she really wished she and Abrams could switch spots. Luckily, Kadence pulled her shit together and wiped her fingers under her cheeks. "I was here, with my boyfriend. I'll give you his name and number. I can't believe...I can't believe anyone would want her dead. She was so sweet."

Grace would have agreed, except she hadn't known Felicia. What they'd found out about her so far was nothing out of the ordinary except the issue with the phone calls, and they really needed to get those records to start putting some pieces together. She'd double-check on that before she left the office for the day.

They finished with Kadence, not finding any other information that they needed. Grace called the boyfriend while Abrams drove back to the station. Sure enough, Kadence and his stories were the same, so she had little doubt that Kadence had much to do with the murder and kidnapping. Grace's stomach growled, and she realized she'd forgotten to eat anything that day. It was nearing the end of her shift, and instead of going home, she had a pile of paperwork she'd have to finish up.

"Do you think Felicia was involved in something no one knew about and got herself into some trouble?" Grace asked.

Abrams shrugged. "Could be, but it's hard to keep secrets like that from everyone."

"True, but we haven't talked to any of her friends yet."

He sighed. "Tomorrow. I'm too tired to go through another interview today."

Chuckling, Grace nodded. "I can get on board with that."

"You hesitated earlier."

"I...what?" Grace turned to him, surprise hanging in her chest. She couldn't follow his train of thought or what he was asking. She hadn't hesitated at all when interviewing George, though he hadn't been present for that. Even with Kadence, Grace had been confident in every question she'd asked. All the questions had been standard. It wasn't an interrogation, so she didn't have to plan or prep for it.

"When I asked if you had kids."

Oh. Grace tightened her hand into a fist and stared out the front windshield. She hated this conversation. People normally never accepted her response and she was always made to feel bad. "What do you mean?"

"You hesitated. Do you want kids?"

"Not really," Grace muttered.

"I can see why you hesitated then."

She let out a whoosh of air from her lungs. "That's not why."

There was no reason for her to open up to him. She didn't know him. She didn't even call him by his first name, but something in his question, in his composure, begged her to share.

"We have a twenty-one-year-old and a seventeen-year-old living with us."

"Foster care?"

"One, officially, now, but not before."

"What do you mean before?"

Straightening her shoulders, Grace risked a glance at him. He seemed sincere in his probing, so she continued. "Peter is twenty-one. I met him on a call, actually, and he kind of stuck around. He was a kid, out of high school but not doing much else with his life, drunk off his ass more times than I can count. We helped him kind of get his life back in order. For a time. He started graduate school last year, but ended up falling off the wagon, so he moved home around Christmas. He's thinking about trying school again in the spring."

"Think he's ready?"

"No." Grace smiled. "But I don't think he'll ever be ready. Addiction is not easy, and he's got an upward hill to climb every day for the rest of his life."

"Seems like you've got the right mindset for him. What about the other one?"

"Kit. My first missing persons case was a pregnant teen who'd run away for an abortion. Kit is her best friend, and got kicked out of her house for being gay—I'm sorry, lesbian, as she would insist I say." Grace rolled her eyes at the last bit, imagining Kit's snarky tone as she corrected Grace's statement.

Abrams laughed at it, too. "So you found her on the street?"

"The mall. The first time. Different places after that. It's been back and forth with her and DCFS, but she's permanently ours now until she's eighteen."

"Think she'll stay after that?"

"Yeah, I think she'll stick around. She likes my dog."

Abrams belted into a full out laugh as he pulled into the station. "Because she likes your dog?"

"It's the small things. She graduates this spring, so if she moves, we're about to have an empty house again, right after it filled up."

"Think you'll do it again?"

"Do what?" Grace undid the buckle on her seatbelt.

Abrams paused. "Foster."

"Oh. I honestly hadn't thought about it. They just needed a home and some stability. We could offer that."

"Halling, there's a lot of kids that need a home and some stability, and a dog too."

"Huh. Hadn't really thought of it like that."

"Give yourself some time with an empty house. Then decide."

"I guess." Getting out of the car, Grace headed inside to finish out her day. Hopefully Paige wouldn't keep her too late this time.

WHO HAS RIGHTS?

"HALLING!" PAIGE shrilly yelled through the unit.

Grace cringed. The day before, when she'd been gone with Abrams, had been the best reprieve she'd had in months. A full eight hours without Paige on her ass, though she'd come back to an angry boss and a mountain of work to unravel.

Getting up from her seat, Grace dragged her feet as she moved into the Paige's office. She'd barely been there five minutes, and she was fifteen minutes late—again. As she got to the door, Paige motioned for her to close it. Worry etched its way into her stomach that she was finally going to be written up for being late all these months. Instead, Paige tossed a notepad at her.

"You need to deal with these grandmas."

"With who?" Grace's mind raced to catch up. She really needed at least one more cup of coffee before she tackled Paige and her weird quirks that morning.

"The grandmas for your case."

"O...kay? What's going on? I just saw Theresa Erikson yesterday and she seemed fine."

"Fine? Grace, she's called in here twice since you left her yesterday and asked for an update on the case. The other one has called three times in the last three days."

"They just want updates on the case?"

"Oh, no. If it was only that simple."

Grace's patience was already running short. She'd noticed that as the months went on with Paige as her boss, her patience for Paige's idiosyncrasies was thin. Not that Grace had much patience to begin with. Everyone on the force knew that. She was the least patient person in the world. Thank God Amya had it in spades.

"If what was simple?"

"They want custody."

"Of Andrew?"

"Of course of Andrew. Who else?"

"I don't know, the body in the morgue."

Paige paled. "I'm pretty sure only Felicia's mom wants that. I'm talking about custody of Andrew."

"We haven't even found him yet."

"Which brings me to another point. What is it you're doing with Abrams all day? Because it doesn't seem like you're actually working on solving this case."

Grace pressed her lips tightly together to try and keep her tongue in check. Saying something stupid that would only piss Paige off would not help either of them in the long run. "Yesterday we interviewed Jonas, like I told you we were going to do Monday night." She didn't add the fact that Paige had interrupted her Thanksgiving dinner in order to have that conversation even though she really wanted to.

"Where are you on the case?"

"Nowhere, really. Still waiting on the full autopsy report back on Felicia. We got the first chunk of it, but not any of the tests run."

"What did it say?"

"It's in the report I wrote up for you to read."

"You know I hate reading those things."

Swallowing down her snide retort, Grace listed out what Paige might need to know about the murder. "Cause of death is stabbing. She was stabbed twenty-two times in the upper torso, in her arms, and three times in her neck. The killer avoided her abdomen and anywhere else on her body completely. The knife was in fact not serrated like the ME thought at first. It was a smooth knife, most likely a very sharp kitchen knife or hunting knife, about seven inches in length. Knife was nowhere on scene."

"Did she struggle?"

"Yes. She hit her head on the floor and on the corner of the counter by her temple." Grace raised her hand to show Paige where.

"It's honestly probably that hit that stunned her enough to let the killer finish the job."

"This killer sounds pissed off."

"Or desperate."

Paige cocked her head at Grace. "Go on."

"The body was left where it fell. We've collected samples and are running them, but like toxicity reports, DNA takes a few weeks to come back, so still waiting on that."

"I hope Homicide is paying for those."

Grace shrugged. "Don't know. Don't care. That's above my pay grade."

Paige shot Grace a sharp look. "I suppose you're right about that."

"Tip lines have been less than helpful so far. Lots of baby sightings, none have been Andrew. I should be getting the reports from the phone records in today or tomorrow, and I will go through them as soon as I get a minute."

"I don't want you spending all your time over in Homicide working their case for them."

"This is a joint investigation, Paige. They're helping me as much as I'm helping them. That's the entire point of doing this together."

"I don't like you being out of the office for so long."

"You never minded before." Grace clenched her jaw hard, biting her tongue when she realized she'd said too much and pushed it a bit too far. Paige used to always want to be out of the office, doing something other than sitting on her butt all day. In some ways, that might have been why she tried to keep Grace in as much as she did, so she wasn't bored and stuck by her lonesome. Still, Grace had a job to do, and she needed to get it done without Paige watching over her shoulder every two seconds.

Paige said nothing, only gave Grace a hard stare for a few minutes before continuing to her next question. "Who are your suspects?"

"None that we really like at the moment. Jonas Erickson is still a suspect. If these grandma's keep up this shenanigan, it'll bump them up the list a bit. We've checked out most of the family in town, and they're not hitting any part of what we're looking for and there have been no signs of Andrew in any of their homes."

"Friends?"

"Can't seem to find any."

"A twenty-year-old just doesn't not have friends, Grace."

"I know. But that's what I need the phone records for. None of the numbers in her phone that she called or texted had names in them. I need the records to know who she was talking to."

"Why wouldn't she add contacts?"

"To hide whoever she was talking to. Or because it was a newer contact."

Paige rested her elbow on her desk as she leaned over the top of it. "Which do you think?"

"I think she didn't want anyone to know who she was talking to."

"Why?"

"I don't know, Paige, that's what I'm trying to figure out. Instead, I'm stuck in here giving you an update on what you could very well read in the report I updated last night before I left."

"Pissy much this morning, Halling? Go have some orange juice or something."

Grace glowered. "I'm going to go to my desk and work through some financials. I'd appreciate at least a few hours before being interrupted again."

Without another word, Grace stood up and walked to her desk. As soon as she was settled in, she turned on her computer and started into her research. Abrams said he'd already gone through it, but a second eye would be helpful. Grace had one idea as to why Felicia was hiding who she was talking to, and she wanted to test that theory before she told anyone what it might be.

Grace had a list of locations based on Felicia's financials that she wanted to check out. She also really needed to talk to Abrams about her theory, since he was the second closest person to the investigation. Glancing around the unit told her most people were in for the day. Jackson and Kline sat at their desks, typing away at whatever cases they had. She was lucky so far to only have one case, which was probably Paige's doing since hers was so high profile and she was unit hopping.

With the list in her notebook, Grace rolled her neck to remove any of the kinks from her muscles after having been bent over her desk for the better part of hours. Office work had never been her preference, but she was getting more used to it as the years went on. She did have to work out more often to keep up her physical fitness, but that had gone to the wayside lately because her hours had been so horrible. She missed working out with Amya.

Grace nodded at Kline as she grabbed a small baggie from her desk drawer filled with dried bananas. She could snack while she walked down to Homicide to talk with Abrams. As she walked down the halls, Grace munched on her banana chips until she stopped short. Abrams was coming toward her, a hard set look on his face.

He glared at her. Grace furrowed her brow, trying to read between the lines and figure out why he was upset, but she couldn't figure out a good reason. He grunted at her. Turning her chin up to look into his eyes, she shook her head.

"What happened?"

"You don't want to work with me anymore?"

Confused, Grace stared at him. "I never said that."

"Delwin asked for another detective to be assigned the case, specifically requesting Honeywell."

"The fuck?" Grace spun on her toes to face the office she'd just come from.

"My captain is in a tizzy over it, thinking I did something to offend you."

"Absolutely not." Grace's jaw hardened. "I need to speak with your captain."

Abrams cocked his head at her. "Why?"

"Just let me speak with your captain."

"I was going to confront Delwin."

"Ignore her. Come on." Grace moved toward Homicide. Everything with Paige seemed to be moving a level up lately, and her resolve to hold out until Paige was once again demoted was thinning.

Abrams and she walked to Homicide. Grace set her crap at Abrams desk before he knocked on the door. "Captain, this is Grace Halling."

The man was hunched over his desk, his silver hair gelled up to make him no doubt look taller than he actually was. Seated, he seemed small, but he was well-built. Thick with muscles, broad shoulders, and a gruff look on his face. He didn't say anything.

Abrams continued, "She wanted to speak with you."

"Fine."

Grace stepped inside, raised an eyebrow at Abrams before shooing him out of the office. Her stomach twisted, her heart rate picking up. Confrontation with captains was something she hated, and she was about to throw Paige under the bus, at least a bit. With the door shut, Grace put her hands on her hips and faced the captain down.

"I don't have a problem working with Abrams."

"Oh?" He leaned back in his chair, his fingers steepled together.

"I actually quite enjoy working with him. He's very smart, experienced in detective work, and I've been learning from him."

"He said the same about you."

Grace's cheeks flushed hot. "Oh. Well, um, I think Lieutenant Delwin is having some issues with me working with Homicide in general, not Abrams specifically."

"Why would she have problems with that?"

"She wants me to stay in Missing Persons."

That bushy eyebrow of his shot upward. "Are you planning on asking for a transfer to Homicide?"

"Not at this time, no."

"Then why would she be worried."

Grace clenched her jaw. "She just is, sir. I can't explain more than that."

"I get the feeling it's *won't* instead of *can't*, but I'll let it pass."

Nodding, Grace moved to the door. "Please don't assign another detective to the case. Abrams is good, and he knows the case in and out."

"Your choice." He watched as Grace left the office. She went to Abrams' desk and crossed her arms. "Let's get to work."

"So I'm not off the case?"

"No."

"Yes!" He pumped his arm like a kid. "Where we going first?"

"Grocery store. I want to see if Felicia had Andrew with her before she was murdered."

Abrams narrowed his gaze at her. "What do you mean?"

"Come on." Grace gathered up her stuff and walked toward the door. Abrams, with his keys and files in hand, followed her. Once they got to the cruiser and were seated, she let out a breath. "We're under the assumption that Andrew was kidnapped at the same time as Felicia being murdered."

"Yes."

"What if he wasn't?"

"What do you mean?"

Sighing, Grace nodded toward the street. "Felicia had money coming into her account. Cash flow. We have no idea where that money came from. But, what if she was thinking about adoption, changed her mind, got the baby back, and someone was pissed about it?"

"Like she was scamming people?"

"Maybe, or maybe she genuinely just changed her mind."

"But what about the cash?"

"Birth mother expenses." Grace rubbed her palm over her thigh. It was the first time she'd voiced her theory out loud to anyone, and Abrams wasn't running from it yet.

"That's a thing?"

"Yup. And depending on how the adoption is set up, the expenses can be quite high or under the table, especially if it's done in cash."

"How did you think up this one?"

"For some reason, Abrams, I know quite a bit about adoption."

"Link."

She smiled at him. "Have we gotten her computer history back yet?"

"No. They're backed up and with the holiday, who knows when we'll get it."

"That would be helpful right about now."

"Sure. But let's get some of this security footage and figure out what we can see."

They spent most of the day going from place to place on Felicia's expense list for the weeks prior to her murder and collecting the footage while watching it in the stores with the managers. By the end of the day, they didn't have much. Felicia had Andrew with her everywhere she'd gone, but for a new mother, she'd gone out a lot. Not only for baby supplies but in general. She was definitely not a woman who could sit still, and Grace understood that need thoroughly.

After spending hours reviewing the footage with Abrams, Grace made her way to her desk. She pulled up the phone records that had finally come in and combed through them. Her phone buzzed on her desktop. A quick glance told her it was a text from Amya. She read it and smiled. Amya was always sweet.

Going to the refrigerator in her unit like Amya told her to, Grace found dinner for her wrapped up in a reusable container. It was leftovers from their turducken, which was by far not what Grace wanted to eat but the rumble in her stomach told her she'd accept it. With her dinner successfully reheated, Grace settled into her chair and concentrated on the phone numbers. The same number would be texted or called for two weeks and then it would stop. It went all the way back to halfway through her pregnancy.

Kline pushed against Grace's shoulder, getting her attention. The woman was at least fifteen years Grace's senior, but they got along fairly well. "You still working?"

Shrugging, Grace nodded toward her computer. "Got a lot to go over. You headed out?"

"Soon." Kline shifted her gaze from Grace to Paige's open door. She lowered her voice so only Grace would be able to hear. "She making you stay late again?"

"She hasn't asked yet, but I figure it'll happen so might as well plan on it at this rate."

Kline snorted. "She sure likes to pick on you."

"That's an understatement," Grace muttered.

Speaking of the devil, Paige stepped out of her office and eyed the both of them. Kline immediately tensed, and Grace had to work hard to keep herself from rolling her eyes. Paige crossed her arms and stared awkwardly.

"You check in on those tip lines yet, Halling?"

"Not since this morning."

"Do that before you leave. You never know what comes in on those things."

"Yeah." Grace wanted to turn to Kline and share a comment of "I told you so" but she resisted the urge, knowing it'd get her into more trouble than it was worth.

"You like your new partner in Homicide?"

Grace smirked. "What new partner?"

Paige narrowed her gaze. "Didn't you get a new partner today? I heard they were taking Abrams off the case."

"Nope. He's still on it."

The annoyance that washed over Paige's face was priceless. Grace couldn't have asked for a better reaction, and she was smug about being in the know the entire time. Paige probably knew it too, but she didn't care. She was tired of the damn games Paige seemed determined to play lately. Maybe she should consider a transfer to Homicide, though it hadn't sounded like the offer was really there for it.

"I must have heard wrong, then."

Grace nodded and turned to face her desk. "If you've got time, Kline, I could definitely use a hand going through those tips."

"Sure."

Paige's lips parted, and Grace knew she was about to offer a hand, but with Kline already volunteering there would be little reason to have all three of them on it. Kline went back to her desk after Paige walked away. Grace finished her dinner and spent the next two hours going through tips like Paige had requested. She'd found absolutely nothing, which she had predicted. The tip line would have called her if there was something good to go on. This was simply busy work that Paige wanted her on to keep her in the office.

Kline came over, her jacket on and her satchel over her shoulder. "I'm taking off."

"Good, go rest."

Paige came out of her office then, leaning against the doorframe. "Taking off, Kline?"

"Yeah. Hey, do you know how the hiring is going for a new captain?"

Shaking her head, Paige came closer. "Not a clue. I know they're interviewing and near the final interviews, but beyond that, not one clue."

"Ah, I was hoping we'd get some semblance of normalcy around here soon. See you tomorrow, Halling."

"You too," Grace answered, still turned toward her computer screen. She wasn't sure she wanted to say anything to Paige because Grace had a feeling Paige was in the interview pool and that she knew a lot more than she was saying.

Once they were alone in the office, every one of Grace's nerves was on fire. She waited for Paige to say or do something that would push the boundaries. Instead, Paige walked back to her office and sat at her desk. Grace had no idea what she did in there, but surely she also didn't need to be working twelve to fourteen hour days every day of the week.

With the numbers and names for the numbers listed out, Grace pulled the records and look through them. It would either confirm or deny her theory. She managed to get through two of them before her yawning was too much. Her brain wasn't working, and she had to re-read a paragraph about three times and still struggled to retain the information.

Her phone told her it was nearing ten at night, Amya had called twice and texted three more times. Peter had texted, asking to meet up for lunch the next day. She didn't answer, not sure if he was even still awake at that point. Shoving her stuff into her bag, Grace turned off her computer. She shouted to Paige from her desk, "I'm leaving! See you in the morning."

"See you, Grace."

When Grace got home, she dropped everything by the door

and stepped into the hallway. Peter's light was still on, so was the one in her and Amya's bedroom. Kit's room was dark, but Grace also knew she liked to stay up late reading, so she could very well still be awake. Knocking on Peter's door, Grace shoved it open as he called her inside.

"Hey, kid."

"Hey, boss."

"What time do you want to do lunch tomorrow?"

"Eleven? I've got to work at one."

"Sounds good." Grace noted the folded boxes shoved against the wall, and she had a feeling she knew what the conversation was going to be about. He still wanted to go back to school in the spring. "Meet you at the diner?"

"Sure."

"Night." Grace stepped out of the room and down the hall to her own room. Amya leaned against the headboard, glasses perched on her nose as she read a file. "And you get on me for doing work late into the night."

"What else should I do if you're not home?"

Grace plopped onto the bed face first, weariness seeping into every one of her bones. "Are you saying I'm the only reason you're not a workaholic?"

Amya snorted. "No, but you've become one."

"And I hate it."

"I know." Amya rustled the papers, and before Grace knew it, Amya was pressed against Grace's side, running hands over Grace's back and massaging the tense muscles in her neck and shoulders. "You've been working a lot lately."

"I have. You'll never guess what Paige tried today."

Amya tensed.

Grace knew she'd misstepped, that she shouldn't have started the conversation that way, not when Amya was already insanely sensitive about everything Paige did or didn't do. "Sorry, I didn't mean it to come off like that."

Turning on her side, Grace pressed her lips to Amya's. "It's not what you're thinking. Might be worse. She apparently called down to Homicide and told them I was having issues with Abrams and needed a new detective on the case."

"She's insane."

"She's protective."

"Controlling."

Grace rolled her eyes. "Yeah, I'll give you that one."

Amya's lips parted like she wanted to ask a question, but she didn't. Grace kissed her again.

"I had a talk with their captain today and set the record straight. Abrams doesn't need to be getting in trouble because of my issues. I think Paige transferring from Homicide to Missing Persons helped a bit. He at least knows her and knows how she works."

Amya hummed her agreement. "Any word on a new captain?"

"No. Not yet."

"Then I guess we wait it out a bit longer."

"Yeah. I'm going to change, and I really could just use some snuggle time tonight." Grace's cheeks heated with embarrassment as she said the words, but she felt so alone lately, lost in the sea of chaos that was her work life, and pulled away from Amya and the family she wanted. Abrams had reminded her, although unintentionally, how she may not have wanted the family to begin with, but the family was hers, and she didn't want to lose them.

"Of course." Amya gave her a soft smile.

"Good." Without another thought, Grace got off the bed, stripped down, and crawled under the covers. At least she knew she'd get a good night's sleep so long as she could keep her brain from thinking and Amya close by.

HOPE SPRINGS ETERNAL

GRACE'S MORNING had been fairly simple, and she'd even managed to get Abrams into Missing Persons for an hour instead of always going to Homicide, though she preferred going to Homicide. Paige had glared at Abrams the entire time he'd been in there. They'd filtered through more of the phone numbers, running simple checks on them.

When it was thirty minutes to eleven, she begged off for her lunch—which she rarely took anymore—and got in her cruiser. Abrams was going to finish finalizing a plan for interviewing the people they thought most likely to be suspicious of murder, and they would get onto those that afternoon or Friday, after Thanksgiving.

Peter was already sitting in the back booth, Grace's favorite place to be. She skirted around the L-shaped diner and slid into the booth across from him. He already had coffee and orange juice ordered for her.

"I'm not even late, kid."

Peter smirked. "Thought I'd get a head start."

"On bribing me? You know it's a felony to bribe a police officer?"

"I know, and I don't think food bribes count when they're from your son."

Grace smiled, warming at the thought that he really considered them his parents even though they didn't know him for most of his life. Grace sipped at her coffee and settled into the seat. "What's on your mind, Peter?"

He grimaced. "Just jump straight to it, don't you?"

"You know I'm not good at being patient and waiting for you to come out with it."

Peter chuckled. "I wanted to talk about school in the spring."

Grace sighed. "I thought you might."

Sally came over, and they ordered their food. Grace settled in to wait out Peter and see what he really wanted. While he was part of their family, they weren't his parents in a lot of ways and he was an adult. He could readily do whatever he wanted, within the law, of course. When Peter didn't talk, Grace decided to prompt him a bit.

"You talk to Amya already?"

He shook his head. "Wanted to talk to you first."

"Why?"

He shrugged. "Don't know, figured it'd bother you more."

"Why would it bother me?"

"Because I'm going back to seminary."

Grace raised an eyebrow at him. "So?"

"So you are adamant God does not exist."

It was as if he sucked the air from her lungs. Grace forced herself to take another sip of coffee before setting the mug down and crossing her arms. Talking to him about God, and her faith, was not exactly something she wanted to do—ever. She barely even talked to Amya about it. It was the one topic they stayed away from with a ten-foot pole. That and Grace's biological family.

"I am not adamant," Grace stated, her voice quiet but firm. "I don't know one way or the other, but I'm not someone who puts all her eggs in one basket, and I don't really want to put all my eggs in the God basket."

"It's so much more than just a basket."

She scoffed. "You know what I mean, Peter."

"But...I don't know."

"What's really bothering you? I don't think it's my lost soul that's getting you this riled up."

Peter gave her a small smile as their plates were set in front of them. He dug into his food, ignoring the conversation they'd left mid-talk. But Grace couldn't let it drop. He'd made a point of bringing her to the diner, of getting her alone and out of the house to talk to her, that meant this was something big, and she wasn't about to leave it alone.

"Peter?"

"Yeah?"

"What is bothering you about seminary?"

"Will you support me through it?"

"Of course I will. I support you in anything you want to do except bad shit. That I'll tell you flat out is a stupid choice."

The echoing curve of his lips put her at ease a bit. Peter rested, looking her direction. "You don't support Amya."

"I absolutely do."

"No, Grace, you don't. You two don't talk about it. It's completely separate from your relationship with her and I see how much it hurts her."

Grace's chest tightened. *Did she really do that?* Did she really force Amya to have to hide that part of her work and her life? In some ways, she supposed she did. Grace moved her fork around her plate before dropping it. "It's more complicated than belief or unbelief."

"It's really not."

"It really is." Giving him a hard look, she hoped he didn't press, but at the same time, this would be good for him to experience. People had been hurt by the church for centuries, and she was no different. When Peter looked confused, Grace heaved a sigh and left her food alone for good. She suddenly had zero appetite. "My father was a minister."

"You're shitting me!"

Grace snorted. "I'm not. And it's because of him that I have very little trust in the church and in people who are religious and especially those who hold leadership in the church."

"So you don't trust me?"

"Peter, I trust you with everything I have."

Peter's cheeks reddened. "Then why won't you trust me when it comes to God."

"It's not you I don't trust when it comes to God."

Peter looked confused again, but Grace wasn't going to elaborate. She and Amya had talked about it at one point, but that had been it. As soon as the conversation was over, they'd never revisited it.

"Why is this so important to you?"

"Because I want to know that when I graduate, you'll be there. When I'm ordained into the church as a minister, you'll be there.

That you'll come and hear me preach if I end up preaching, that you'll support me through it all."

"I wouldn't miss it for anything." She stared directly into his eyes, hoping her words and the meaning she wanted conveyed got through to him. "I won't. I'll be there for everything, kid. You're family, and that's more important than whether or not we believe the same thing. I'm sure you and Amya don't agree on everything when it comes to God and the church."

His snort told her she'd hit the nail on the head. "We don't."

"Exactly. What I'm worried about in terms of you going back to school has nothing to do with what you'll be learning and everything to do with the fact the last time you went to school you started drinking again, and it wasn't until you'd been here for four months that you finally sobered up. I want you to have a plan to deal with stress, to deal with anxiety, to deal with the social pressures of being twenty-one and sober." She pointed her finger at him. "Without that, I guarantee you'll be back at this house drunk off your ass again. Or worse, and it's the 'or worse' that really worries me, Peter. I'm serious. I don't want to have to launch an investigation into your disappearance, your murder, or something else."

"You won't." He gave her a grin. "I'm making a plan. My sponsor is really helping me with it, and I've already gotten a list of meetings out there for me to attend."

"And what happens if you don't?"

Peter sighed. "Then I have to make some serious decisions about how I want to go to school, but if I can't handle school or living on my own, then I don't have much of a life to live, do I?"

"But are you ready to test that theory out?"

Pausing, Peter looked from his food to his hands to Grace. He gave her a very small nod and then a quirk of his lips. "I think I am."

"Good. You stick with that, and you call me when it gets tough. I'll answer any time you need me."

Peter looked far more relaxed than he had earlier. Grace finished her coffee and started in on her orange juice. At one point she used to drink more orange juice than coffee, but Amya and lack of sleep had changed that. They spent the rest of the hour chatting about his plans for school and the new apartment he was looking at renting. He, at one point, whipped out his phone to show her. Grace was impressed even if she doubted he'd be able to afford it while going to school full time and wondered just how much he was planning on taking out in student loans.

As she got up to leave to go back to work, Peter gripped her in a hug, holding her tight. Grace wrapped her arms around him after hesitating for only a moment. She was never the kind who was touchy feely and Peter had never really wanted physical affection before. When he pulled away, he was grinning at her.

"You going to help me move out there again?"

Grace groaned. "Do I have to? You know how much I hate moving."

He laughed. "Yeah, sure, whatever."

"Doesn't Amya have a sister out there?"

"Connecticut? I don't know, I'll have to ask. She's got so many sisters that I lose track."

"Right?" Grace laughed at their inside joke. "I think Beth lives there, or maybe it's Jenessa. I can't remember. Forget I said anything. Ask her. I bet her sister will help you move or even keep you on the straight and narrow."

"Great." He elongated the syllables. "Another parent to watch over my every move."

"Hey, you need all the help you can get."

"True."

Grace waved him off, as she got in her cruiser. Lunch had been a welcome respite, and she really did need to do it more often. Maybe she could even steal Kit away from school one day before Christmas to have lunch with her. She might like that. No, she'd probably hate it. Too much parenting for their independent teenager. Laughing at the thought, Grace drove to the station, ready to focus all her attention on Andrew's case for the next few hours.

Everyone was out, no doubt trying to finish up whatever they were working on so they could take Thanksgiving day off. Grace was stuck working Thanksgiving, though she'd already put her name in to work at the mall for Santa's big appearance in two weeks, and no matter what Paige said, she was going to be there.

Sighing, she sat at her desk and pulled up the list of people she wanted to check out. Phone calls would be easier than going door-to-door especially when she didn't know if they were going to be there and there wasn't a major reason to suspect them. Still, door-to-door was appealing. She picked up her cell phone to call Abrams and see if he was up for it when Paige stepped next to her desk and glowered.

Putting her phone down, Grace turned her face upward.

"What's up?"

"You took a long lunch."

"Not really. Wasn't even late coming back."

Paige's jaw muscles tightened. "What are you working on?"

"Finally got those phone records. Abrams and I spent last night and this morning matching the names up and doing a basic background on them."

"And?"

"Felicia is the only one with connections to them. From what we can tell no one else on either side of the family has a connection. It's three people, well families. Two couples and one single woman."

Paige cocked her head to the side before standing up. She grabbed the chair from the desk next to Grace's and dragged it over so they could sit next to each other. Paige put a hand on Grace's thigh, making Grace jump from the contact. This was not what she had wanted to happen.

"What were they talking about?"

"The texts seemed to be mostly them checking in on Felicia and her pregnancy, on Andrew after he was born."

"Seems benign."

"It does." Grace kept her gaze locked onto Paige's when Paige moved her thumb back and forth subtly under the desk. "Abrams was supposed to pull financials while I was out. I'm just waiting on his email."

"Financials for what?"

"Felicia was getting cash somehow. I want to see if the amounts match up with what she was depositing and what they were withdrawing."

"You think she was scamming them for money?"

"Maybe. Won't know until I investigate." Grace's words were harsh, but she was tired, and she really wanted Paige to move her hand.

Paige sighed. "Do you mind if I join in? I could really use the distraction."

"Distraction from what?"

"Long story."

Grace snorted. "Break up with another girl?"

"Haven't had a steady girl in months, Halling. I figured you knew that."

"I don't pay that much attention, Paige. And I've been swamped with cases lately, so I really haven't paid much attention."

"Fair. I've been swamped with work, too. I never thought

running my own unit would feel so much like a ball and chain."

Grace chuckled. "There's a reason I never want that job."

"Never say never."

"Fine. But still, don't want it. You could always give it up and come back to the dark side of investigating. You're good at it, so it'd be worth it for everyone if you did that."

Paige worried her lower lip, glancing from Grace to the computer screen. "I may not have a choice soon enough."

"So you did apply for the position, then."

Paige shot Grace a sharp look, clearly caught red-handed and not knowing what to say in response. "You know I can't talk about it."

"So that's a yes."

Nodding, Paige shifted in the seat, her voice lowering. "Yes, I did apply for it, but I don't know if I'll get it. There are other applicants who are much more qualified than I am, and who have a steadier temper."

Grace snorted at that. She would hope so. Paige was definitely not known for her patience. "You'll do great."

Moving her leg out of Paige's grasp, Grace shifted a folder so Paige could look at it. Paige took it, skimming the report while Grace grabbed her phone. She texted Abrams to tell him she was going to call the people on the list to see if they were even in town for an interview before just going to their houses. He agreed it was a good choice. Picking the most recent name, Grace dialed the number and put the phone to her ear. It rang three times before there was an answer.

"Hello?"

"Hi, is this Paulina Dutroit?"

"This is she."

"I am Detective Grace Halling with the Sheriff's Department. I was wondering if you had a minute to talk with me about one of our ongoing investigations."

"Is this about Andrew?"

Grace's stomach clenched, and she sent Paige a look. Paige immediately leaned in closer to try and hear the other side of the conversation, but Grace shifted away. She wasn't about to put the call on speaker phone in the middle of the room where anyone could walk in and hear, and she didn't want Paige that close to her.

"It is."

"Have you found him?"

Grace tightened her hand into a fist. "No, ma'am, we haven't found him. Can you tell me why you thought this call was about him?"

Paulina sighed. "I met Felicia a few months ago. We'd been texting a lot lately, and I figured I might get called because of that."

"Where did you meet Felicia?"

"When she was pregnant at the doctor's office. We always seemed to have appointments close together, and our due dates were similar."

"Due dates?" Grace swallowed as she waited for an answer.

"Yeah, I wasn't expecting to get pregnant either, but I at least had my husband to go through the process with me. Felicia had her mom with her at some appointments, but mostly it was just her. We checked in on each other to make sure everything was going okay."

"Did you see her outside of the doctor's office?"

"We got coffee a few times, but between my work schedule and hers, it was hard to find time to meet up. I know she was worried about Jonas."

"Why would she be worried about him?"

Paulina sighed. "He didn't want anything to do with the baby or her pregnancy. She couldn't even get him to talk to her about it. She was worried she'd have to raise Andrew on her own."

Grace wrote down notes on a legal pad, Paige reading over her shoulder. "When's the last time you saw Felicia?"

"Before she had Andrew. She kind of stopped texting me after he was born, I'm not sure why. I never got a response from her on that one. I had Gabriella about a week after Andrew was born, and I haven't been able to keep up or reach out to her. Guess I don't need to now."

Thinning her lips, Grace drew in a deep breath. "Was Felicia always planning on keeping Andrew?"

"I'm pretty sure she was. She'd talked once about considering adoption, but it didn't seem like something she was super interested in."

"Do you know if she'd contacted an agency about adoption?"

"No, I don't know."

"All right. Did she mention anyone else when she was talking to you, anyone who might have worried her?"

"No, just Jonas, and maybe his mom. She said his mom is an odd one."

Grace could agree with Paulina there. Theresa Erikson had not stopped calling about Andrew. "Okay, well thank you for talking to me. I may call you again if I have any other questions."

"Absolutely. I'll answer anything you need to know. I was so sad to see that on the news."

Wrapping up the conversation, Grace settled her phone down. Paige looked at her curiously, obviously wanting some kind of answer. Paige's hand on her arm had her attention. "What'd she say?"

"Nothing useful." Abrams text came in with perfect timing. Reading it, Grace moved it over so Paige could also read it. "She hasn't been the one giving money to Felicia."

"Then who has?"

"I don't know. It's not easy to get releases for that kind of information, especially with tomorrow being Thanksgiving."

"You'll have to work on that one."

"I am working on it, Paige." Grace barely managed to keep the anger out of her tone, but Paige's proximity was setting her on edge. She didn't want Amya to randomly walk in and see them, and she really just wanted to focus on her case and nothing else, even though she could tell Paige needed a break and a win that day, which was why she was picking the low hanging fruit with Grace.

"Who's next on your list?"

"Um...the number is registered to Collin Mullins. He is married to Carla Mullins."

"Call them."

Grace did, but her conversation was eerily similar to the one she'd had with Paulina. It wasn't the doctor's office that they'd met, but Carla had been a support to Felicia throughout the latter half of her pregnancy, contact also ending when Felicia had given birth or shortly before it. Either these were fast friends she didn't want to continue a relationship with or something had happened between them and Felicia to cause the breaking point.

"The third number is registered to a single woman out of Johnson County."

"Really?"

"Yeah, I'm going to call Blake in a bit and see if she's heard anything."

"Thinking you might want a trip down there?"

Grace raised a shoulder and dropped it. "If something pops up that would warrant it, yes. That would be ideal. But if you want me to not go, I'm sure Blake can handle it."

Paige frowned, her fingers wrapped around Grace's bicep. "I don't want to keep you from your work, Grace."

"Seems to happen often."

"All you do is work."

"Yes, and all you do is ask for updates."

Paige straightened her shoulders. "I didn't realize I was being so imposing."

"It's a little annoying, Paige. I do know how to do my job at this point, and while you hold your temporary position—whether you get it permanently or not—you're not my partner anymore."

"I get that," Paige whispered. "I just hoped we could still be friends."

"You want more than friends, and I've told you many times that won't happen."

Paige's eyes widened. "You're right. My apologies."

Without another word, Paige shoved back the chair she'd brought over and stalked to her office. Finally alone, Grace called Blake. "Hey."

"What's up, Halling?"

"Still working that missing baby case."

"No shit."

"Yeah. You hear anything about it?"

"Nope."

"Figures." Grace grumbled. "How's work down there?"

"Busy. I got stuck with the Thanksgiving on-call shift."

Chuckling, Grace smiled. "Me too. Amya is thrilled."

"I bet. I was wanting to spend the time with my girlfriend."

"Oh?" Grace's eyes rose up at that. She glanced to Paige's office, finding the door closed. "When did that happen?"

"Month or so ago."

"What's her name?"

"Tiffany."

"Nice. You'll have to bring her up some time."

"Plan on it when we get around to it."

Smiling again, Grace clicked through her computer, planning her next call while she finished her conversation with Blake. It would be helpful to get out and see Blake, not just for professional reasons but for personal reasons. They had really hit it off and become fast friends. Even Amya liked her.

"You let me know if you hear anything about my case, will you?"

"Absolutely, Grace. You know me better than that by now."

"I do. See you around."

With one more phone call for her day, Grace made it. She was shit out of luck when Elizabeth Novety didn't answer. She'd run her name, figured out where she worked, called there only to discover she'd quit over a month ago. Sighing, Grace pressed her fingers to her temple. She was done for the night. Logging out and closing everything down, she left the office without even telling Paige she was going home for the night. She needed space, time, and a break from work.

OVER COMMUNICATION

THANKSGIVING MORNING started out slow, which was a surprise for Grace. Normally she raced around the house trying to get everyone ready and going, mostly Kit, who habitually took an hour to get ready. She was still dressed in her pajamas as she sipped at her coffee on the couch, Amya curled into her side. It was the first down time they'd had in as long as she could remember.

"Are you still going to the mall for Santa?"

"Every year," Grace said, the happiness seeping into her tone. "I wouldn't miss it."

"Good. I signed up, too."

"Thank God. You in a uniform is exactly what I need for Christmas."

Amya giggled and wiggled even closer to Grace. "What time does Kit have to go in?"

Grace glanced at the clock on the wall. "Two hours."

"When are you going to check in?"

"On and off, but I plan on staying right here as long as I can."

"I'll take it." Amya's lips brushed against Grace's neck just as Kit walked out of her room.

Kit groaned, rolled her eyes, and scrunched her nose up. "Could you not?"

"Not what? Kiss my partner of three years? Almost four at this rate." Amya giggled. "You should get used to it, Kit. Why is it so odd for you?"

"My parents never did that."

"Yeah, well your parents are weird and not a fine example of humanity." Grace said the words before she could stop herself, and the look in Kit's eyes and the jab from Amya's elbow to her ribs told her she'd way overstepped. "I'm so sorry, that just...that came out."

"It's true," Kit stated, her voice quivering, but she still had a hard look to her face.

"Doesn't mean you don't love them or that it doesn't hurt when you think about them. I'm so sorry, kid." Grace tried to grovel as best as she could. She shouldn't have said any of that, and the fact she did, told her just how close she was to the edge. "They're your parents. They brought you into this world and they raised you for sixteen years."

"And then they kicked me out when they caught me knuckle deep in a girl."

Grace froze. Her gaze was locked on Kit, her lungs holding the air tightly in her chest. *What the fuck was she supposed to say to that?*

"Kit," Amya stepped in. *Thank God.* "One, that is not appropriate to say. Two, you will not get kicked out from here for doing that, though if you are going to do that, we need to set some serious conversations about how to have safe sex."

Kit groaned and rolled her eyes again, stalking into the kitchen to pour herself coffee. "I got enough of that last week."

"Last what?" Grace's brow furrowed as she was confused. If Amya had to have the sex conversation with Kit, then she had missed out on way more than just taking her to and from school and work every day.

Amya shook her head at Grace, telling her it wasn't a big deal before raising her voice so Kit would hear her. "You are free to love whoever you want in this house, Kit. And so are we."

"But do I have to see it?"

"Yes!" Both Amya and Grace answered in unison.

It took a minute, but they settled into the couch cushions together. Grace sipped at her coffee until Kit stalked back into her bedroom, closing the door behind her. She turned on Amya. "You had a safe sex talk with her?"

"At the school." At Grace's continued blank stare, Amya elaborated. "For the after school program, when you couldn't go. I told you taxes were not my arena, so I talked to them about safe sex and healthy relationships and boundaries."

"Oh."

"Did you forget?"

"Completely." Grace buried herself in her coffee, not wanting to think about how much she had missed because it was more than she ever wanted to admit. When her phone rang, she groaned, but it wasn't Paige. It was dispatch. Grace showed Amya the number before holding it to her ear. "This is Halling."

"We've got a lead for you on Andrew Erikson."

"Give it to me." Grace stood up sharply and stepped straight to the kitchen to grab a pen and paper. She wrote down everything dispatch told her. As soon as she hung up, she pointed at Amya. "You're taking Kit to work."

"Really?"

"Yup. This is about my case."

"All right."

Grace called Abrams while she changed her clothes. She'd text Paige after she was done that way. There'd be no chance of Paige jumping in her cruiser and heading over to the scene. It was a breech in protocol but one Grace was willing to risk.

She met Abrams at the gas station on the far side of town. They stayed back, watching the car in question. The uniforms had staked it out before they got there, their radio telling them no one had come in or out of the vehicle since the call had been placed.

Grace snuck out of her SUV and over to Abrams car, both choosing to take private vehicles instead of cruisers to keep their identities a secret for a bit longer. He rolled down his window to his sedan as they chatted.

"You having a good Thanksgiving?"

"Not likely. Anyone come in and out yet?"

"Nope."

"Want to approach?"

"I'll tell the uniforms." Abrams got onto the radio in his hand and called it over. Grace felt around her side for her weapon just in case, unzipping her jacket so she'd have easier access to it. Like true midwest, snow started to fall as soon as Abrams opened the driver's side door. They walked together, uniforms pulling up in the parking lot to block exits if necessary and provide backup.

Grace peeked through the back window of the green Subaru. The infant was buckled neatly into the car seat, perfectly contained. The blanket was laid over the feet to keep the baby warm. And there was not a peep as the baby slept the entire time. Grace tried the door handle, but it was locked.

Well, there was that at least. Grace sent Abrams a glance, trying to determine what he thought of the situation. Grace nodded to one of the cruisers and a uniform came over. "Stay here. We're going in."

"Got it."

Abrams walked next to Grace as they stepped through the doors to the gas station. For a holiday, it wasn't busy, which Grace had suspected. She was pretty sure he wasn't Andrew. They had the same coloring, but this baby looked different.

The gas station was one truckers frequented because there were showers in the back. With the other trash that had littered the seats, Grace had a sinking feeling whoever mom was or whoever had the baby didn't have a place to live. She stepped close to the counter, flashed her badge as Abrams watched the rest of the building.

"I'm looking for whoever came in that green Subaru out front."

The cashier nodded. "I'm the one who called. She's in the back taking a shower. The third door. Here's the master key."

Grace took it. Great, she was likely going to deal with a naked suspect. That was something she had gladly avoided since she'd become a detective and wasn't taking daily calls. Abrams walked two steps behind her. Grace closed her fist and drew in a breath. Abrams flanked the door, his hand on his weapon.

Pounding her fist on the door, Grace drew in a sharp breath. "Open the door! Police."

"What? Hold on!" the woman's voice called through the closed door.

"Ma'am, I need you to open this door immediately."

"I'm just getting dressed. Hold on."

Grace shot a glance to Abrams. Too much could be hidden in a few seconds. "Open the door now or I do it."

"Fine." The door flung open, revealing a young woman in her mid-twenties, pants on but chest wrapped in a towel, her damp hair clinging to the skin at her shoulders and back.

"We have some questions for you."

"Can't it wait until I'm dressed?" Her attitude was hitting close to over the top.

"Get dressed now, where I can see you."

"Everyone else can see me!"

Grace drew in a deep breath. "Turn around and do it. Door stays open."

It didn't take long, but she emerged with a shirt on and her hands on her hips. "What the hell is this about?"

"Do you own the green Subaru parked out front?"

"Yes."

"Did you leave your baby in the back seat?"

She paled. "Y-yes."

"That's what we're here about." Grace beckoned the woman out with a curl to her finger. "Let me pat you down. I don't want any surprises."

"Are you arresting me?" Her voice quivered.

"Not at this particular moment. I just don't want to get stabbed unexpectedly."

"I don't have anything on me."

"Good. Then this will be quick." Grace had her put her hands against the wall, and skimmed her fingers over the woman's body. Sure enough, she had nothing on her. "All right. Turn around. What's your name?"

"Daria Winthrop."

"Who is the baby?"

"M-my daughter, Jasmine. I'm so sorry. I just...I needed to take a shower for this job interview tomorrow, and she was sleeping, and I didn't want to wake her up."

"Daria, calm down." Grace shared a look with Abrams. "My partner here is going to get your stuff, and we're going to go talk outside, okay?"

"Okay," Daria muttered.

They all walked out together, Abrams carrying Daria's bag. Grace slid the key over the counter to the cashier, and they stopped at the Subaru.

"Where's the key to the car?"

Daria pointed to her bag. "Second pocket on the front."

Abrams looked in the pocket before he stuck his hand in there. With the key between his fingers, he handed it over to Grace. She unlocked the car, opened the door and pulled the carseat out, setting it on the trunk of the vehicle.

Muttering to the uniform, she said, "Call DCFS, would you? Also request a bus just to check this little one out, though I'm pretty sure nothing is wrong."

He nodded and walked away. Grace checked over the baby as best she could without taking her out of the carseat. She could save that for later. Daria looked like she was going to cry. Grace's heart went out to her, but it was clear she shouldn't have left the baby alone in the vehicle.

"You have no place to stay?" Grace asked suddenly and quite out of the blue. Abrams wrinkled his nose.

Daria nodded. "I can get into a trailer as soon as I get a job and can prove income. Until then we've been living out of my car."

"No family?"

Daria stilled. "None I can trust."

"All right. I'm going to have a paramedic come look over Jasmine. I'm not planning on arresting you today, Daria, but I've got to tell you, this isn't good."

"What's going to happen to my baby?"

Grace drew in a deep breath. "That'll largely be up to DCFS and the district attorney if they want to charge you with anything."

"With what?"

"Neglect," Abrams said, his voice low and a grumble coming from behind Daria.

Daria turned her head to look at him. "I didn't neglect her. I let her sleep."

"Alone. In a parked car in a parking lot. You can't do that."

"What was I supposed to do?"

"Take her with you." Grace's gaze hardened. She did have a heart, but Daria's mistake had been a stupid one to make.

Daria broke down. Grace let her. Maybe the reality of the situation and the danger she'd put Jasmine in would set in a bit. As soon as the ambulance arrived, Grace took the baby to them while Abrams watched over Daria and continued to talk with her. Grace got into the back of the bus and settled in next to the EMTs.

"I need to make sure this baby is a girl," she stated.

"What?"

Grace sighed. "This was called in not because she was left in the car but because she matches the description of a missing baby."

"Andrew?"

"Yeah."

"Got it." The EMT stripped the baby down, undoing the diaper. Definitely not baby Andrew. Grace sighed at that. She hadn't thought the baby would be, but it still would have been nice to find him, especially since her case seemed no closer than it was before.

It took an hour for DCFS to show up, and another two hours to get all of that straightened out. By the time Grace made it in to fill out her report, she was dead tired. She rebraided her hair down her back, realizing it was way too long and needed cut, but she'd never find the time for it. Paige wasn't there, thankfully, and she had a quiet blissful hour while she filled out her paperwork, checked messages, waited for another call to come in before she gave up and headed home.

Amya was surprised Grace came home so quickly from the call. She had just figured she'd get sucked into work or Paige would insist she stay and she wouldn't see her again until they woke up in the morning. Grace dropping her keys into the bowl by the door was welcome.

"How was it?"

"Not Andrew."

"That's a pity."

"I guess." Grace flopped onto the couch, closing her eyes.

Amya ran her fingers over Grace's arm, longing to see into those brown eyes. "Was the case okay?"

"Tough one."

"What happened?"

"Woman stuck in a rock and a hard place made a stupid decision that will likely follow her the rest of her life."

"I'm so sorry." Amya leaned against Grace's side. "You know, I didn't expect you home this soon. We have the whole house to ourself."

"Oh?"

"Peter's at work. Kit's at work for another two hours."

"Why didn't you expect me home so soon? I came as soon as I finished."

Amya balked. The tone Grace was giving her was a strange one, and she couldn't decipher it just yet, not with her only being home for a few minutes at most. "I figured you'd work late."

"I don't like to work late."

"I know you don't." Amya touched Grace's shoulder. "But you seem to always work late."

"Not always," Grace muttered. "I'm home today, aren't I?

"You are."

"And I came home Monday. I was here for our Thanksgiving."

"You were, but Grace, you were on the phone half the time talking to Paige or Abrams. You might have been here, but you weren't here."

Grace scoffed and stood up, every muscle in her body rigid. Amya should have known better. She just wanted to spend time with Grace, something they hadn't been able to do in forever. She missed her partner.

"Grace..."

"I don't want to hear it, Amya."

"Hear what?" Her tone was sharp, but she didn't care. She was so tired of this, of living a basically single life without her partner, without the woman she loved.

"I don't want to hear about your issues with Paige."

Amya's chest rose and fell sharply. Standing up, fire in her chest, she glared at Grace. "My issues with Paige?" Her voice rose at the end as her anger pooled.

"Yes, Amya. This damn jealousy you seem unable to deal with."

"I'm unable...I'm unable to deal with it?" Amya stepped close to Grace, getting into her face. "You're the one who hasn't done a damn thing about it. You're the one who refuses to file a report, who refuses to consider a transfer to another department, who keeps trying to play these stupid games so that you can...what? Not piss anyone off?"

Grace's gaze hardened. "Be careful."

"No! I'm tired of running this house by myself. I'm tired of being the only parent here. I can't do this without you, Grace. I don't want to."

"This is ridiculous. I need to be able to do my job, and that requires me to go in on days off sometimes and stay late sometimes."

"But not all the time." Desperation clung to Amya. If Grace didn't understand what she was begging for this time, she wasn't sure Grace ever would. The hope she'd held on to that they could talk this out rationally fled. A year ago, when Amya had first told Grace about her jealousy where it concerned Paige, Grace had brushed it off, and here she was doing it again.

"I don't work late all the time."

"Yes, you do!" Amya lost control. She'd done so well at keeping it tight in her grasp, but Grace had pushed her to the edge and shoved her over. She had to get this out, had to let it loose because keeping it balled up inside wasn't helping anyone. "You work late all the time. You even know it. You're exhausted. You can barely function most days. You drag your feet. You hate work."

"I love my job!" Grace punctuated every word. "How dare you tell me I don't?"

"Because you don't. Not anymore. You may love being a detective and being on the force, but you hate your job. This isn't how you wanted your job to be, and it's written all over you."

Grace growled, stepping around Amya and heading toward the

kitchen. Amya had no idea why, but Grace turned and spun as soon as she reached the island. "What do you want from me? I can't be this perfect girlfriend who is here every minute and still has a job and is a fantastic parent to our two wayward kids. That's not me. I told you I didn't want a family, and here we are."

Amya paused. She cocked her head at Grace as she studied her, trying to figure out what Grace was thinking and feeling. But she got nowhere. This was the first time Grace had thrown the foster care situation back at her, and they'd been foster parents for nearly a year at that point. Amya shook her head, walking forward. "I want you to come home at night with enough time to actually spend with your family."

"I can't do that. I have cases to solve. I have a baby I need to find."

Amya bit her tongue. "Is he more important than your family?"

"What family?" Grace spat the words out in anger. "The family here? The one that's leaving in a few months. Yeah, sure, some family."

"Grace—"

"No. We're not doing this. I can't do this."

"Do what? Admit that this isn't what you wanted?"

"I never wanted a jealous girlfriend."

"To be fair, Grace, did you even want a girlfriend?" Amya planted her hands on her hips. She'd known she'd pushed Grace, but at the pace Grace moved, they'd still be in the awkward beginning dating stage if she'd had her way.

Grace's jaw dropped. "What do you mean by that?"

"I mean you don't exactly treat me like your girlfriend. We live together, but we don't do anything together. You don't even text or call to tell me you're going to be late anymore, you just show up, crawl into bed, and leave in the morning. Every night is like that. I'm tired of it."

Grace remained silent, her eyes glued to Amya's.

Amya stepped closer, trying to break the argument, trying to calm it down so maybe they could come to some sort of resolution, but Grace seemed so distant. "I don't want you to be any further away from me."

"Like hell, Amya. You don't want me to end up with Paige."

"Of course I don't!" Amya's voice raised again. So much for control. Cursing herself, she slammed her palm on the top of the counter. "Why would I? She treats you like crap. She doesn't respect your boundaries. She's your boss, Grace, and still she's pulling this kind of crap. She's playing with fire, and she will get burned."

"What are you going to do?" Grace's eyes widened with fear.

Amya shook her head. "I should probably report it myself. I should probably march myself up to IAB and file it since you don't have the guts."

Her head hurt from the argument, from holding back everything for so long and releasing it in such a rush. Amya relaxed her jaw and rolled her shoulders. When Grace said nothing, did nothing, didn't even bother to move, Amya shook her head and let out a sigh. Having the last of her hopes dashed, she turned on her toes and walked into their bedroom, shutting and locking the door behind her.

Amya sat on the edge of the mattress, her hands covering her face as the tears released. She couldn't be the strong one anymore, the one who stood by and watched as Grace refused to do anything to change the situation she found herself in. Grace had to make some decisions, and Amya wasn't sure how much longer she could hold on and wait for her to come to the conclusion that Paige wasn't going to change, and that if Paige ended up permanently a captain in Missing Persons that nothing would change, nothing would be different, except Grace would absolutely loath the one thing in her life she might have loved more than Amya herself.

She didn't move when she heard the front door open and shut hours later or the car in the driveway start up. It took exactly twenty minutes for them to come back, Kit chatting as the door shut, her voice carrying in from under the doorway.

As much as she wanted to go talk to Kit, see how her day at work went, she couldn't bring herself to walk out into the living room. Amya pulled the blanket over her shoulders as she turned on her side and curled into a ball. She didn't bother unlocking the door, didn't care for Grace to try and grovel and snuggle against her. She couldn't even think about Grace against her right then. Her stomach churched, her head ached, her eyes were dry.

When Peter came home, she could hear him ask Grace why she was sleeping on the couch. She couldn't make out Grace's response, but she did catch him telling Grace that Amya wasn't wrong. Poor kid didn't need to be in the middle of it, which she was pretty sure was what Grace told him, since he walked down the hall and closed the door to his room with a loud click.

Amya laid still for hours, finally glancing at the clock on the nightstand. It was two in the morning. She should have known it was late since Peter wasn't off work until after midnight. She'd laid in the bed alone with the door locked for hours. Drawing in a shuddering breath, she closed her eyes and begged for sleep to come and take her away. She just needed to not think, to not feel, to not worry about what might happen if Grace and she couldn't talk this one out.

With her heart in shambles, her mind whirring up a storm, Amya closed her eyes and pushed everything to the side. She said a prayer, drew in deep mediating breaths, and got out of bed. She stripped her clothes and pulled on pajamas before heading to the door. Her hand hovered over the handle for a brief second before she flicked the lock and opened it a crack. The rest of the decision would be Grace's.

The dogs walked through, finally allowed in the room. Roslin curled on the floor, too old to jump on the bed anymore, and Izzy curled on the bottom corner that she always claimed as hers. Amya patted her head as she got under the covers again and sighed. The ball was in Grace's court now. Grace had to make the next move.

THE LONER

GRACE GOT to the office late Friday morning, and her back ached after sleeping on the couch all night. At some point, Amya must have unlocked the door, which had been enough for Grace to go get dressed in the morning. They hadn't spoken. Amya stayed home with both Peter and Kit, and Grace had driven around town in the newly fallen snow, trying to figure out where they'd gone wrong.

Their argument played over and over in her head until she just had to leave the house to get some of her thoughts straight, though that hadn't been very successful. But she also knew that if she walked into work and Paige picked up on the fact that she and Amya had fought, she would push boundaries even more.

Grabbing Abrams from Homicide, they got into Grace's cruiser. It wouldn't take them too long to do what she wanted that morning, but it would at least keep her out of Paige's hair while still getting her job done. Kline was watching the tips to see if any more came in that were relevant and would jump on calling Grace if there was one.

Abrams sat quietly in the seat next to her, his hard exterior not swaying Grace much more than it had the first day she'd met him. She drove through the slush filled streets to the other side of town where Kadence lived. They'd interviewed her once, but Grace wanted to double-check everything. She had a list of homes from immediate family members that she was planning on doing a door-to-door search and see if anyone had seen Andrew in the last week and a half since his disappearance.

When she got to the first apartment complex, Link stepped out of the cruiser without a word. He wasn't normally chatty, but they did at least have a comfortable relationship where they would talk, but today he seemed off. Grace thought about asking him what was wrong but avoided the entire topic instead. If he wasn't going to share what his issues were, then she wasn't going to share hers.

They went separate directions from Kadence's apartment. Knocking on the first three doors got Grace nothing. The fourth door got her an answer at least. She flashed her badge, planted a smile on her face, and straightened her shoulders.

"Hi, I'm Detective Halling with Missing Persons. I was wondering if I could ask you a few questions about an ongoing investigation."

The small woman nodded.

"Have you seen anyone around here with a baby recently?"

"Like baby Andrew?"

Grace gave a sharp nod. "Yes, like baby Andrew."

The woman bit her lower lip and looked around the other apartments. "No. No one who shouldn't have a baby, anyway."

"Have you seen any strange people coming and going from apartments lately?"

"No. Everything has been fairly normal."

"Fairly?"

The woman shrugged. "It's been normal."

"All right."

Anyone she got hold of at Kadence's complex pretty much gave her the same story. There'd been no sign of a baby being in Kadence's apartment either when they'd interviewed her, so Grace felt fairly confident crossing her name off the suspect list, or at least putting it way down to the bottom.

She and Link rendezvoused at the cruiser, Grace leaning against the door. "Find anything?"

"Nope."

"Me either. To Jonas'?"

"Yup."

He got into the cruiser just as Grace did. This was the part of detective work that wasn't as much fun as chasing the bad guy, but at least it got her away from her desk and walking, which was something she enjoyed.

"Did you have a good Thanksgiving outside of getting called in?"

Link gave a small shrug. "Could have been better eating with the family instead of being stuck at a scene, but the food was good."

"Better than the leftovers I heated up in the microwave."

"No doubt." His tone was dry.

Grace had to sigh. She didn't need to be best friends with the man, but some camaraderie that day would be a very welcome distraction from Amya and the jealousy that seemed to always find a wedge between them. Grace hadn't actually eaten dinner the night before. The last thing she'd eaten had been breakfast, and her stomach was currently telling her that had been a mistake. But she couldn't bring herself to stomach food or think about anything other than the argument.

"Do we have the full autopsy report yet?"

"ME said we should have it back by this afternoon."

"Good. I'm interested to see what's in it."

"From the prelim...not much."

Grace shrugged. "You never know what you might find."

"That's true. Did you get hold of that third person who Felicia was calling and texting?"

"No. The number is no longer active, and she's in Johnson county, so I'll have to convince them to make a stopover or Delwin to let me go."

Link snorted at that. "She keeps you on a short leash."

"You have no idea," Grace muttered.

They finished up the door-to-door by Jonas' and his parents with no new information. There was still no sign of Andrew anywhere. All Grace could hope was that since it was proven when infants were taken from the home they were generally cared for that he was still alive somewhere, but with the list of who might have taken him narrowing, her hopes thinned.

She pulled onto the road by Felicia's parents' house. They had talked to them several times, Grace talking to the mother so many times she honestly couldn't count them all. They'd done the door-to-door once already within a day or two of Andrew's disappearance and Felicia's murder, but it wasn't that hard to hide a baby and bring him home when things calmed down a bit. Luckily, no one was home.

Grace parked down the road from the house, eyeing the driveway. Link walked across the street to knock on doors there while Grace stayed on the side with Felicia's parents' house. The first two houses netted her nothing, but at least the residents were home. When she got to the third, she found no one there, and then she came across Felicia's parents' house.

Stepping up to the door, she knocked to prove her suspicion the house was empty. It was a single story ranch-style house, so this would actually work to her benefit. She stepped to the front window and peered inside, her hands coming up to block the sunlight from the reflection so she could see better.

The house was messy, which it hadn't been when they'd interviewed them the first time, but that didn't bother Grace. It wasn't a disaster. It looked like a normal amount of mess after a holiday or after having such a traumatic event happen.

Walking around to the side of the house, Grace got up on her toes to peek in through the side windows. The blinds were drawn, thankfully in a bedroom, but it sported nothing but a bed in the corner and a dresser and some dated decorations on the walls. The next window was definitely the bathroom, and Grace couldn't see anything in there.

The third window at the back of the house was another bedroom, this one had a small fold-up crib in the corner. Something tugged inside her, and Grace looked around the room even more. There were diapers stashed in the corner, a changing station. This was set up for someone who had a baby. It didn't prove they had Andrew, but it was definitely a good lead to go on.

Stepping away from the window, Grace jumped when she came face-to-face with Link. He raised one gray, bushy eyebrow at her. "Done snooping?"

"They've got a crib in there and a changing station."

"Does it look used?"

"No?" She furrowed her brow and rubbed a hand against the back of her neck.

"Is that a question?"

"It could be used or not. It's not messy if that's what you're asking."

"Rest of the house is."

"True." Grace put her fists on her hips. "Find anything with the neighbors?"

"Nothing, and one in particular who has been watching like a hawk because she *feels so bad for them.*"

Grace rolled her eyes. "So our regular nosy neighbor."

"You got it."

Link glanced in the window before they walked toward the cruiser. Grace got into the driver's seat, realizing she'd forgotten her phone in the car when it buzzed in the cup holder as soon as she opened the door. Grabbing for it, she stopped short when she saw Paige's name on it. She didn't answer.

When they were settled inside, she started the engine to try and get the car warm again. Winter hadn't hit full force yet, but she knew it was coming. She could feel it in her bones. "When do you want to interview them again?"

"This afternoon if they show back up at home."

"Want to stick a uniform on it?" Grace asked.

"I can have one drive by to see when they get home and then call me."

"Sounds good." Grace stared down at her phone. "I've got to call her back."

"Who?"

"Delwin."

"So call her."

Sighing, Grace put the phone up to her ear. "Hey, what's up?"

"Where have you been?"

"Canvassing. What's going on?"

"New case."

"You're kidding me."

"Nope. Everyone else has two cases already. I've held off on it as long as I can. You're up, Halling."

"Fuck," Grace muttered, hopefully quiet enough neither Paige nor Link heard. A glance at Link told her she'd at least been loud enough for him. "I'll be back in twenty."

"Make it quick."

Hanging up, Grace shoved the cruiser into drive. "I've got another case."

"Another case?" Link turned to her surprised. "You get more than one?"

"When it's busy, which is during the holidays, yes. The most I've had at once is three."

"That's insane."

"Why? Do you only get one?"

"Unless it runs cold."

"This one is about to," Grace reminded him. "Unless we find some leads soon, they'll hand it over to the FBI to continue the investigation, working *with* us, of course."

"Of course," he echoed. "I'll email you over the autopsy report when it comes in, but we should look at it sooner rather than later."

"Agreed. Want to work tomorrow?"

"I'm on call anyway, so it won't hurt."

Grace snorted. She always worked weekends, and whether or not he was going to join in, she had no doubt she'd find herself at the office, going through files and doing more for her investigation. Though, she wasn't going to tell him that. The drive back to the station was mostly quiet. They tossed ideas around about who else Felicia might have connections to but hadn't come up with anyone who skyrocketed to the top of their list. It seemed as though the case for Andrew was going cold faster than the winter coming in.

Kline was waiting for her when she walked in. Grace gave her an odd look and a glance toward Paige's office door, which was shut with the lights off. "Where's Delwin?"

"Out."

"Really?"

"Said she couldn't wait for you. I'm giving you the update."

"Anyone working with me?"

Kline cocked her head to the side. "I am."

"Nice." Grace smiled. "What have we got?"

"We got a call in from a law firm about one of their employees. He hasn't shown up to work in over a week and they are concerned. They did a wellness check this morning, managed to get a good look inside the house, but there didn't seem to be anyone there. Mail piled up for over a week."

"All right." Dropping her stuff onto her desk, Grace took the file Kline handed over. In it was a driver's license photo of a heavier set man, bald, with bright blue eyes. He had on a suit and tie in the picture—he definitely fit the profile so far of someone working in a law office. "So he hasn't been seen since when, exactly?"

"Tuesday the week before Thanksgiving."

"That's way more than a week, Kline."

She shrugged. "They didn't have office hours yesterday or today, and one of the other lawyers seemed concerned, tried to call him, he didn't answer, went to his house and it was the same, so they called us."

Scratching her head, Grace stared down at the picture. "So he's a lawyer?"

"One of the partners at the firm."

"Wonderful." Grace slid into her chair and booted up her computer. "Family?"

"None in town from what we can tell so far. I just managed to run the basics on him before you got back."

"Thanks." Grace turned to her computer. "Let me get a bit more information and I'll make a few calls and see what we come up with."

Kline nodded sharply. "I'll be working on my missing teen."

"Catch up with you in a bit, then."

Focusing entirely on her computer screen, Grace ran through a few more searches that Kline hadn't managed to get done. She pulled phone records that she could get hold of, listened to the call in for the wellness check, and figured out where Leon Gross lived. She'd check the house herself, just to be sure the uniforms hadn't missed anything. And they hadn't talked to the caller except to report back about the initial wellness check. She'd have to do that too.

Grace wrote down names and addresses in her notebook that she wanted to check out. She'd take Kline with her for this first round, especially since she had no idea what she was going to run into yet. Once she had her list compiled, she picked up the phone on her desk and called Leon's cell phone and house number. The cell went straight to voicemail, and the house rang until it went to a full message system.

She started on the family next. Kline was right, he didn't have anyone in town, but she did manage to track down a sister, which would be a good starting point. Her first call, however, was to the two hospitals in town. The first one answered right away. Finally getting the right person on the phone, she sighed and pulled open her drawer and her stash of snacks. Picking the dried peaches, she munched while she waited for the person to pick up.

"This is Jessica Lewis."

"Hi, I'm Detective Grace Halling. I work in missing persons. I was wondering if you had any John Does come in or if you had a patient there by the name Leon Gross. Either in the last few days or the last week and a half. Any time up to Monday before Thanksgiving."

Clicking echoed through the line. "No one here by that name, but we did have one John Doe come in just three days ago. He was released, it seems, AMA, two days ago."

"I'm looking for a man who is six foot three inches, about two-hundred-thirty pounds. White, bald, with blue eyes. There are no tattoos on his body that I'm aware of, and no scars known at this time."

"Hmm." Some more clicking. "Doesn't seem to match the description of the individual we had here."

"All right. Will you please keep a look out for Leon Gross and anyone matching his description should he come in?"

"Absolutely."

"Thanks."

The second hospital was the same. No one of that description or name was a patient there. Grace's head was hurting, her back gave a few sharp pangs to remind her she'd slept on the couch all night. Her next call was to the initial caller.

"Hello?"

"Is this Harvey Rowe?"

"Yes."

"I'm Detective Grace Halling. You called this morning about your friend, Leon Gross."

"He's not really my friend." Harvey corrected. "We work together. Leon doesn't exactly have friends."

"Oh?"

"He's a bit of a loner."

"Ah. When was the last time you saw him?"

"Tuesday night, the Tuesday before last. We were both leaving the office late. He had court the next day, so when he didn't come into the office, we all assumed he was there. It wasn't until the client called in a panic we realized he wasn't. He never showed back up after that."

"Why did you wait so long to call it in?"

Harvey paused. "We thought his sister would call it in.

"And she didn't?"

"Don't know. I got tired of waiting and called."

"Well, I'll be handling the case from here on out, so if you hear anything from Leon, please do let me know."

"Yes, ma'am."

"Did Leon seem to be in a normal state of mind when he left work Tuesday?"

"Yeah, I guess. We'd talked about his case, about court in the morning, and that was it. He doesn't talk a lot about his personal life, so I can't say there was any change there."

Grace nearly snorted but held it back. Seems this guy really was a loner based on his coworkers description. "Had he said anything about going away?"

"No, and he would have since he'd had court."

"True." Grace wrote random notes down to keep herself

focused. "Does Leon only have his sister or is they any other family?"

"I think he's got a cousin or two, but other than that, I don't know. Like I said, he never much talked about his personal life."

Grace sighed. She wrapped up the call, leaving her name and number with Harvey. She called Leon's sister next, and luckily, she answered.

"Hello?"

"I'm looking for Linda Gross."

"This is she."

"I'm Detective Grace Halling from the Sheriff's Department. I'm calling in regards to your brother, Leon."

"Oh my God, is everything okay?"

Grace's stomach clenched. She should have opened that conversation differently, although there wasn't really any good way to start this conversation. "We received a call earlier this morning from one of the partners at the firm concerned for his welfare. Have you heard from your brother in the last few weeks?"

"No, but we don't talk very often. We're not exactly close."

Grace's lips thinned. "When was the last time you talked to him?"

"September, I think. For his birthday?"

Jesus. Grace wrote the date down. "Have you exchanged emails, texts, anything else with him since then?"

"No, like I said, we don't talk much. Often we only talk on birthdays and Christmas."

"Okay. Do you know if he had any friends that I could talk with?"

"What's wrong with Leon? Why are you're calling?"

Sighing, Grace wrinkled her nose. "The partner who called in today was asking for a welfare check on your brother because he hasn't been to work since Tuesday before last. When our officers performed the welfare check this morning, your brother was not at the house. His vehicle was there, but he wasn't."

Linda's voice trembled when she drew in a deep breath.

"I'm so sorry to have to tell you like this, ma'am. We're just starting our investigation and will be putting our full effort into finding your brother, though at this time, we don't suspect foul play."

"I knew I might get this call someday."

Grace froze at that. "Why would you say that?"

Linda paused, dragging in a deep breath. "Leon has always

struggled with depression, since as far back as I can remember. I always thought he was bipolar, but he never went and got diagnosed or saw a therapist. Anyway, I just always assumed I'd get a call someday that he was dead and that would be it."

"Ms. Gross, we haven't found your brother at this time. He's only been reported missing. We plan on thoroughly investigating and not stopping until we find him."

"I know. I just...let me know what I can do to help, Detective."

"When Leon struggled with depression, he was suicidal?"

"Yes. He has three previous attempts, though I don't think he's had one in fifteen years."

Grace's stomach tightened. She hated finding people dead. She always wanted to find them living, and typically held on hope that she would until the inevitable came. "How did he try to kill himself in the past?"

"The first time he slashed his wrists. The second time he tried to crash his car, but the airbag and seatbelt saved him—ironically. The third time he tried to shoot himself in the head, but at the last minute he moved his hand and so it grazed his skull instead of doing any more damage."

"Does he have a scar then?"

"Yes. It's along the side of his head, the right side. It's barely visible, though."

"That's helpful to know. Did he have any tattoos or piercings?"

"No."

"All right." Grace made a few notes on the paper in front of her. "Did he ever have in patient hospitalization for mental health?"

"Only on the last attempt, and it was not helpful for him."

Things like that always depended on the hospital. Grace would have to try and pull the past reports and see what was written up and what she could glean from them. "We're going to do our best to find your brother, Ms. Gross. I promise you that."

"Thank you."

Finally off the phone, Grace pulled the previous reports about Leon Gross and skimmed them over. Linda had been fairly detailed and correct in what had happened, but it had been fifteen years since the last attempt. She bit into another dried peach as her stomach rumbled loud enough that the neighboring detective glared at her. Her next step was going to be to collect Kline and go through Leon's apartment and see if she could figure out where he was. The coming weekend had just taken a turn.

COLLIDING CASES

IT WAS quiet in the apartment. Grace heard Kline rustling through the living room while she'd volunteered to take the bedroom. She half-expected the apartment to be clean and pristine, but this guy was a bit of a slob. Clothes were strewn about on the floor and on half the bed he clearly didn't use. With her gloves on her hands, Grace rummaged through the closet, which was another mess.

The shelves inside it were lined with crap that looked like it hadn't been touched in months. A thick layer of dust coated everything. The dry cleaning he'd picked up the week before he'd gone missing was laid on top still wrapped up in the plastic it came in, completely untouched. The closet had a few more suits hanging in it, but Grace's best guess was they weren't ones he typically liked to wear.

Law books covered a shelf in the corner of the bedroom. None of it was fiction. Grace sneered at the options. She loved a good book herself but not a law book. She pulled a few of them out and checked them over but didn't find anything interesting. The computer sat on his nightstand, not a desk in sight in the entire small one bedroom apartment.

She opened the computer but found it locked and requiring a password, so she'd have to hand that off to someone else unless she found the password somewhere in the apartment. Sighing, Grace stacked it with the stuff they were taking. She almost missed it, but his cellphone was tucked into the messy comforter. Kneeling on the bed with one knee, Grace plucked it and tried to power it on but got nowhere. The battery was completely dead, which shouldn't surprise her.

Closing her eyes briefly, Grace stacked that on top of the laptop. It was going to be a long search through the apartment. Thus far, Grace had found absolutely no sign of where Leon might have gone or even what he'd been thinking. She found remnants of his work in his bedroom, in his bathroom—which had been odd. He hadn't taken anything with him. No suitcases that she could tell since there was a full set stashed into the back of the closet. No toiletries since the travel sized ones and full sized ones were still in the drawers in the vanity.

Sighing, Grace wiped the back of her wrist against her brow. The apartment was still warm because he'd left the heat on above eighty. If he'd been planning to leave and go on a trip, one would think he'd turn that down to lower his electric bill at the very least, but then again, lawyers made a whole lot more money than she did. Maybe they didn't care about those kinds of things.

She had her lips pressed hard together when Kline stepped into the room, her graying red hair and baby blue eyes catching Grace's attention. "Find anything?"

"Not a thing. You?"

"He's messy?"

Grace snorted. "Yeah, at least recently. Who knows if he was always like that."

Kline shrugged. "Find anything on the computer?"

"It's locked. Phone is dead. I'll have to drop both off when we get to the station and wait them out."

"Wonderful," Kline murmured. "The fridge is full. Pantry is full—mostly."

"Mostly?"

"Looks like he ate a lot of those pre-made meals. The ones you buy and they ship all the ingredients to you and you cook it in thirty minutes or less."

"That's a thing?" Grace asked.

"Yeah. Where do you live? Under a rock?"

"Sometimes," Grace muttered. She and Amya always switched off who cooked until recently. Amya had done the cooking, and when Grace had been home for it, more often than not, she'd order out. Never before would she have thought about dropping that amount of cash on food, but if it was cheaper than eating out, it might actually be a good bet for her own house.

"Did he take anything with him?"

"Not that I can tell. He picked up dry cleaning the Monday before the last sighting. It hasn't been touched."

"This guy is weird."

"He looks consumed by work and not much else."

"I'd agree with you there," Kline answered. "Work everywhere but not one sense of what he does other than work."

"Right? No hobbies. He's got a television, but it's not even plugged in."

"I'll be curious to see what's on his computer, especially his search history."

"Yeah." Grace stretched her back. It had been a long few weeks, and sleeping on the couch was the tip of the iceberg for her. If she and Amya didn't talk soon, she wasn't sure she could take another night on the couch. Sighing, Grace stretched her triceps next. Kline didn't seem phased, which was good.

"Should we search his office next?"

"Yeah, after a little door-to-door. See if anyone saw him leave."

"Didn't the uniforms do that?"

Grace lifted her shoulders and dropped them. "Yeah, but does a second pass really hurt?"

"Probably not."

They finished up their search of the apartment, still coming up empty handed. Grace put the electronics in her cruiser before going back to join Kline in the door-to-door. She knocked and knocked and knocked, finding no one home who knew the good lawyer. He apparently came and went and that was it. She did learn he never came and went with anyone, which she supposed was a good thing, but it was also bad. She had no one to contact next to ask about him.

Soon enough, Grace found her way to the lawyer's office. Kline stood slightly behind her as they walked in and spoke with the secretary. They were shown to Leon's office, which was far cleaner than his apartment. Things weren't exactly orderly, especially on his desk, but everything else was clean. Grace pulled open some of the drawers, another lawyer—Kenneth Judberry—standing right by to watch them as they worked and to protect any information they might potentially and accidentally see.

Grace decided to begin the second part of their investigation while they were there. "You worked closely with Leon, right?"

"I'm a junior associate, so yes, I worked closely with him."

Grace nodded to herself. "Were you working on any particularly distressing cases?"

Kenneth shook his head. "No, nothing out of the norm. We don't take high profile cases or anything that would be upsetting. We're not that kind of law firm."

"Did he have too many cases piled on him at once?"

"Leon is one of our best partners. He can handle anything thrown at him with quick efficiency. We all love him around here."

"Is he a good boss?"

"For the most part. He's a bit rough around the edges, and you don't really want to piss him off, but it takes a lot to actually piss him off."

Grace made sure she was going to remember absolutely everything Kenneth was saying because she knew the request of Leon's work computer was not going to go over well.

"Did he have any friends in the office? Anyone he talked to more than someone else?"

"Leon?" Kenneth snorted. "Leon didn't have friends. He worked. That's it. He didn't have personal conversations with anyone. All he did was work."

"Not even watercooler gossip?"

"Nope."

Grace raised an eyebrow in Kline's direction, surprised in one way and not in the other. Everything they'd learned so far about Leon said he worked and only worked. "We'll need to talk to some of the other associates and partners here."

"Everyone is willing to talk to you. They want to find Leon. He's a good guy, thorough in his work and everything, but he's a good guy."

Grace wasn't going to mention that while he might be a good guy and the office seemed to like him for the most part, it still took them over a week to report him missing or really delve into why he was missing.

"We'll need to take his computer. Make sure he didn't buy plane tickets or something on here."

"I'll have to talk to the other partners about that."

"Please, do."

Kenneth nodded his head as he left the office.

"What are you thinking?" Kline asked, finally breaking her silence.

"I'm thinking Leon was all work and no play and maybe, just maybe, he got tired of it."

With everything for Leon with the experts and she was waiting to hear back, Grace walked down the long hallway toward Homicide. It was becoming a regular route for her to take. She was passing the Chaplain's offices when she stopped short and stared at the door.

Amya should be at the station and not at the jail that day, though that didn't mean she wasn't with someone in a session or something. Grace stood still, staring at the door, every muscle in her body frozen on the spot. People moved and walked around her, but she didn't pay any attention as she stared at the closed door. Grace felt a world away from Amya and all she wanted was to be close.

"Halling?"

Grace spun around at the sound of her name right next to her ear. Link stood in front of her, his hand on her shoulder. She hadn't even noticed. She cocked her head at him. "What's up?"

"You okay?"

"I'm fine." Her voice was terse even though she didn't mean it to be.

"Are you sure? You've been staring at that door like you expect the devil to walk through it."

Grace's lips quirked at his phrasing. "I didn't realize how long I'd been staring. I was just coming to find you."

"Okay, but really, Grace, is something wrong?"

"I'm fine. I promise." Grace put on a brave face. "It's something I can deal with later. Did you have any developments on the case?"

"Yes, actually. One of the neighbors finally came back from vacation and one of the uniforms talked to her. She's got an interesting story. Thought you might want to check it out with me."

"Oh. Um...sure."

"Grace, are you sure you're okay?"

"It's been a tough week," she finally admitted.

Link pointed at the door. "Do you need to go talk to her?"

"No. It can wait. I'm sure she's with someone, anyway. It just reminded me that I need to talk to her sooner rather than later."

"I hear you on that one." They walked together toward Homicide. "What's the other case you ended up with?"

"Missing lawyer. Absolutely no foul play suspected. Pretty sure he just ran off somewhere, but he hasn't left many clues. I just dropped his tech off, so maybe by the time we get back, I'll have a few more answers."

"Maybe you will." Link's lips curved upward at her. "And for what it's worth, Halling, make sure you always make the time to talk with Amya. Don't neglect it."

"I'm not avoiding it, just really don't want to have that conversation at work."

Link snorted. "Oh, sometimes it's unavoidable."

"Are you married to a cop, Sergeant Abrams?"

"Worse."

"What can be worse than that?"

"I'm married to an assistant district attorney."

"No way."

"Yes." Link's lips pulled tight. He grabbed his keys, and they made their way to the cruiser. "It's been interesting in some ways, conflicting in other ways. We try very hard not to work the same cases and keep that as separate as possible, and never when I'm the lead on a case."

"I can't imagine. At least Amya and I don't have those issues."

"It's a whole new layer." He got into the driver's seat. "But we also deal with issues at work sometimes when they come up even though we try not to."

"There's just so many rules sometimes." Grace sighed as she clicked her seatbelt into place.

Link sent her a long look. "What do you mean?"

"There's rules to when and where we can talk, what I can and cannot do, and it's frustrating sometimes."

"You're talking about Delwin."

Grace's jaw clenched, and she stared forward, not really wanting to look at him.

Link snorted. "She transferred from Homicide because of a similar issue."

"What do you mean similar? I haven't said anything."

"You didn't need to, Grace. Spending this case with you, I can see what she's doing and her having the power now to do it makes it worse."

"I don't know what you're talking about," she muttered, but she did know. She knew exactly what he was saying without saying it. Link drove in silence for a while, and when they came to a stop at a light, Grace sighed. "It's making work miserable."

"You can always report it."

"Since when has reporting *that* gone well for anyone?"

Link shrugged. "The other option is to transfer. The captain was talking about reworking our budget to bring on more people since our case numbers have been up all year."

"I love missing persons. The majority of missing persons cases are teenagers in a shitty spot."

"I can see why those particular cases would interest you."

She kept her mouth shut, her fingers clenched tightly into fists. Grace needed to figure out what she was going to do because after six months of the way work had been, she wasn't sure she could handle it much longer. Especially if it kept affecting her and Amya the way it had, not to mention the rest of the family. She'd missed out on so much lately.

They pulled up outside the apartment, and Grace didn't wait to get out of the cruiser. She needed to focus on work and stop thinking about what a mess her life was right now. Link followed her as they walked up to the third floor of the apartment complex. Grace knocked. They heard someone call from the apartment, and Grace listened as heavy footsteps came closer.

When the door opened, they were met with a short, portly woman, who had less hair on top of her head than she did on her chin. Her eyes had this gray quality to them as if she couldn't really see them. Grace was about to speak, but Link stepped in.

"Mrs. Ramusken, we're here to talk to you about your neighbor."

"Oh right, come in." She waved them inside.

Link stepped through the doorway first, and Grace followed. When the door shut, her muscles tensed. She always hated being stuck in an unknown apartment and only one way out. At least she had Link with her. They moved over to sit on the aging couch while the woman took the big fluffy chair that was obviously her preferred place to sit.

"I was so sorry to hear about Miss Felicity. I was visiting my sister in Chicago and saw it on the news briefly. That baby was cute as a button."

Grace was once again about to speak, but Link shot her a look. Apparently he was taking charge on this interview.

"Mrs. Ramusken, you told our officers on the phone that you had some information about Felicia and another neighbor?"

"I do. I always watched out for her, pretty girl like that. You can't be too careful with the perverts living in this place. When I figured out she was pregnant, I made sure to check in on her as often as I could. She was such a sweet thing."

"So you visited her often?" Link asked.

Grace took out her notebook and started scribbling things on it in case anything they talked about was helpful.

"About once a week until I left to visit my sister. It's such a tragedy what happened to her."

"It is," Link answered. "What would you talk about?"

"Oh this and that. She was getting ready for the baby and didn't seem to have much family support. No husband to speak of. No daddy for that precious little baby."

Grace tensed unwillingly. Even though there was a dad, and Felicia didn't seem to be partial to women, the assumption being there always got her back up. She let it go.

"What specifically would you two talk about?"

"I'd bring her food sometimes, just dinner here and there to help her out. She was working a lot until a few months ago when they put her on bed rest."

Grace wrote that down even though she already knew it. Felicia was unemployed and had been for three months due to medical problems according to her old boss, and with the hospital records, they could readily see she'd been told to go on bed rest.

"Did Felicia ever mention Andrew's father?"

"Only that he wasn't interested in the baby."

"Did she ever mention the potential for adoption?" Link asked.

Grace perked up at that question. She'd wanted to ask it, but she hadn't been sure Link would pursue that line of questioning.

"Only once or twice, briefly. I don't think she ever truly considered it."

Link nodded. "All right, was there anything else you wanted to tell us?"

"I called because of Felicia's neighbor just below her."

"Oh?" Link asked, leaving the question open for elaboration.

"He has been obsessed with Felicia since she moved in here last year. I've caught him taking pictures of her through the windows, peeking in her windows. He follows her around the complex when she goes on walks."

Grace wrote more notes as she listened carefully.

"This guy gives me the creeps. I've reported him to management several times, but they never do anything. Can't be bothered to lose a good paying tenant because he might be off the wall a bit."

"Do you know his name?" Link pressed for more information.

"Hal, I think. I only met him once, and that was three years ago when he moved in."

They spent another ten minutes with Mrs. Ramusken before making their way down a floor to Hal's apartment. They'd run the address to get his full name and check for any priors, of which he had nothing other than one speeding ticket and a couple parking tickets. Nothing that would tip him off to being a sexual deviant like Mrs. Ramusken was convinced.

Link also took lead this time, which Grace didn't seem to mind since they were working more his case than hers. When no one answered the door, he knocked again, this time a little more forceful. Finally, on the third knock, Hal opened the door. He looked like they'd woken him up, his black hair tousled, his cheeks red from sleep.

"Are you Hal Galveston?"

"I am. Who are you?"

"I'm Detective Link Abrams, this is Detective Grace Halling. We wanted to talk to you about your neighbor Felicia Erikson."

"Uh...yeah, sure." He brought them into the dim apartment, hitting the light so they could see.

Hal moved to the kitchen to make coffee before sitting on the couch. Grace and Link took the chairs nearby.

Link looked Hal right in the eye. "What do you know about Felicia?"

"She was sweet. We dated a while back, until I found out she was pregnant because it definitely wasn't mine."

"And she was okay with that?"

"We'd only gone on like three dates before she found out, and she was completely honest with me. She'd rebounded with her ex shortly after their divorce was finalized and got a nice surprise for it. He didn't believe her that it was his."

"Did you?"

Hal shrugged. "Didn't see any reason she'd lie to me, and she didn't seem like the kind of girl who would jump into bed with a bunch of different guys either. She barely kissed me on our second date."

Grace looked around the apartment, taking in what she could see of it. He had a camera settled on the kitchen table. When the coffee was ready, Hal got up and poured himself some.

"Are you into photography?" Grace asked. "My daughter is thinking about learning."

Hal sat back down. "I'm a photographer for the newspaper. It's why I was sleeping. Most big events happen in the evening, at least what I'm sent to."

"Do you ever do portraits?" Link stepped in, following Grace's train of thought.

"Sometimes. I did some for Felicia if that's what you're asking. She couldn't afford maternity photos and wanted some. It seems to be the new hot thing on the market right now. Not really my style or my thing, but I know some photographers make bank doing those kinds of shoots."

"Did you take any photos of Andrew after he was born?"

Hal nodded. "I did. I went up to her apartment when he was only a week old and took some. I hadn't even gotten them back to her yet. I suppose I could send them to her mom or her ex. He'll end up with Andrew, right? When you find him?"

"We have to find him first, Mr. Galveston," Grace stepped in. "Did you see anyone else going to visit Felicia since she had the baby?"

"See? No. Hear? Yes."

"What did you hear?"

"Floors aren't exactly insulated well here, and since she's right above me…I heard her talking with another woman, a voice I didn't recognize. The conversation was heated, including some yelling. Andrew must have been a little over a week old at that point. I'd already done the photos. I didn't hear a lot of what they were saying since everything is muffled, but they were not happy."

"Did you see the woman leaving?"

"Yeah. She got into some big black SUV thing. I didn't pay too close attention to what because I wanted to make sure Felicia was okay and I had to go to work. I checked in on her, she was fine. Upset, but fine, and didn't want to talk about it. So I went to work."

"Did you get a look at the woman?" Grace asked, interrupting Link.

"White. Brunette. Hair midway down her back. She was wearing a winter jacket and jeans. That's about it."

"That's helpful, thank you."

When they were back in the cruiser, Grace read over her notes while Link drove. As he pulled into the station, she let out a sigh. "So now we have a mysterious pissed-off woman."

"We do."

"You want to take on that one? I could use the extra time to find my missing lawyer."

"Sure thing." Link smiled at her. "Want to meet up tomorrow

to talk about it?"

"We can do that. I'm sure I'll be here all day again."

Link snorted. "Think about a transfer, especially because I'm pretty sure Delwin will get the captain position."

"You're shitting me."

Link shook his head. "I'm not. She's wanted one from the get-go, and it was never going to happen in Homicide, especially after...well, it was never going to happen in Homicide, which was part of why she transferred."

"Do you know who else is interviewing for it?"

"A sergeant from Warrants, but that's quite a leap for a change, and one of the Captains who still works the streets, so he has no experience in detective work."

"Oh. No one else?"

"No one else wanted it, not with the way Humbard left it."

"Great." Grace tightened her jaw. She hadn't thought about that. Moving up had never really been on her radar, so she hadn't put much thought into the politics behind it all. "I'll consider it."

"I'll put a word in with my captain, if you want."

"Sure, why not? What harm can it do?"

"If Delwin finds out?"

"On second thought, you're right. Let me think on it first."

Link smiled at her again. "You got it."

They walked into the building together and then went their separate ways. Grace was definitely going to find time to talk to Amya as soon as she got a chance. They needed to reconnect.

ROAD BLOCKS

"YOU GOT a minute, Halling?"

Grace glanced up from her desk toward the door that led into the hallway and to the rest of the station. Link stood, leaning in the doorway, staring right at her. She shuffled over to him, and they moved into the hall and away from Missing Persons.

"What's up?"

"I got another lead."

"Oh?"

Link shrugged. "Forensics finally got back about the computer. Seems she was dating someone or trying to date someone. One of the phone numbers she was texting matches up with a name on a dating website she had her profile up on."

"Oh really?" Grace crossed her arms. "Which site?"

"Does it matter?"

"Maybe. Was she only on one?"

"So far as we can tell. You want to go check this guy out?"

Grace glanced at her desk through the open doorway. "Sure. Let me wrap this up in the next five minutes. I can meet you out at the cruiser."

"Sounds good." Link turned and walked away.

It didn't take Grace the five minutes she'd thought it would to finish up the research into Leon Gross. He really had just vanished.

He'd pulled cash from his accounts, but as soon as he were on a cash only trail, it was far harder to track him. Grace left a note on her desk that she was going out with Homicide to check on a lead rather than telling Paige because she knew how that would go.

When she got into the cruiser, Link handed her a handful of papers with a driver's license photo on it, name, physical details along with his record. Grace skimmed it as Link pulled out of the parking lot.

"So...do we think this is a decent lead or not?"

"It might turn into it. He doesn't have any priors, at least, nothing that might put murder and kidnapping on the radar."

"I see he was arrested for public indecency."

"Five years ago."

Grace moved on to the next piece of paper, which was the actual arrest record and report that Link had pulled from their system. It was a standard arrest, and he hadn't put up a fight. He'd been drunk, downtown, young, and idiotic. Grace snorted. The number of men in particular she had arrested for pissing in public was higher than she had wanted it to be, but she'd worked nights for a long time before switching to days when she was in uniform.

"You think this might be the guy?"

Link shrugged. "I'm not really sure yet. Won't be until we talk to him, but I'm betting it's not. I do want to know what happened with him and Felicia, however. If she was up on a dating website, it means she was trying to date. With a new baby in the picture? That seems odd to me."

"It could." Grace stared at the picture of their newest suspect again. He had green eyes, shaggy black hair that looked massively unkempt, a chiseled chin and pointed nose. He was not the most attractive man she'd seen, but he seemed to fall into Felicia's type for men, based on Jonas, Hal, and now this man. "She did try to date Hal."

"Before she was showing."

Grace pressed her lips together. "Just because he broke up with her because she was pregnant didn't mean she wanted to break up because of her pregnancy. If she didn't want to keep the baby..."

"There's no evidence to say she didn't."

"None that we've found yet, but I imagine the thought crossed her mind on more than on occasion. She's young, single, newly divorced, and about to be a single mom to a baby who's dad wants nothing to do with him."

"Jonas hasn't been given a fair chance to be a dad yet."

"Bullshit." Grace's voice rang through the cruiser, her tone harsh and jaded.

Link turned to look at her curiously. "Did I hit a nerve?"

Grace's cheeks reddened. He had. She had. And she hadn't even anticipated walking right into that one. It had been years since she'd been truly angry about her own father, but the thought of a dad just walking away? Yeah, that had hit a nerve.

"Sorry," Grace muttered. "But she told him about the pregnancy. He choose not to be involved, not to go to appointments, or talk to her or support her."

"Why would he if he can't prove the baby is his?"

"You've been married to someone for years, and you don't trust them to at least give you that decency? Nothing about Felicia has told us she was running around on him or he was running around on her. They were both young and stupid when they got married, but they've known each other so long, would you not even give one ounce of attention to what she might have said, one moment of maybe she is telling the truth?"

Link's lips parted, then he locked them shut. Grace huffed and pressed herself into the seat, willing the conversation to end. She hadn't anticipated it would go this direction, and she was trying to defend her point without bringing her personal life into it.

Grace barreled forward, trying to defend her argument. "I think we need to look more into why Jonas truly might think the baby wasn't his. There's more to it than that."

"There might not be," Link stated, his voice quiet.

Clenching her jaw, Grace held her tongue, though it was hard and more out of self-preservation than to make her point. She didn't want to have to talk to Link about the shit her father had pulled, and that was clearly where the conversation was headed if she didn't shut up.

They arrived at the small apartment complex on the east side of town. It was one of the mid-level complexes. Grace shoved the reports on the dash board as she stepped out of the vehicle right into a pile of slush. Drawing in a deep, slow breath, she closed her eyes. It had been ages since she had done that. Link had gotten her so upset that she hadn't been able to think about where she was stepping and going.

Shaking her leg off to try and get the cold snowy water out of her shoe, Grace groaned. With a sloshy shoe, Grace followed Link to the apartment and let him take the lead. She wasn't in the right mindset to do it anyway. As they were led inside to the small living room, Grace noted everything in the apartment. It was pristine, everything put in its spot.

Link sat on the couch with the thin, lanky man. Grace stood near the door, her arms crossed as she observed everything. Link's voice was clear and precise as he spoke. "How do you know Felicia Erikson?"

Luca sighed and brushed his fingers through his hair. "We went on a date."

"How many dates?" Link asked.

Grace hardened. She had to pull herself out of her own anger, it wasn't going to be good if she couldn't get out of her own head and focus on the case. Listening to every word Luca had to say, Grace took it all in. Perhaps this would help them get some answers.

"One." Luca closed his eyes. "I knew you'd be by eventually."

"There were hundreds of text messages exchanged between the two of you."

Luca nodded. "She didn't tell me she was pregnant, and it took about a month of talking before she was willing to meet up with me for the date. She told me the day of our date. What was I supposed to do? Cancel it just because of that?"

Link raised an eyebrow at him. "Might have been the better option."

"I didn't want to hurt her. She was so sweet and cute." Luca brushed his hands through his hair and sighed. "I didn't think she'd end up dead. I saw it on the news. I can't—I can't believe that happened."

Grace ground her molars. Every story was the same, and they were getting no closer to any answers. They hadn't found any clues as to who might have murdered Felicia or who might have taken Andrew. Link pulled out his notebook.

"What did you tell her after your date?"

"That I wasn't interested in continuing anything with her. I really wish she'd said she was pregnant. Carrying another man's baby? That's a huge turn off, you know?"

Link didn't comment, which was wise. Grace wouldn't have either. Link moved forward with his next question. "When was the last time you saw her and spoke to her?"

"Um..." Luca closed his eyes. "She said she had a month left to her due date? Or something like that. The last time I spoke to her was the night after our date. I called her and told her I didn't want to date her."

They spent another thirty minutes with Luca before they left.

Grace jumped into the cruiser and heaved a breath while Link got behind the steering wheel. With the engine running, Grace glared. "That was a complete waste of time."

"We have one more person knocked off our list." Link's tone was quiet.

"We have no more list."

Link sent Grace a glance. "You're right, and we need to remedy that."

"I'm never going to find this kid."

"Don't give up, Grace. Babies are relatively easy to hide for a short period of time, but the older they get the harder it is."

"Unless they completely change everything about him. It's not hard with a baby, no one knows what they'll look like in a few months or a few years."

Link sighed. "Who is most likely to take a baby?"

"From a home? Someone the victims knew. Kidnappings by strangers don't happen like this."

"Then it's someone she knew, and we need to cast a wider net."

"I suppose," Grace murmured, sinking into her seat. Link drove back to the station in silence.

With the cruiser parked, Grace had her hand on the door when Link's fingers on her shoulder stopped her. She jerked with a start, and he pulled his hand away sharply. "Sorry."

"No, I am." She shook her head. Her reactions that day were all over the place, and she couldn't figure out why. "What'd you need?"

"Don't give up hope, Grace. We've just got to be more persistent."

"You're solving a murder investigation, Abrams. What hope can you have? Your victim is dead."

His lips thinned. "And don't you think Felicia's family deserves some answers? That Andrew deserves some when he gets older?"

Grace shot him a glare. "I have to find him first for that to happen."

"You'll find him, Halling."

She snorted.

"Have some hope, and some faith in your abilities."

"I'm working a kidnapping case with no leads. Every way we turn is another road block. Everyone we've interviewed has led us nowhere. The more time passes, the more impossible it'll be to find him."

"Grace."

His tone made her glare again. It was gentle, but there was a patronizing undercurrent to it she didn't like at all.

"You have to have some hope. Seriously."

"Fine," Grace grumbled, mostly just to end the conversation. "I'm going inside to see if I can find us some real leads."

"You and me both."

Once they were in the main doors to the station, they parted ways. Grace passed by the chaplain's offices, but the debate over whether to visit with Amya didn't even occur to her. She'd probably just mess that up even more too. With heavy feet, Grace walked to her desk.

Collapsing into her chair, Grace sighed. Her head hurt, her heart hurt, her body hurt. Link may have wanted her to have some hope, but she wasn't sure where to find it anymore. Everything in her life, work to home life, seemed to be going wrong. Amya and she had barely spoken since their argument, and while they weren't fighting, they were still fighting. Grace hadn't been able to resolve anything with Amya in the meantime because she'd been so caught up in work and finding Andrew.

She pulled out her messy bun, letting her hair float around her shoulders, the blonde strands way too long. She couldn't even remember the last time she'd managed to get it cut, but it was way past regulation length. She always followed regulations. Growing up with no rules, Grace had thrived as soon as the rules were in place and she had something to follow, something to guide her. It had been why she'd loved working for the Sheriff's Department, although it wasn't the only reason.

Looking up, Grace glowered. Kline and Jackson both sent her pitying looks, and she wondered why. *They couldn't possibly know what she was thinking, right?* Grace pulled up all the reports she had on Felicia and Andrew. There had to be a hint somewhere. She could work on it at home or even back here after she went to the school. It was Friday, after all, and she wanted to go down to the school. Amya had been right. She'd missed way too many of her Friday afternoons with the kids. She needed the rejuvenation for herself.

Checking her watch, Grace noted the time. She had an hour before she had to be there. She could at least start making lists of the connections Felicia had. She was going to leave none of them unturned. Time for baby Andrew was running short.

She spent thirty minutes starting her list from scratch. It was pointless in some ways, but it did help focus her. She was just getting to names with those she hadn't visited or interviewed yet when the alarm she'd set on her phone went off. Ending it, Grace stretched her back and neck. She would go down to the school, spend some time with Kit and the other kids, and then come back and finish out her work for the night.

It'd mean she'd work late, but at least she'd get to spend some time with Kit and the others. It might rejuvenate her, which was exactly what she needed. Grace pulled her hair back up into its messy bun and put her desk into order. She was just pushing out her chair to stand up with Paige's cool tones hit her.

"Where do you think you're going?"

"Uh...Hamilton High School."

"For the case?"

Grace tilted her chin up, her spine resting against the hard back of her chair. Paige looked unmovable. She'd seen that look before, many times, but usually it was turned on suspects and not on fellow officers of the law. Grace crossed her arms. "No, for my class."

Paige shook her head. "You're not going."

"Paige, I haven't been in weeks. I can't keep finding substitutes to cover for me."

"You shouldn't be doing it anyway since you have to leave the work early. I never approved it."

Grace's heart raced. "Humbard approved it."

"And I'm not Humbard. He hasn't worked here in months, Halling. He got fired. You really think his ethics were in line."

"You really think yours are?" Grace clenched her fist, not quite believing those words had come out of her mouth, but they had. She was finding her limits with Paige were far closer than she'd thought. Months of this bullshit was enough.

Paige glowered. "That is over the line, Halling."

"You want to talk about being over the line. Let's talk about it."

Paige glanced around the room, the sudden stillness and quiet of it setting Grace on edge. She knew she was making a scene, one she had vastly tried to avoid, but if she was going out, then she was going out with a bang. Paige needed to hear what she had to say.

"That's quite enough." Paige's voice was calm, cool, and collected. Everything Grace was not, and it made Grace even more on edge knowing she couldn't even keep her shit together. Paige quieted her tone, leaning down so only Grace could hear her. "If you have a problem, Grace, you can speak to me in private in my office."

Shivers ran up and down Grace's spine, Paige's breath on her face. Being alone with Paige in her office was the last thing she wanted. Closing her eyes slowly and opening them to stare right into Paige's green eyes, Grace pursed her lips. "My issues with you are well known throughout this unit. They all see how you treat me, don't think it's gone unnoticed."

Without another word, Grace pushed her chair out from her desk and stood up. She turned sharply, headed for the door, and didn't intend to utter one more word to Paige that night.

Paige gripped Grace's forearm, holding her in place. "Where do you think you're going?"

Ripping her arm away, Grace glared at Paige's offending hand. "Somewhere to cool down, and somewhere I can find a replacement for my other obligations."

Paige released her. Grace let out a snort as she twisted around and stalked out of the room. Her anger didn't subside as soon as she was in the hallway. Every nerve in her body was on fire with rage. People walked through the halls, officers, captains, victims, and perpetrators. Grace had no mind for them. She knew where she had to go, the only place she could.

The first door revealed Khloe. Grace gave her a hard look. "Is she—"

"Go on in."

At Khloe's worried tone, Grace knew she must look a mess. Nodding sharply, Grace stepped around the main desk and straight for Amya's office. The door was open, and as she moved inside, she shut it, locking the door. Amya looked startled as she turned in her chair and stared up, her crystalline eyes watering with tears. Grace hadn't realized how bad it had become.

Sighing, Grace leaned over Amya's chair, cupped her cheek, and pressed their mouths together. She closed her eyes, putting all of her pent up frustration into the kiss. Amya resisted at first, but within seconds, she'd given in. Her hand curled behind Grace's head, holding her in place. Grace tangled their tongues, slid a hand against Amya's breast before settling it on her waist.

Grace's anger seeped away from her, just like she'd hoped it would. Grace moved down to her knees, pulling Amya's face toward her as the angle changed. Amya's hands were in her hair, pulling the strands from her bun as their mouths remained locked together. Grace didn't want to pull back, didn't want whatever they were doing to end. She needed this comfort only Amya could give her. She needed Amya.

She had a few moments in her life since they'd been together when it was as clear as day that she needed and wanted Amya. This was one of them. Nipping at Amya's lower lip, Grace ended the kiss and pressed her forehead to Amya's.

"I need to go to the school today, don't I?" Amya's voice was sad, resigned.

Sitting back on her heels, Grace looked up into Amya's eyes and pleaded with her silently. "Paige won't give me the time."

"She never does."

"I know." Grace was resigned, her heart shattered. Her mentor had planned for this program before he'd died, and she'd so desperately wanted to keep his memory alive and honor who Daniel was in helping those kids who desperately needed the help and attention. That was why she'd started the program to begin with, to help the kids who desperately needed it, to lighten her case load because she got to them before they went missing.

"Grace." Amya's eyes were sad. She brushed a thumb over Grace's lips.

"I promise you, I'm working on it. I promise."

"You can't keep doing this. It's not good for you."

"You're right." Tears pricked at Grace's eyes, but she didn't want to cry. She was tired of feeling this way, tired of feeling like her whole world was falling apart piece by piece and no matter how desperately she tried to hold it all together, it wasn't working. "I'll figure it out."

"You don't have to figure it out alone."

But everything Grace had ever done, she'd done alone. Every decision she'd made since she was sixteen she had done on her own. Daniel had given input, but she had been the one to make it. Not sure what to say, Grace nodded. "I need to get back."

"All right. Can we talk last weekend, please?"

"Yeah. We need to."

Amya's fingers against Grace's cheek tilted her chin upward again. Leaning down, Amya pressed their mouths together in a sweet kiss. "I guess I better get going, then."

"Probably. Tell Kit I'm sorry."

"Always."

Standing up, Grace moved to the door as Amya shifted around her office and gathered her things. Grace said nothing else as she went back to her desk, plopping into her chair. There was a stilted silence in the room, people sending her looks over their shoulders and computers, probably wondering when she'd break again. Paige didn't dare come out of her office–thank God.

Grace pulled out the list she'd started earlier, she went to work on continuing it, but she found it desperately hard to keep focused. When the clock hit five, Grace grabbed her bag after shoving her work in it and left. She couldn't stay there any longer than necessary, and even if she had to work from home, she would. At least she'd be able to concentrate there and not wonder what Paige had up her sleeve this time.

INTERFERENCE

GRACE WAS barely up Saturday morning when her phone buzzed. She sipped at her coffee slowly before glancing down at the device, debating whether or not she even wanted to see who was calling. The possibility that it might be someone with information on baby Andrew made her pause. She had to answer it.

"This is Detective Halling." Her voice wasn't as confident sounding as she'd hoped, but it was still early in the morning and she'd barely been awake more than five minutes. Amya was up, blessedly had made the coffee already so Grace didn't have to, but it wasn't even seven in the morning and after the last few weeks, Grace didn't care if someone thought she was unprofessional.

"Grace. It's Paige."

Furrowing her brow, Grace pulled the phone away from her ear and looked at the number. Where the hell was Paige calling from? "What's wrong?"

"I need you to come in today."

"No."

"This isn't optional, Halling. This case with Andrew needs to be resolved immediately. I spoke with the FBI this morning, and if we don't make any progress on it in the next few days, they're going to take over the investigation."

Grace froze with the coffee mug halfway to her lips. She closed her eyes and sighed. She didn't want the FBI to take over the investigation. *Who would want that?* But maybe it would be for the better. She would be able to sleep again that was for damn sure. No, she had to stop thinking that way. She'd never wanted to give up on a case before, and even though she thought about it now, it wasn't because of the case itself. It was because of the woman she was on the phone with.

"When?" Grace asked.

"I need you here in the next hour."

Grace flicked her gaze up to the clock on the microwave. *Seven-twenty-one.* She pressed her lips together tightly. "I will be there before noon."

"Before ten."

"No. Noon, Paige. I will stay as late as I need to tonight, but I won't be there before noon."

"Halling, get your ass in here before ten."

Sighing, Grace gritted her teeth. "Fine."

She hung up the phone and set it on the kitchen counter and walked away. If Paige called back, she could easily wait an hour and a half until Grace was in the office to deal with it. There was no need to talk to her again so quickly. Taking her coffee into the bathroom, Grace shut the door and turned on the shower, staring longingly at the bathtub. Oh she missed the days when she had time for a hot bath after work. Even if she had to do it without the whiskey because Peter was still there it would be a welcome respite.

Sipping her coffee while she showered, Grace prepared herself emotionally for the day. It would be quiet in the office on the weekend, most likely her and Paige, but hopefully Abrams would have been called in to help too. He had as much stake in the case as Grace did. If he hadn't been called in, maybe Grace would call him herself—although, maybe she'd also give him the day off too, like she wasn't able to have.

Washing her hair and rinsing it out, Grace got out of the shower, finding Amya staring right at her as soon as she opened the curtain. She raised an eyebrow in Amya's direction as she took the offered towel and dried herself off.

"You're going in to work, aren't you?"

"Please don't argue with me, Amya. I don't have the energy for it."

Amya sighed, leaning against the bathroom sink as she watched Grace finish drying off and wrap the towel in her hair. Grace grabbed a second towel and wrapped it around her middle. Before

Peter and Kit, she would have walked unabashedly naked in her own house down the hall to her bedroom. Now she had to be more careful.

Picking up her empty mug, Grace gave Amya a pointed look. "She said the FBI is going to take over the investigation soon if we don't make any progress on it."

"Andrew's case?"

Grace nodded.

"What about your other case?"

Shrugging, Grace walked to their bedroom, Amya hot on her heels. "I don't know. Paige doesn't seem to care much about that one."

"Are you still working at the mall next weekend?"

Grace paused as she reached in their closet for clothes. "I plan on it. I wouldn't miss it for anything."

"Good." Amya crossed her arms over her chest. "I guess I'll see you for dinner?"

"Probably not." Grace stepped over and kissed Amya gently, although there wasn't much energy in the embrace. She finished getting dressed, grabbed herself a travel mug full of coffee and headed in to work.

Snow had been falling all night, so the tires on the cruiser crunched as Grace pulled into the parking lot at the station. It had been plowed at one point, probably hours before, but there was enough of a dusting on top of it that it covers the soles of Grace's boots. Grabbing her shit, she made her way inside. One day without seeing the inside of that building would do her some good.

Kit was about to be on winter break soon, and Christmas was coming up, as Amya had so kindly pointed out that morning. Grace and she still needed to do some shopping, though Grace figured Amya would end up doing all of it. Walking into her unit, Grace stopped short. No one else was there. The light was on in Paige's office, but that was it.

Great, this is going to go well. Grace settled into her desk, turning on her computer and sipping her coffee. She would try to get out of there as soon as possible because the prospect of being alone with Paige all day was not one she wanted.

"Halling! Good, you're here. We got some tips in about Andrew." Paige slid over a stack of tips, and just from a glance, Grace could tell they hadn't even been gone through for the first round of weeding, which meant she would have to do it. Whatever Paige had been doing in her office all morning, Grace had not a clue as to what it could be.

Grace barely acknowledged Paige, diving straight into the tips. She was able to eliminate over three-quarters of them as she went. The last quarter were the ones that stumped her, and she spent a good two hours on the phone calling about them, eliminating all but two. She sent uniformed officers to check them out.

Paige sat next to her, plopping down a takeout meal while she dug into her own. "How's it going?"

Grace pressed her lips together hard. Everything she was doing here she could have done at home. There was no emergency that Paige insisted she come in for. Yes, if the case went on too long with no advancements, then the Federal Bureau of Investigation would come in and work with them before taking it over, but there was still time before that might happen. Besides, the extra help might be useful.

"This case is slow. There are literally no clues. Someone came in—she let them in—they stabbed her, took the baby and ran. No immediate family member has the baby, and it is so rare for a kidnapping like this to happen with a stranger, but we're going to be forced to look in that direction soon."

Paige nodded. "Boyfriends?"

"She didn't have one." Grace sighed, building the fajita Paige had bought her before shoving it in her mouth. "She dated. But no one at the time of her death that we know of."

"There's got to be something."

"There's nothing. That's what I'm telling you. Whoever did this is like a ghost. There's no contact with random people she didn't know. Yes, she considered adoption briefly, but that didn't last long and didn't get further than a talk with a social worker. Her finances were in order. She even had the DNA test Jonas insisted she get to prove he was the baby daddy in her kitchen ready to be mailed back."

"Think he could have killed her in order to prevent her from mailing that in?"

"And done what with the baby? Killed him? It's possible, Paige, but I don't get that sense from him. You're thinking too much like a homicide detective."

Paige snorted. "Always suspect the spouse, kid. Most often it's them who did it."

Grace sighed and took another large bite of her fajita. It was warm, good, and just what she needed. Paige and she had worked well together at one time, and this was very reminiscent of that. Yet,

Grace still felt this underlying tension they had never been able to resolve, the tension of Paige's growing crush on her and Grace's refusal.

"I'll look into him again. Link and I can go over it Monday. I'm not coming in tomorrow, Paige."

"Fine."

Grace pursed her lips. "And don't forget next weekend I'm not coming in Saturday. Santa's at the mall, and I signed up for it."

"All day."

"Every year. You know that."

Paige groaned. "Don't remind me. Once was enough."

Grace smirked at that. The one time she had convinced Paige to go with her had been enough for the both of them. It was much better if Paige stayed at the office or home. She was not a people person but definitely not a kid person. It wasn't much longer until Paige's phone rang in her office. She vanished behind the door.

When Grace was alone again, the tension eased from her chest. She had to get that under control, and she had to figure out a way to get Paige back on track with the way they used to be. Telling her no wasn't getting them anywhere, it seemed, so it might just take a report being filed up IAB. Grace finished her fajita and turned back to her computer to double check everything with Jonas, like Paige had suggested, before she moved on to the next suspect to look at. She still felt as though she were blinding fumbling in the dark when it came to this case.

Hundreds of interviews, hundreds of hours watching security footage, scrolling through phone, texts, email records, and there was no connection to Felicia and someone who may have taken Andrew. But they were working under the premise that Andrew was the target. Maybe Paige was right, maybe killing Felicia was the purpose, and Andrew had already been taken, killed, and dumped. Why the killer would do that, she didn't know. Why Andrew wouldn't have just been killed in his crib and left with his mother? No idea.

Or even why Andrew was killed at all. No newborn would be able to identify a killer—at least not in conventional ways. Either way, she had loads of work to get done, and since she was there for the day, she might as well get to it.

Amya had the kitchen was so spotless that Grace would know something was up when she came home. If she was awake enough to even notice when she got there. Amya abandoned the kitchen, picked up the living room, and then tackled the bathroom. Somewhere in there she had driven Kit to work. By the time she was done with the bathroom, she still hadn't worked off all of the angry energy she'd hoped.

What could she do? Grace was stubborn as they could get, and there was no way to convince her to put in for a transfer or file a report. Grace was stuck in her ways, and she was nearly immoveable. Amya had run into that side of her so many times throughout the years, and while she did convince Grace to move sometimes it took years of strategic planning.

Amya couldn't be strategic or logical about this. Paige crossed boundary lines in every direction, and Grace just took it. But something had to give, something had to make it stop, and that something might end up having to be Amya. She didn't want to have to be the one to file the report, but she just might have to. But, God, she didn't want to.

Putting all the cleaning supplies away, Amya washed her hands in the kitchen sink and collapsed into the couch, tears in her eyes. She grabbed hold of the pillow and held it to her chest, holding back the tears that wanted to spill over her cheeks. She had done so much crying lately, so much raging, so much cursing the situation she found herself in.

What could she do? She couldn't control Grace, that was for sure. She didn't even want to. What Amya wanted was her girlfriend back. She wanted time with Grace, time as a family, the lack of stress, the lack of worrying might happen when she was on shift. What she would give for the days when she worried more about Grace getting hurt than their relationship ending because of one woman.

"Amya?"

Turning her cheek, she looked up to see Peter standing in the doorway. Tears streaked down her cheeks, her vision blurring over. He dropped whatever he was holding by the door and rushed to the couch. Wrapping his arms around Amya's back, he tugged her into his chest and held on tight. Amya sobbed. There was no cure for her jealousy. She'd tried to pray it away so many times, tried to sit in the emotion, tried to distract herself, but it was always there, sitting right in the pit of her belly and waiting to strike.

"What's wrong?" Peter whispered, his voice so full of concern.

How could she tell him, though? How could she confess that their relationship was failing not because of Paige and Grace's refusal to transfer out of Missing Persons, but her own damn jealously.

"Amya, tell me. What happened? Is it Grandma? Grandpa?"

She shook her head. "No, no, it's nothing like that."

Sniffling, Amya wiped her nose. She drew in a deep breath and tried to get control over herself. It was one thing to lose her shit when the kids weren't home, but when they were? Peter didn't need to see this, and he didn't need to be the one to pick up the broken pieces of her either.

"I'm fine. Really."

"You're not fine." Peter took his thumbs and wiped the still falling tears from her cheeks. "What happened?"

"Nothing happened, to be fair. This is just me having my breakdown." She snorted. "Did you know at one point I told Grace we couldn't break down at the same time?"

He shook his head, still not moving too far from her.

"Yeah, well, I think if you don't get back to school soon, you might be witness to it."

Peter chuckled wryly. "I have never seen you lose your shit, Amya. You're the calmest person I know."

That at least brought a small smile to her lips. "I do. I'm not perfect, as you have seen from living here no doubt. I can be every bit of a jerk as Grace or anyone else."

"Maybe, but you being an ass is limited to scary silent looks."

"Is that the mom-look you're talking about?"

"Yes. Definitely yes. Kit will agree with me."

"I'm sure she will." Amya tried to move herself away from Peter, but he held on and pulled her in for another hug. This one lasted longer than the first, and when Peter moved away, he glanced toward the kitchen.

"I see you've been cleaning."

"It's Saturday. That's what we do on the weekend."

Peter's lips pressed together. "Sure, we scrub every surface of this house until it doesn't exist anymore because it's so fucking clean."

"Language," Amya muttered. "And shut up."

Peter laughed. "You've got to get over whatever it is that's bugging you."

Amya sighed. She knew that already, but it had been nearly eighteen months of this feeling living in the pit of her belly and all it had done was grow. She'd attempted to stunt it, and even kill it, and it had gotten her nowhere.

"Want to talk about it?"

"Not with you. Thank you for the offer, though."

"I get it. You think I don't have any experience in this arena. That I don't know what it's like to feel alone and ditched."

Amya's gaze riveted to Peter's eyes. She supposed he did have a point, and that was all he saw from the relationship issues between her and Grace. Everyone saw that. It was next to impossible to miss. He hadn't shown any signs of knowing what the root of the problem was, however. Which, for Amya, was a good sign. They had managed to hide it even from the kids who lived in the house with them.

"I suppose you do have some experience with that."

"I do. My parents? My friends? My ex when I decided to get sober again. I've been left so many times I came to expect it until you and Grace."

Amya's mood shifted. She went from dwelling in her jealously to listening to probably the most honest Peter had ever been about his past in all the years she had known him. She gripped his hand and held on tight, encouraging him with silence to continue.

"I hated it, Amya. I did. Living that way was the worst experience of my life, but you know what it got me? It got me you, a Chaplain, someone I can admire and look up to, someone who shares in that belief with me."

She smiled then, and tears welled in her eyes but for a completely different reason.

"It got me Grace. This bitchy, strong ass woman who never looks back when she makes a decision and who loves with everything she's got. She loves you Amya. I see that every time she looks at you. But she also loves her work."

Snorting, Amya brushed her fingers over her eyes. "She does. I'm her second wife."

Peter laughed, shaking his head. "No, you're her first wife. Her second is definitely work. I think it took her a while to see that."

"Maybe."

"Feeling better?"

"A bit. Thank you." Amya cupped Peter's cheek.

"I've got just the thing to get you all the way there."

"What's that?"

"Cookie bake."

Amya out right laughed.

"You have to help me make it."

"Fine." She waved her hand. He jumped up from the couch. Amya followed him into the kitchen, the dogs at their feet as they moved. They were going to destroy her newly cleaned kitchen, but that was the point, wasn't it? Having family meant things didn't stay clean. It meant she had to deal with the heartache and pain that came with some conversations and some emotions.

Peter pulled out all of the ingredients they would need. They chatted aimlessly about him going back to school, studies, Kit, and hopes for the future. Amya kept her own fears at bay, leaving Peter out of that part of the conversation. He didn't need to know it. He didn't need to be worried about what might become of them if Amya didn't figure out how to resolve her own issues.

TIT FOR TAT

THE HOUSE had been tense all weekend, but they hadn't had a moment to talk through it. As Grace checked her email Monday morning, she eased into the work week. Although, to be fair, it hadn't really ended either. She'd successfully worked every weekend for over a month straight.

She'd gone through as much of the reports and information she'd gotten back over the weekend. Grace had hop-skipped between both her missing persons cases, trying to keep up with them and keep a balanced glance on both of them. She never had a case as big as Andrew's, and it was so easy for her to get sucked into that one and forget about Leon, but she couldn't. He deserved her attention as much as anyone else, although he wasn't a critical missing.

Not getting anywhere on either of her cases and spinning her wheels was getting to her. She didn't need Paige's reminders about working or finding something. The guilt in her chest was already enough. So when the next email she hit was her assignment for Santa day, the smile that lit her lips was welcome.

She needed that day. After putting in so many hours, sacrificing for her family, she needed the hours of doing something for someone else to relax and soothe her weariness. Grace knew Santa day was the perfect day for that. The whole family was supposed to volunteer actually. How Amya had managed to convince Kit to do it, she had no idea, but she was going to take it. Kit was slowly coming out of her shell and finding her feet. Grace was pretty sure she'd make it.

Before everything got started on her day and she wouldn't have any hope of catching Amya, Grace snuck out of her unit and down the hall toward Amya's office. Santa day had always been something they could share together, ever since that first one Amya had done when she'd started at the Sheriff's Department three and a half years ago. Perhaps this could be one of those connections that would get rid of the space between them.

Opening the first set of doors to Amya's offices, Grace waved at Khloe. "Hey, Khloe."

"Hey, Grace! You're looking much better than the last time I saw you."

Guilt twisted in Grace's stomach. She had been coming less and less, and usually only for specific reasons or quick moments to try and convince Amya to do something for her, like her Friday program. "Yeah, I've been slammed with a tough case."

"I figured as much."

At least Khloe wasn't in on the fact Amya and she barely saw each other lately, and it wasn't all because of work. Grace could finally admit that. Grace wasn't making the family a priority, and that did have to change. She had to find a way to redraw the boundary lines and have more family in her life. Grace plastered a smile on her face, "She got a moment?"

"The next hour."

"Good." Not hesitating, Grace walked to the farthest door from the front of the offices. She knocked, waited for Amya's sweet voice to call her to come in, and slipped inside. Shutting the door behind her, Grace's stomach muscles tightened even more. Even after nearly four years, this woman was still amazing and gorgeous. Grace needed to remind herself of that more often.

When Amya turned to look up at her from her desk, Grace smiled—genuinely—for the first time in, she couldn't even remember. Amya had her light brown hair pulled up into a high pony tail, and the lilac colored suit she'd chosen to wear that morning was a statement to who she was—confident, beautiful, close to being one of the higher ups, but someone who could walk lines and did it often.

"I got my assignment for Saturday." Grace gave her a smile, trying to ease into the conversation or any conversation. Why was just talking to Amya so hard lately? Everything in their relationship had become difficult.

Amya sighed. "Do you think you'll even be able to go?"

"I told Paige I'm not coming in for anything. I need it. I think we all need it."

"I couldn't agree with you more there." The underlying snarky tone in Amya's voice set Grace on edge.

Here she was, coming to Amya with some sort of weird olive branch, and all she was getting in response was attitude. Maybe their relationship was further gone than she'd thought it was. Grace rubbed her lips together, biding her time to try and figure out how to respond. She could give equal attitude back, but that likely wouldn't get them anywhere.

Drawing in a deep breath, Grace held her ground. "I miss you and the kids. I feel like I'm never home anymore, and I think next weekend will be good for us."

Amya rolled her eyes. "You feel like you're not home because you aren't home. Even if you are, your phone isn't more than two inches from you and Paige is texting or calling or emailing about something to do with work, drawing you back in."

There it was again. That tone. What the hell was Grace supposed to do with that? She was the cause of it, but there was no way they could resolve this issue in one five second conversation about volunteering at the mall. Grace shrugged. "You're right."

"I...of course I'm right." Amya's words were vicious. Grace was glad she'd shut the door. "I'm the one who has had to pick up all the slack at the house with zero support from you, but that's not even the worst part."

Grace looked directly into Amya's crystalline blue eyes. She tried to hold back some of her own snark, but she was pretty sure it snuck in there anyway. "And what is the worst part?"

Amya stood up, getting right into Grace's face, so close but not touching. "You."

Grace's heart stuttered. Her voice was surprisingly calm when she spoke. "Me?"

Tears filled Amya's eyes but didn't spill over. Grace wanted to reach forward and wrap Amya in her arms, but she was pretty sure Amya wouldn't want that at all. Dragging in a ragged breath, Grace waited for Amya to talk, anything so they could work on whatever was going on between the two of them.

"You don't want to do anything to try and fix this."

"Fix what?" Again, Grace managed to remain calm. How? She

had no idea, because she was never the calm one.

"Us!" Amya nearly screeched. One small tear fell from her eye. Grace went to reach forward and brush it away, but Amya jerked back and shook her head. "Don't touch me."

"Amya...please talk to me."

"No. All I've done is talk and sit in this, and I can't do it any more, Grace. I really can't. Something has to give, and right now it's me."

"I don't want you to break." Grace reached out, skimming her hand down Amya's arm until she could tangle their fingers. Drawing Amya in, they shared a quick hug before Amya stepped back, that anger still in her eyes.

"You need to do something about it."

"About what?"

Amya snorted. "Like you don't know."

"I don't know which is bugging you the most right now." As soon as Grace said it, she regretted her choice of words. Because she did know what was bugging Amya. The one thing Amya had told her about that they had then successfully avoided for a year. Amya was jealous, and it hadn't gone away. The more hours Grace spent at work with Paige, the more jealous Amya became. The cycle was vicious, and Grace was pretty sure there was only one solution—she just didn't want to do it.

"You know exactly what the problem is. It's her."

"Paige."

Amya gave a snort nod. "Yeah. Not just how she treats you, but how she's always keeping you at work. She has no boundaries, Grace, and she gives you those nasty habits."

"I can't quit my job."

"I don't want you to quit your job," Amya shot back. "And if you think that, you haven't been listening all year."

Grace cocked her head to the side. "I can't transfer. There aren't any openings."

"IAB—"

"No!" Grace's voice rose. "I won't do it, and you shouldn't even be asking after I told you my answer. I won't go there."

"Then condemn yourself to living in this hellhole." Amya stepped away and turned toward her desk.

Grace's fingers itched to do something, anything, to take that pain away from Amya, but it wasn't working. There was nothing she could do right then and there that would ease the discomfort. Not a kiss, not soft and gentle words, not promises or even words of love.

Amya was so wrapped up in her own jealously that anything Grace said wouldn't be heard.

Saying nothing, Grace turned on her toes and walked out of the office. She shut the door behind her, plastered a mask on her face, one she had been wearing for months. Everything was fine. Everything was going to be fine. Nothing was wrong. She nodded at Khloe, chatted with her for another minute like nothing was wrong and walked out of Amya's office.

They had been on the edge of whatever that was for months. The turmoil made Grace's stomach hurt, her chest tightened with pressure. Everything hung on whether or not Paige got the promotion permanently, but even then, Grace wondered if they could go back to the way they were. Paige had started some of this before then, before Humbard had been fired and she'd been given temporary leadership.

Staring at the door to her unit, Grace let out a sigh. She couldn't worry about it right now anyway. She had two cases on her plate, both needed her undivided attention. But she also knew, somewhere deep in the back of her heart, she couldn't keep putting this off. She had to do something, *anything*, to makes amends for this past year.

When Grace got to her desk, the weight of everything pressed down on her. Yes, Amya had to do some work on her issues, but Grace really needed to make a change or a decision or do something. They couldn't keep living in the world of stagnation they'd found themselves in, no doubt mostly Grace's fault, since she was so slow to make any big changes in her life anyway.

Furrowing her brow, she stared at her computer. Leon might have been the same way. Everything she had learned about him so far was routine, routine, routine. He came in to work the same time every day, left and went home. Everything was in order at his desk, perfect, easy to find the next day. He didn't have much of a life outside of work. Grace snorted. She and Leon definitely had more in common than she'd realized at first.

She pulled up his financial records on her computer and stared at them, cocking her head from one side to the other as she scrolled through. *What if he had a break?* Amya had once told her that it was rare for her to break, but when she did, it was bad. What if Leon broke? What if he'd literally just stepped away from his life and went to do something else. Who would he tell? Because as far as she could figure, it'd be no one. He had no one. His sister, yes, but it didn't seem like they were all that close.

Grace got to the one part of his financials when they stopped. The cash withdrawal not huge that it would trigger the bank to be worried, but it was large enough for him to buy a gun and some bullets at a pawn shop, get some drugs if he wanted, hire a prostitute, buy a plane ticket. Scratching the back of her head, Grace reached into her bottom drawer and pulled out a small bag of dried apricots. It was a good thing she'd restocked her stash over the weekend, because she was going to need it.

With the conversation with Amya playing in the back of her mind, Grace munched on her snack while wondering just what Leon Gross had done with all that cash. Felicia Erikson had been particularly short on cash. Seems her two missing had opposite problems, although Felicia wasn't her missing.

Rent was going to be a problem for Felicia to pay. Yet she had taken the time to purchase a private paternity test kit for Jonas. Felicia wasn't working, yet she was the one making all the accommodations for Jonas to be a father. Curious, Grace pulled up Felicia's financials again. There were small purchases here and there, but one stood out to her. A coffee shop over in Johnson County.

Grace knew that place. She'd been there with Blake a few times when she'd been down for an investigation or to pick up a kid Blake had found who needed transport back to Grace's county. What was odd about this purchase was it was the only one outside of their city. Felicia hadn't done anything else in Johnson County, not even gas up her car, so she'd only been down there and back after the coffee.

Felicia getting a coffee wasn't abnormal—at least according to her financial records. They'd stopped when she had Andrew, but picked up again two weeks after he was born. Felicia really had no money to her name. Those medical bills were going to hit hard and fast without her having a job, but she wasn't even going to have a place for her and Andrew to live before that happened. What would a young, unwed mother do in order to provide stability for her newborn child?

In Grace's opinion, she'd do just about anything, especially if she wanted to keep that child, yet Felicia hadn't asked anyone for money so far as Grace could tell. They'd asked on and off during interviews, depending who they were talking to, and no one had mentioned Felicia having financial difficulties. Even her own mother had said Felicia had a nest egg, which she clearly did not.

But that led Grace back to Johnson County, to the coffee shop.

Who had she met with? Grace sent an email to Link, asking him to check it out while she focused on Leon. As much as she'd like to focus on Felicia, there were at least two detectives working that case, whereas Leon's case relied solely on her.

Flipping back to Leon's financials, Grace stared at them as if by osmosis she would know where he'd spent the cash. Cursing under her breath, Grace popped another dried apricot between her lips. This was hopeless. How was she supposed to track cash spending without any hints as to where he had spent it?

Sighing, Grace pulled the Internet on her computer and did a wild search. She looked for businesses in her county that accepted cash only. There were very few. Most were small startups or businesses that took cards but only cash when they were at some sort of event, which during the holiday season there were tons of. That had been pointless.

She closed out the search and rubbed the bridge of her nose. She had to think like herself. Leon was used to routine and structure. He was slow to make decisions, but when he made them he went all in. Sure, it was a huge assumption on her part to make, but he seemed to fit the bill at least for now, and it was a running theory she was going to go with.

With pen in hand, Grace took her notebook and scribbled on it. If she had to leave and give up her life, if she was at the point that she needed to make a huge change, what would she do? She wouldn't get rid of the house because that was still a safety. Leon still had his apartment, his car even, though he'd left it at the apartment. He'd left everything there, like he intended to come back or he intended to never come back. The latter of which was the scarier scenario.

Say he was coming back, he couldn't get far on foot, although Grace was pretty sure he hadn't done that. Unlike Grace, Leon didn't take care of his physique. He wasn't a runner or a jogger or a gym buff. In fact, nothing about him said he ever went to the gym or ate healthy, meaning he wasn't going to go for a marathon run into the next county just for shits and giggles.

He would have most likely left in another vehicle. Grace perked up at that. He didn't have any friends to take him anywhere, so he would have gotten hold of someone he didn't know, some kind of service. The number of companies that could have taken him were endless, but Leon was a man of routine and comfort, so that did help in one way.

Once more scanning Leon's financial records, Grace looked

for one specific item. Some type of ride-share or taxi. Since the dawn of technology and smart phones really taking over, the amount of services had skyrocketed. Grace skimmed through each line item, hoping one stood out to her as a company she knew or heard of. If Leon had none in his personal records, then she'd call the firm and see who they used. Surely they used someone, right?

"Fuck."

There, right in the middle of the previous month was a ride share, a glorified taxi company, and one Grace knew very well. Drawing in a deep breath, she closed her eyes and centered herself. She'd arrested the owner last spring and had assumed the business had gone completely under since it was pretty much there already.

Rolling her neck, she popped it. Then she rolled her shoulders to get rid of some of the tension. Picking up her phone, Grace dialed the number and waited as it rang.

"Taxi Services, where can we take you today?"

The voice sounded vaguely familiar to her. The slight accent, the crisp words as if he was trying to hide an accent. Going for it, Grace spoke firmly. "This is Detective Grace Halling, I would like to speak with the owner."

"Detective Halling?" His voice wavered.

In an instant, Grace knew who she was talking to. Joseph. Matteo's dad, the kid who had been in ICU in a coma for years and no one knew who he was until Grace had gotten the case. This was a nightmare. "Uh...yes. Is this Joseph?"

"It is." He sounded like he was going to cry.

Grace sighed. "How's Matteo doing?"

"We took him off life support a month ago."

"I'm so sorry to hear that." And she hadn't heard about it, which was shocking. She should have. It was her former case, but she'd been so wrapped up in work and the Ping pong with work and family life that she hadn't even gotten a chance to really watch the news and stay up-to-date on life in her city.

"Yes, it was the right decision." Joseph sniffled.

Grace cursed inwardly. She hadn't meant to bring up a slew of emotions for him, but there was no way even her mere presence wouldn't do that. "Did you take over Angel's company?"

"Yes. We did. He'd run it into the ground. It's taken some time, but we're nearly in the black every month now."

"Good for you." She was happy for him, even if it had necessitated this call. "I was actually calling about a case."

"Oh? Anything we can do to help you, Detective Grace. It'll be our pleasure."

Grace smiled to herself. At least he was happy with her, though she was still sure talking to her was a mixed bag of emotions. "I'm calling to see if you drove a man named Leon Gross a few weeks ago, right before Thanksgiving."

"Let me check."

A keyboard clicking echoed through the line. Grace waited patiently as she was sure Joseph was looking up what she needed. He hummed through the line, and Grace waited with bated breath for another thirty seconds before Joseph finally answered.

"We didn't. But if the customer paid cash, we wouldn't have his name, just a location."

"Oh, can you look up by address?"

"Yes."

Grace rattled off his address and waited again. This was a hail mary if she had ever seen one, but humans were typically creatures of habit, and Leon was no different except that he excelled in his habits.

"Here it is."

"You drove him?"

"It seems we did. The Wednesday before Thanksgiving."

"Can you tell me where he was taken?"

"No. There was no address given when he called it in. But I remember that one. My driver took him to Johnson County because I had to call in a second driver to replace him while he was gone. A large fee for a ride."

Grace's heart thumped. This might just be the break she needed. "Can I talk to your driver?"

"No."

"What?" Grace's shoulders stiffened.

"He went to Mexico for the week to visit his mother. He won't be back until just before Christmas."

"Will you give me his name and contact information? I'll need to talk to him as soon as he's back."

"I can email that to you."

"Perfect." Grace sighed. "Thank you, Joseph, this was very helpful."

"You're welcome, Detective Grace. You brought us answers when we had none."

She smiled lightly, bidding her goodbyes and hanging up. She hoped she'd have to call him again, but either way, she was glad that Joseph was at least adjusting well to all the trauma she had brought to their family. With a light of hope on one case, Grace settled in to see if she could figure out just where Leon had asked to go in Johnson county, and it may just give her the break she needed in his case. She might even call Blake up and see if Blake wanted to join her on the adventure.

PROFILING SHAME

GRACE WOKE up early. She had spent all of the previous day lost in financials, trying to figure out what Leon could have possibly wanted in Johnson County. There wasn't much there as it was a much smaller county than hers, though some of the laws were more open and liberal. Perhaps he had knocked up some teen who needed an abortion. Snorting at the thought, she shook her head. That seemed very unlikely, but she wouldn't put it past him. Anything was possible.

Everyone in the house was still sleeping. She sipped at her coffee, the wooden dining room table cool under her fingers. Yesterday had been the longest day ever, and Amya hadn't wanted to talk when she'd gotten home from work. Their argument had been on Grace's mind all day and all night. She'd barely been able to sleep, although she hadn't been locked out of the bedroom this time, which she was thankful for.

The snick of the door in the hallway caught her attention. Kit sometimes woke up early, but when Grace turned to see who it was, she was glad to see Amya sneaking out of the bedroom instead of Kit. Maybe now they could finally talk. Amya stalked down to the bathroom then shuffled her way to the kitchen and dining room. She eyed Grace suspiciously as she moved slowly.

Shit, I'm in trouble.

Taking a long sip from her coffee, Grace set it in front of her as she waited for what fresh hell she was welcoming into her life with this conversation. They needed to have it, but that didn't mean she wanted to. It was going to be tough, and no doubt it'd take them a few rounds to figure out how to listen to each other. They seemed to be out of practice doing that lately, not that Grace was ever very good at it, but Amya was.

Amya made her own coffee, sitting across from Grace. She barely looked her in the eye. Grace waited patiently, something Amya should be proud of her for since normally she bulldozed her way right into the conversation, but Grace knew Amya had to lead this conversation.

"About yesterday," Amya started. "I'm sorry."

"Sorry for what...exactly?" Grace's shoulders stiffened, but she needed an answer. She needed to know just which part of yesterday Amya was sorry for.

Amya sighed. "I'm sorry for arguing with you at work."

Grace wanted to cry. That had been the last thing she'd thought Amya would apologize for. Whatever was happening between them, it must be bad if Amya thought Grace was mostly upset because they'd argued at work. Grace was probably the one of the two most likely to start an argument there. Clenching her jaw, Grace closed her eyes. "Well, thank you for apologizing for *that*."

What Grace really wanted an apology for was the outlandish out of nowhere problem Amya had brought up. When Amya remained silent, Grace sighed. She only had thirty minutes before she had to be at the station. Amya's shift started later than hers, although lately, Amya still finished first.

When they sat in silence for ten minutes, Grace took a step to end the agony. "Are you working at the jail today?"

"Yeah."

"Then I guess I'll see you tonight."

Amya didn't answer as Grace pushed her way up from the table and walked to their bedroom. She was dressed and ready for work in record time. Amya had brought up a point in their argument the previous day that they needed to talk about, but if she wasn't going to talk, then Grace couldn't even begin to have those conversations and find resolutions.

When she got into work, Grace sat at her desk and stared at her computer for a full five minutes before she picked up her cell phone. Her lawyer definitely had gone to Johnson County. She had no idea if he was still there or if he'd left, but she'd called Blake the day before and now the two of the were working on it.

Grace had a phone call to make, one she should have made well before now. Grabbing a clean notebook and two pens in case one crapped out on her, Grace walked to the back of her unit where the interview rooms were. Sitting down, she set her notebook up and took a deep breath. Why was it she always seemed to call Morgan for work help when she and Amya were arguing?

Dialing the number, Grace listened and prayed Morgan would answer so she wouldn't have to leave a message or risk having to call again. Morgan didn't answer. Grace rubbed her eyes as she debated what to say when leaving a message, but the phone in her hand buzzed. Pulling it away from her ear, she saw an incoming call from none other than FBI Special Agent Morgan Stone, Amya's oldest sister.

Grace ended the voicemail and answered the call. "This is Grace."

"Grace? You called?" Just like Morgan, always short and to the point.

"I did. I wasn't sure if you'd heard about the case I'm working." Grace felt stupid as soon as she said it. It'd be a toss-up if Morgan had heard about it. She wasn't necessarily working that case on their end, and it had been in the news, local and national, and they lived decently close, but that still didn't mean Morgan would have heard about it. "Baby Andrew who is missing. Mom murdered in her apartment before the baby was taken."

"Oh." Morgan's tone raised up. "I didn't realize that was your case."

"Yeah. Um...you're not working that one from your end, are you?"

"No. Then I would know it was your case."

"Right." Grace clenched her fist, digging her nails into the palm of her hand. Morgan's know-it-all tone wasn't helping Grace's confidence. "Do you have a minute?"

"I'm on the phone, aren't I?"

Either Grace was striking out, or something had crawled up both their butts. She'd talked to Morgan several times even though she'd never met her in person. Apparently she was the sibling who knew everything about the family, according to Amya. Grace wondered briefly if Morgan was aware of their issues. Pushing that thought from her mind, she realized she had to stop wasting Morgan's time.

"Right, anyway, I need help with a profile. I'm a bit stumped.

I'm used to missing teenagers, not babies."

Morgan snorted. "These cases are rare enough as it is."

"Yeah. We've checked out everyone in the immediate family thoroughly and don't suspect any of them at this time. Not ruling them out. I know most of these cases are done by family, but could you give me a little more insight into the mentality of someone who would kidnap a baby?"

"Uh...sure. Got some paper?"

"Yes."

Morgan drew in a deep breath, and Grace caught sounds of someone talking to her. Morgan sighed. "Hold on."

The line went quiet. Grace held on as she waited. Patience was apparently the name of the game for the day. It took Morgan two full minutes to come back on the line—Grace had checked to make sure they were still connected several times.

"Sorry, Pax needed something."

"Your partner?"

"Yeah. You gotta get out here some time to visit. Amya says we'll get along."

"I'm pretty sure she says that about everyone."

Morgan snorted. "I think you're right. Always the perpetual optimist."

Except for lately, Grace thought. Bringing the conversation back around to the purpose of the call, Grace asked, "So the profile?"

"Yes. Like you said, the kidnapper for infants in this case is typically a woman, a young woman, someone who is related to the family."

"Immediate?" Grace asked.

"Most often, yes, but even then related far more often than not. It's very rare for stranger abductions to happen in the cases of infants from the home."

Grace wrote down a few notes, surprised Morgan knew this abduction had been from the home since the case wasn't hers. If the kidnapper was family, then her search needed to be expanded drastically to all cousins, aunts, uncles, and perhaps even friends one might consider family.

Morgan continued, "If she took the baby from a hospital or store or whatever, she usually is in a relationship with a man, and she tells people she has lost a baby frequently. Whether or not she has isn't really the point. She could have had miscarriages or they could all be in her head."

Grace had most of this information already, but hearing it

from Morgan gave her confidence that her research hadn't been wrong. "Does she often have other kids?"

"Um...she can. Not necessarily though. Usually if she does, it's likely that the man she's currently with isn't the father of the other kids. Because she's usually trying to provide his baby as motivation for him to stay with her."

"That's shitty," Grace muttered. When Morgan laughed out loud, she realized she'd spoken instead of just thought it.

"Yeah, real shitty. But these people aren't right in the head. If they were, I wouldn't need a profile for them."

"Agreed."

Morgan sighed. "Whoever she is, she's damn good at lying and manipulation. She'll be able to twist stories and lies with the best of them, so you have to be on your toes."

"Great."

"However, since this case happened in the home, whoever did it is actually most likely to be single while claiming to have a partner. She wants to have the house with the white picket fence and two point five kids. So she says she has a partner when she doesn't."

"Interesting that there's a difference."

"Yeah, most research is done on abductions of infants outside the home since they happen far more frequently. The profiles are often blurred accidentally."

Grace had made the same mistake. The profile she'd researched had given her the wrong information just like Morgan had said it might.

Morgan's voice quickened. "I've got to run, but one last thing. When the abduction is out of the home, it helps to not look at family, too. A social worker or nurse, basically someone who is claiming to be in that profession even they aren't. Look at distant family, too. Not everyone follows the profile perfectly, and without details on the case, I can't tell you one way or the other."

"Right. Thanks, Morgan."

"Any time, Grace. And I meant it about visiting. It's been too long since I've seen Amya in the flesh, and I'd like to meet this girl she's been hung up on for three years."

Grace smiled. "Sure, we'll make it happen as soon as we can."

As Morgan hung up, Grace let out a sigh. She only hoped there was enough of a relationship in the end that she'd actually get to meet Morgan. With the new information in hand, Grace went back to her desk to expand her list of people to check on. She still had a lot to learn, and it was good to have someone like Morgan to talk to when she needed.

Grace grabbed her notebook from her conversation with Morgan as soon as she'd been able to put a little more of her thoughts and papers in order. Leaving her unit, she walked down to Homicide, finding Link at his own desk, hunched over his computer.

Sitting on the edge of his desk, Grace smiled down at him. "Find anything?"

"Not a fucking thing." The edge in his tone was one she hadn't heard before.

Cocking her head to the side, Grace stared down at him and waited for an explanation.

Link heaved a breath. "It's like this killer vanished or never existed to begin with."

"That's impossible."

"I know." Link narrowed his gaze at her. "We have all this evidence and no one to even think about matching it to."

"Maybe this will help." Grace flopped her notebook down onto the desktop with a loud snap.

Link leaned back and stared at it. He turned his head at it as he read some of what Grace had written, then he turned his head the other direction. "What is this?"

"I called my sister-in-law."

"Because that makes sense."

Grace chuckled. "She's a profiler for the FBI out of Chicago. I asked her for the basic run down on a profile for someone who would kidnap an infant in the home."

"Oh!" Link grabbed the notebook and pulled it closer to him. "So, anything new?"

"Yes. These are not commonly stranger abductions, which we knew, but when they're out of the home, they're meticulously planned." Grace pointed to the notebook. "She said the woman who is often the kidnapper will most often know the victim, is a master of deceit, and she's often working up to kidnapping for a long time."

"All right, but this isn't exactly big news."

Grace snorted lightly. "When it's done in the home, the kidnapper is often single versus when it's done in the public. What that means is we had the wrong profile all along."

Link shifted his gaze from the paper to Grace. "So who are we looking at now?"

"So glad you asked, Detective Abrams." Leaning forward, she flipped the top sheet on the notebook up to reveal the sheet underneath. "This is a list of those involved with her at the hospital that we know about, including social workers. I took the time to call her mother earlier and ask if there were any social workers who stopped by the house and there was one social worker and one home nurse. Their names are listed here, and I think we should start there."

"You were busy."

"Always." Grace smirked. "I also put together a list of her more distant relatives who are young women with or without partners."

"With? You just said she's most likely single."

"Yup. But master manipulator, remember? She lies, and in this case, not uncommon for lying about partners."

"Ah." Link skimmed the list of names.

Some of the people they had talked to briefly already, but Grace wanted a more in depth conversation with a few of them, and she was pretty sure Link would as well. "I should have thought to call Morgan sooner than I did."

"Maybe, but this might help us. Did you check the licensing for these social workers and nurses?"

"I did. They're all on there. So I'm not sure if they're our targets or not, but definitely worth a more in depth interview."

"You're right. Let's get started on this." Link pushed away from his chair and grabbed his jacket.

Grace followed suit, letting him lead the way. When they got into the cruiser, they strategized who they were going to talk to first. They went from home to home, from work to work, striking out at every turn. As they crossed more names off their list it was a relief to be making some progress, but a frustration to not be finding any suspects. Grace wanted to find this baby, and she knew Link wanted to find this killer.

Sighing as they struck out again, Grace rolled her shoulders and buckled her belt in the passenger seat as Link did the same in the driver's seat. Grace asked, "So what now?"

"Now we go home, get some shut eye, and try again tomorrow. There's still ten people easy on this list. And as we have more time, we'll add to it."

"I guess," Grace muttered. "I'm not a patient person to begin with, Abrams, and this case is trying what little patience I have."

Link laughed out loud. Grace turned on him, somewhat

appalled but how funny he thought her comment was. It wasn't that amusing. He shook his head at her. "I was thinking the same thing about me."

A smile hit Grace's lips. At least the two of them were on the same page for now. "I'm going to go to Johnson County soon for another case, so if we find any relatives there, I could hit them up while I'm in town."

"Good idea. I've contacted my counterparts in other counties to do some interviews, but I'd much prefer to have you or me conduct them, detectives who actually know the case and care about it."

"Agreed." Grace watched as the city around her passed by the windshield of the cruiser. "You know, I have a thought. You up for one more interview today?"

"Sure."

"Head over to Jonas' apartment."

"You sure?"

"Yup."

The drive didn't take them very long. Grace took the lead, since this idea was hers. She knocked on the door. Jonas answered after a minute. The room behind him was dark, all the blinds drawn, and he looked like he was just waking up.

"Everything all right, Jonas?" Grace asked, taking in everything about him. He looked completely disheveled, half-asleep still, his eyes had dark rings under them, but his eyes were red too. Could be drugs, but it could also just be lack of sleep or crying.

He shook his head silently, his dark curly hair moving. Jonas opened the door wider and invited the two of them in with the movement of his hand. That was a good sign at least. Grace stepped into the apartment, the stale scent hitting her first. It was messy, take out boxes left everywhere, nothing cleaned. Jonas sighed as he went to sit on the couch. Grace followed him, sitting next to him while Link stayed standing since there was no other place for him to go.

"What happened, Jonas?"

"I can't believe she's gone."

Ah, so it had finally hit him that his ex-wife was dead and his son was missing. "I know it's tough. We're here to talk to you a little more about Felicia and Andrew."

"She named him after my brother who died when he was born, you know. Andrew. That was my brother's name."

Grace's heart clenched at the thought. Felicia must have been certain that the baby was Jonas' for her to do that. Although, it could have also been a manipulation tactic to get Jonas back. "Did she tell you that?"

Jonas shook his head. "I knew it when she told me his name. Did those test results come back yet?"

Grace glanced at Link, who shook his head. "No. There's a backup at the lab because of the holiday. We should have them by the beginning of next week I think."

"I want to know if he's my son, for real." Jonas turned his dark eyes on Grace. "But I'm pretty sure I already know."

Nodding, Grace reached out and touched Jonas' arm lightly. "That's why we're here, Jonas. We want to talk to you about Andrew."

Jonas drew in a ragged breath. "Anything I can do to help, I will. I want my son. I want to honor Felicia by raising him."

"Good." Grace smiled at him, glad to see he was turning around. There'd still be a whole investigation by child protective services and social workers to make sure Jonas was fit and ready to be a parent and take custody, but if he wanted to parent, he could from what Grace had seen. "I wanted to ask if you've been dating anyone."

Jonas shook his head. "Not seriously."

"So you are seeing someone regularly?"

Jonas shrugged. "I guess you could call it that. I haven't seen her in a few days."

"When did you meet her?"

"In high school."

Grace's lips thinned. Another connection to that damn high school. "All right, how long have you two been seeing each other?"

"Well, we're not. Not really. We're more just friends with benefits."

"Ah. I'm going to need her name so we can talk to her." A glance at Link told her he was ready to take the name down.

"Ashton Haverson."

"Does Ashton know about Andrew?"

"Who doesn't at this point?" Jonas rubbed his hands over his face. "I can't believe Felicia is dead. We had her funeral a few days ago, just a private thing with the family, but I can't...I can't believe she's dead."

Grace squeezed his arm to try and give him as much comfort as she could. "Have you dated anyone else since you and Felicia split?"

Jonas nodded. "A few girls."

"We're going to need all their names."

Sighing, Jonas looked at Link instead of Grace. "I don't know all of them."

Grace wanted to roll her eyes. Of course he had gone a bit wild since they'd split. She should have expected something like that might happen. They took down what names they could, starting a brand new list of women for them to interview. They took down phone numbers when Jonas had them, descriptions of women he'd picked up where he only had first names and no other information.

Link and she were going to have to do a lot of running around and following up to figure out who these women were. It seemed as though Jonas had gone a bit crazy once the divorce went through, well, even before it finalized. They wrapped up their interview with him after asking about family members. The list for Grace and Link to check had grown by nearly fifty people. They would have to split it up to check them all out in a timely manner.

Grace stretched her back as they walked out to the cruiser. That had been an hour well spent. Checking her phone, she saw missed calls from Paige, missed texts from Paige, missed emails from Paige. She sighed. She'd check it all when they got back to the station and find out what drama she had happened while they'd been out working the case.

"That was a good idea, Halling."

"Thanks," she muttered as she got into the cruiser.

Link drove them back to the station as they split up the list and who was going to look at what. If they were going out to interview, they agreed to go together, though Grace couldn't figure out why. She was capable of interviewing someone on her own without him there.

When he pulled up, he stopped her from getting out of the car with a hand on her wrist. "I need to tell you something."

"What is it?"

"The reason I'm insisting on going on interviews with you isn't because I don't think you know what you're doing."

Confused, Grace shook her head. "Why are you doing it then?"

Link smirked. "Boss is checking you out and wants my opinion on how you work. He's thinking about trying to convince you to transfer."

"To Homicide?"

"Yup."

Grace's stomach twisted. *Could she work Homicide?* She loved working Missing Persons, and working with all the troubled teens who ran away. It was her favorite part of her job. Pressing her lips tightly together, Grace gave him a short nod. "What if I don't want to transfer?"

"Then you don't, but I think you've got the skills to be in Homicide, and I'd really like to work another case with you. You're smart, Halling. Real smart."

Grace flushed. "Uh...thanks?"

"Don't mention it." Link opened the door and got out. Grace followed suit. He said nothing else as they walked into the station and down the hall before going different directions to their respective units. All in all, her day had been far more productive than she'd anticipated.

ALONE

AMYA STOMPED around the kitchen, her feet heavy on the tiles. Grace watched her carefully from her spot at the kitchen table where she finished her breakfast. They hadn't really spoken since their argument at the office the other day, but with the weekend coming up and Santa day tomorrow, they had to figure out some balance. The kids were starting to notice.

The air around them had become so tense it was impossible for Grace to ignore it any longer. She had to do something, but she also knew that what Amya wanted her to do was impossible. She wouldn't work for IAB, even though she'd been promised a position there if she ever wanted to transfer. Her entire life she'd been the pariah, the outcast, the awkward one who didn't quite fit in, and it wasn't until she joined the academy that she felt she belonged someplace. Grace wasn't willing to give that up.

"Amya," Grace started, her voice calm and quiet. She hoped this wouldn't turn into a yelling match like the office incident. Kit and Peter didn't need to hear about it when they were already worried about what was going on between the two of them.

Amya shot a glare over her shoulder before she went back to emptying the dishwasher Grace had forgotten to do the night. Tension built in Grace's chest. She rose from the table and stepped up to the dishwasher, stilling Amya's hands and taking over.

"Amya, we need to talk."

"I have nothing to say to you."

"This is ridiculous." Grace set the plate on the counter a little too hard.

Amya cocked her head at Grace, the glare still very much alive and present.

"Yesterday you were apologizing for the argument and today you're mad again."

"I was still mad yesterday."

Grace sighed. Instead of continuing with the dishes, she tried to figure a way to break into this conversation. Deciding to just go for it, Grace grabbed Amya's hand and squeezed her fingers. "You know I'm not doing anything with Paige, right? There is no funny business going on. I'm not dating her. I'm not cheating on you."

Amya stilled. Her gaze flicked over Grace's shoulders, and Grace had to pray neither Kit nor Peter had walked in without her sensing it. When Amya's crystalline eyes were locked on hers again, Grace held all the tension in her chest.

"You need to transfer departments."

"I can't right now."

"I don't think this is going to be negotiable." Amya's shoulders were stiff, and she pulled her hand from Grace's grasp. "You might be able to live like this, but I can't. And I won't. I won't be second to your job."

Grace faltered. "You're not second to my job."

Amya rolled her eyes, the glare back in place. "I am. We are. And I won't stand for it anymore, Grace. I am more important than your job."

"You are. You absolutely are."

"Then why doesn't it feel like it?"

"I don't fucking know!" Grace threw her hands up in the air.

"Keep your voice down," Amya hissed.

Shame rattled through Grace. She'd wanted to keep this from Kit and Peter and there she was yelling and screaming. Clenching her jaw, Grace eyed Amya. "I'm in the middle of two cases, Amya. I can't just up and quit."

"I'm not asking you to."

"Why do we keep going around in these damn circles?" So much for keeping her cool. Grace had already lost that bet with herself. "And why do you keep thinking you're second to everything? You're not. I swear to you, Amya. I would never do anything to put you second."

Amya stiffened, her glare morphing into something else, something unreadable. Grace stayed put, staring and waiting. Silence—Amya would laugh right now if the situation wasn't so ridiculous because Grace was finally using it to her advantage against the woman who taught it to her.

"I understand this job comes with odd hours, Grace. That's not what I'm talking about. I'm talking about the fact that I don't see you anymore. The kids don't see you. Kit is graduating this year, and she needs us right now."

"Of course she does," Grace countered. "This has nothing to do with you."

Amya's lips parted in surprise. She shook her head. "This isn't about me."

"Bullshit!" Grace's voice boomed through the kitchen. "It's always been about you, about us. Why the hell are you going back on that now?"

Sighing, Amya stepped away from the dishwasher and folded her hands in front of her. "Who is it, Grace?"

"Who is what?"

"Is it going to be Paige or me?"

"That's not even a question and you know it." Grace's brow furrowed, confused again as to why they were on this train of thought.

"Do I?" Amya raised a single eyebrow in Grace's direction. "When is enough going to be enough?"

Grace wanted to answer, wanted to have a good come back, but no words left her lips.

"That's nice, Grace. Real nice." Amya slammed the dishwasher door shut and stalked away.

Grace stood, stunned into silence. Slowly, she turned and opened the dishwasher, emptying one piece at a time like she was supposed to do the night before. Her entire appetite was gone. She couldn't believe what Amya had accused her of. Did she really think she was second to Grace's job? *To Paige?*

As soon as she was done, Grace gathered up her breakfast and cleaned those dishes. She didn't need Amya mad about something else. Grabbing her bag, she double-checked she had everything she needed in it. With her jacket on and her bag on her shoulder, Grace left the house without another word to Amya. They'd have to talk again, but hopefully it wouldn't be as explosive the next time.

The entire drive to the station, Grace's stomach churned, the coffee adding to the acidity and making her stomach hurt. When she got to her desk, she dropped into the chair with the weight of the world on her shoulders. She wasn't sure she'd be able to make it the entire day without talking to Amya and remedying what she'd fucked up.

And there was no doubt about it. Grace was the one who had fucked up. It was always her. Amya was perfect compared to her. Dragging her files out for her two cases, Grace put baby Andrew's to the side. She focused on her lawyer, a case she figured she might be able to solve over the weekend if she had the time to dig a bit deeper.

Leon was her first priority of the day. She wanted to find out where he was. She ran his cards again, to find out if he'd used them even though she was pretty sure he hadn't. While the reports were running, Grace pulled up the retreat center's information. It was too early in the morning to call, but she searched through it to glean as much information as possible.

It seemed to be the complete opposite of where Leon might want to go, but that might be why he was there. Grace rubbed her thumb over her lip as she stared at her computer screen. Relaxation, meditation, therapy—it all seemed very froufrou. Not anything she'd want to attend, ever.

The retreat center was on the edge of Johnson County, on the far south side of it and as far away from Grace's county as possible. It was going to be a pain to have to drive down there, but she would if she needed to. She'd hoped a simple phone call would be enough to at least get a definitive location on Leon before she made the trek.

Blake would helpful no matter what, but Grace was also looking forward to spending some time with her friend again. They hadn't seen each other in person since the past summer when Blake had come up for a barbecue at the house.

Grace waited impatiently for the time to be little better. Leon's financials came back, and sure enough, he hasn't used any of his cards or his accounts, so there was nothing new there. Deciding not to wait any more, Grace picked up the phone on her desk and dialed the retreat center.

It rang four times before someone answered. "Deep Breathings Retreat Center, this is Cindy."

"I'm Detective Grace Halling with the Sheriff's Department. I was calling to see if you have a guest there by the name of Leon Gross."

"We cannot give out personal information on our guests."

Cindy's voice was saccharine, and it grated on Grace's nerves.

Grace curled her hand into a fist, her nails digging into the flesh. "Ma'am, with all respect, I am with the Sheriff's Department. I need to know if Leon Gross is there since we are looking for him in connection to one of our cases."

"We cannot give out personal information on our guests."

Groaning, Grace rolled her eyes. If this was going to be the canned line she got with every question she asked, it was going to be a long and frustrating phone conversation. "Cindy, I'm not looking to cause issues or even arrest Leon. He is a person of interest in one of my cases, and I need to know if he is there, nothing more."

"With all due respect, Detective, we cannot give out personal information on our guests."

Grace held back the curse she wanted to shout into the receiver. This was obnoxious. "Can you tell me if he is a guest there?"

"I cannot confirm if anyone is a guest here. It is part of our policy to withhold information on anyone who may or may not be here to respect their privacy."

Grace narrowed her eyes at her computer. This was going nowhere fast. Nothing would go wrong if it was confirmed Leon was or wasn't there, but the fact these people thought they could withhold such information might impede another investigation if there ever was one.

"Look, Cindy, I just need to know if he is there or not." Grace's tact was certainly lacking, probably left over from her argument with Amya that seemed to be never ending lately. Her patience had vanished and her skill for precise wording was gone.

"Ma'am, I can't help you." The line went dead.

Grace stared at her phone in awe. It was rare anyone ever hung up on her, especially in her official capacity, but now she wanted more than ever to drive down to Johnson County and take Blake with her to see what the hell was up with that. Unfortunately, it was going to have to wait until Monday because she was stuck in town for the weekend. Her favorite day of the year was the next day, and she'd planned to make it perfect even if she and Amya were arguing. Kit and Peter had agreed to volunteer for Santa day, and it was going to be their first big family to-do.

All day, Grace had spent on the phone doing interviews and going out with Link. When she got back to the station, she was ready to collapse. Her feet hurt, her body ached, and her mind was still stuck on the never-ending argument between her and Amya. Not to mention, they were no closer to finding baby Andrew than they had been the day prior.

Every person they'd interviewed had been helpful but not full of useful information. She'd gotten a few more names to add to her list and crossed off even more. They still had more people they needed to find before she could feel as though they'd fully done their job, but that could wait until Monday.

Dropping her down jacket onto the back of her chair, Grace sat down heavily and turned on her computer. She wanted to write up her report of the day and fill out her log before she headed home for the weekend and Santa day. She needed the time with the family. Amya was right, she had spent way too much time at the station lately, and maybe a sabbatical from the case and work would do her mind well and she'd be able to catch a break in Andrew's case.

She got an email from Link and smiled as she opened it up. He was always so prompt. She read it over, responded in kind, and then started on her notes. She'd type them up, exchange with Link and then fill out her reports fully. She was halfway through her own notes when Paige's hand on her shoulder shocked her. Jumping a little, Grace turned around and stared up at Delwin.

"Got a minute?" Paige asked.

"I was finishing up my notes."

"Come on." Paige didn't give her an option as she headed for her office.

Holding in her groan, Grace followed her inside. Paige shut the door, and Grace managed to hold back her shudder. "What's up?"

"I could ask you the same." Paige sat on the edge of her desk, arms crossed, and faced Grace. "You've been in a mood all day."

Grace glanced at the clock on the far wall. "But the day is about over, so it doesn't matter. I got the job done. I just need to finish up my notes, and I'll be out of your hair."

Paige shook her head. "Not how it works in here, Halling."

Eyeing Paige, Grace tried to find a way to get out of the conversation. She didn't want to be there, and she didn't want to be having this conversation, not with anyone but Amya. Staunchly, she kept her mouth shut and decided to wait Paige out.

"What's going on today?"

"I went out with Link and we did some interviews. I'd like to bump up my trip to Johnson County to Sunday if that's all right, so

I can do some interviews there and maybe find my missing lawyer."

Paige's head moved side to side. Grace's stomach dropped. Paige would never make this easy, would she? "That's not what I meant."

Grace shrugged. "I'm close to solving the case for Leon Gross. I couldn't get confirmation via phone that he's at Deep Breathings Retreat Center, but the cagey attitude of Cindy makes me think he is. They would just deny him being there if he wasn't there rather than trying to protect his information."

Paige's green eyes locked on Grace's. "I meant at home."

Sighing, Grace shoved her hands into her pockets. "Nothing is going on at home, other than I'm not there and I'd rather be there for dinner tonight instead of here."

"We have to talk about that in a minute."

Grace swallowed hard. The rock in the pit of her stomach doubled in size. "What do you mean?"

"Tell me what's going on at home."

"No."

"Halling." The warning tone in Paige's voice was there, but Grace ignored it.

"No. Are you saying I have to stay late tonight?"

Paige issued a sigh. "First, home. Then we'll talk about tonight."

Grace's heart raced.

"You know you can talk to me, Grace." Paige's voice softened.

Sure, Grace could talk to her, but it would come back to bite her in the ass just like it did every time, add in that Grace just didn't want to talk to her about it. She wanted to keep this as professional as possible as much as she can—that was always what she wanted.

"I know," Grace replied. "About my case, if I can go to Johnson County on Sunday, then I can—"

Paige shook her head. "You can't go Sunday. You can go Monday."

"All right. Fine." Grace crossed her arms and stared at the floor. "What did you need to tell me about tonight?"

"I need you to work overtime on this case. Not just tonight, but tomorrow."

"I can't work tomorrow."

"It's not an option."

Grace's lips parted. "No, I can't work tomorrow. Paige, I volunteered at the mall tomorrow, to work the Santa arrival and photos. I can't work tomorrow."

"It's not an option." Paige raised an eyebrow at Grace. "If you don't solve this case by Monday, the FBI is going to take over it. It's been too long without any progress."

"Too long?" Grace's voice rose. She rubbed a hand over her forehead. This better not have to do anything with the phone call she'd made to Morgan the day before. Pacing back and forth in front of the door. "What did they say?"

"They said they're going to take over the case if you don't bring someone in by Monday."

"Who said it?" Grace stopped short, waiting for Morgan's name to be dropped.

"The FBI."

"Who in the FBI?"

"I don't know, Grace. The orders came down from above me. I don't know specifics. Just get the case solved.

Grace's heart raced. "No, tell me who!"

"I don't know, and you need to calm down, Halling. Get ahold of yourself. If you're having issues at home, you need to find a way to deal with them, because they're affecting your job. It's got to stop."

Clenching her jaw, Grace glared. "Amya and I had a fight, all right. It's fine, we're fine, we'll figure it out, but it is *not* affecting my job."

"It is," Paige fired back.

"It's not." Grace put her foot down, firmly. "I can't work tomorrow, Paige. I'm serious. I've had this scheduled for a year now."

Paige shook her head. "Like I said before, this is not an option. You will be at work tomorrow or you will receive a disciplinary action."

Grace held her breath tightly in her chest. She didn't want that to happen, and Paige would know it was a way to get her to come in. Saying nothing, Grace turned toward the door and wrenched it open to leave.

"Halling, you need to finish your reports for tonight, and you need to stay at least three hours of overtime, preferably more until you have a solid lead on this case."

Tossing a glare over her shoulder, Grace slammed the door shut as she stomped toward her desk. She glared at anyone who dared to look at her. Speaking to no one, she sent Link an email to tell him she'd be working overtime and the weekend if he wanted to do any more interviews during that time.

She typed furiously, her fingers punching every key pointedly as she typed out the rest of her notes and finished up her reports. Everyone else filed out of the office one at a time, leaving Grace alone with Paige. This was exactly what Grace didn't want to happen, and she was pretty sure it was exactly what Paige designed to happen.

"This is bullshit," Grace muttered. Not to mention, how the hell was she supposed to tell Amya why she wasn't going to be home on time tonight, but better yet, why she wasn't going to be there tomorrow. It was only going to feed into the argument they were still having. Cursing again, Grace grabbed her phone and shoved it into her pocket.

She walked all the way down the hall to Amya's offices and stopped in front of the door. She couldn't go in there. This problem was her problem, and she needed to resolve it. She just had no idea how that was going to happen. Still, Grace needed to figure out something.

Pushing her way through the front door of the offices, she noticed Amya's private office door was closed. Grace smiled at Khloe. "She busy?"

"Just started a session."

Grace nodded. "Got a pen and paper?"

Khloe handed it over. Grace scribbled on it, writing an apology along with her reason for not being home that night. She'd tackle tomorrow when she did manage to get home and could talk to Amya in person. Last minute, Grace wrote down "I love you" on the paper, folded it and handed it over to Khloe.

"Thanks," Grace muttered. "Catch you next time."

Walking back to her desk, Grace sat down a little more settled than before. She still didn't like being forced into overtime, again, or the fact she was missing her favorite day of the year, but if it kept her out of receiving a disciplinary action, she'd have to go along with it. Although, she did plan on making Amya call Morgan to see if this was all her doing or not. It was one of the reasons she hated the FBI. They always came in, took cases without second questions—or first questions—leaving her in the dust.

Grace pulled up the profiles she'd created for the interviews she'd done so far. She started to file them in order of those who most likely fit the profile of their murderer and kidnapping, assuming still they were one in the same person. She bent over her desk, working hours on the case and losing sight of what time it was even.

When she finally surfaced, her stomach gurgled, and she realized she'd forgotten to eat all day. That never happened. She was the queen of snacks, but when she thought of it, she'd barely eaten anything lately except when she was at home. She checked her desk but didn't find any snacks there. After nixing the idea of going to the vending machines, Grace stretched her back. She needed sleep, rest, some sort of break from being in the damn station.

When her three hours of overtime were up, Grace went to check in with Paige to see if she could leave, only to discover she couldn't. Groaning, she went back to her desk and poured over the interview she'd done. She planned out the ones for tomorrow and figured out exactly what questions she wanted to ask, then she planned her interview for whenever she might find their suspect. At that point, she was just finding work to do because Paige wouldn't let her go home.

At ten, Grace stomped into Paige's office, her face set. "I'm leaving."

"Did you solve your case?"

"No."

"Then why are you leaving."

"Because I'm fucking tired, Paige." Spinning around, Grace grabbed her jacket and keys and walked out of the station. She didn't care if she got disciplinary action for insubordination at that point. Paige would have to be crazy to try and make her stay any longer when she'd been there since seven in the morning already. Rest wasn't a privilege. It was a requirement.

Dragging her weary body into the house, Grace stripped her clothes, locked up her gun, and collapsed into the bed with Amya. "I'm so sorry."

Amya didn't say anything.

Tears stung Grace's eyes. She knew Amya was awake, listening. She always was listening. Drawing in a deep breath, Grace choked back the words she didn't want to say. Ever. "I have to work tomorrow."

Amya remained silent. With an aching heart, Grace turned on her side and closed her eyes, begging sleep or something to take her because this was not the life she wanted or the one she thought she was building. Lying awake for hours, Grace stared at the wall in the dim moonlight until exhaustion took her in its grasp.

SANTA DAY

GRACE DIDN'T wake up until eight, and the house was already a bustle of movement. The far side of the bed was cold, which pained her. She didn't expect Amya to wait for her to wake up, especially when she had to go to the mall to do her volunteer duties, but it still hurt. Tossing a hand over her eyes, Grace drew in a deep breath.

How was she going to explain this one to Amya?

Was it even worth it to try?

Grace had no explanation. Paige was making her work over time all weekend but refused to let her do the one thing that could potentially solve both her cases. It would more than likely solve one of the two, then she could focus all her attention on baby Andrew. She was stuck between a rock and a hard place, and Amya probably thought she willingly put herself there by not transferring departments.

In some ways, that was true. But Grace hadn't been in Missing Persons for very long, and she loved it there. Not the environment, but the cases. These were the kinds of cases that she wanted to work, people she wanted to help. Was it really worth it to give all that up because of the environment?

For Amya's sake, she might have to. Although, change was not something Grace dealt with graciously, and all she'd wanted by going into detective work and getting promoted was stability and to avoid so much change, and maybe a job that was a bit easier on her body. So far, she wasn't sure that last one was the case. She'd gotten less sleep in the last few months than at any other point in her life that she could remember. It'd been constant.

Dragging herself up, Grace sat on the edge of the bed, her feet planted firmly on the floor. Peter's loud voice boomed into her room, and she closed her eyes, a headache forming right between her eyebrows. She was going to need caffeine and medicine for that one.

Every muscle in her body ached, as if she'd been up for days running. Which, in some ways, she supposed she had. Running off coffee and annoyance. Even her beloved orange juice had fallen to the wayside as she drank the dark bean brew to keep herself going.

The door opening startled her, Grace grabbed the blanket and covered herself as best as she could in case it was someone other than Amya, but Amya's bright eyes greeted her. Grace sighed and held the blanket in place, casting her gaze over Amya as she tried her best to judge Amya's mood. She was nearly unreadable.

"I'm sorry about today," Grace started.

"No way to avoid it." Amya opened the closet door and pushed aside her suits to reach for her uniform.

Grace's stomach twisted. That was by far one of her favorite parts of this day—Amya in uniform—and Grace was only going to get to experience it for the next thirty minutes before they left. Unabashed, Amya stripped her pajamas and started getting dressed for the day. The tension between them was so thick. Grace's chest felt as though a weight had settled on it.

She realized all too late when Amya turned around that she still held the blanket to cover herself, which was not something she normally did. Amya raised a single eyebrow in her direction, and Grace knew she'd just been caught in the odd action. Huffing a breath, Grace cringed. She just wanted everything to go back to normal, to the way it was. The space between them was too much to bear.

Amya finished dressing in silence, and Grace stood, pulling on a pair of jeans and a T-shirt. She was tired of dressing up for a job she didn't feel deserved it lately. All she could hope was that Paige wouldn't be there today. That would at least give her some respite and a calm day. Perhaps she could talk with Blake or Link.

Grace followed Amya out of the room a minute after she left. Peter and Kit stood in the kitchen with their jackets already on and ready to go. Amya finished filling a travel mug with coffee and shot Grace a sharp look. Shuddering, Grace sighed and hoped there was still coffee left.

"Have fun today," Grace said, trying to be as upbeat as she could, but it was next to impossible. She was defeated. Paige had managed to do that over the last few months. If Grace were honest, it was longer than that. This had started nearly right after Paige had transferred into the unit.

Tears stung her eyes again, but Grace held them back. She was done crying over her favorite day of the year. She'd just have to learn to live with it since for the first time in her thirteen years of service to the Sheriff's Department she was missing out on it.

"You're not coming?" Peter asked.

"I have to go in and work my cases," Grace muttered, shooting a sidelong glance at Amya, who rolled her eyes in response. "I'll catch it next year."

"That's bullshit!" Kit shouted.

Both Grace and Amya cut her a sharp look and said together, "Language."

"What? It is." Kit shrugged.

While Grace agreed with her, she wasn't about to voice that problem to anyone. Amya didn't need the confirmation and the kids didn't need to be dragged into it.

"Let's go," Amya stated firmly, a hand on Kit's back to push her toward the front door.

Grace didn't even have the energy to ogle Amya in her uniform. As soon as they were gone, Grace brushed away the one tear that slid down her cheek and turned to the coffee pot. Sure enough, it was bone dry.

"Fucking figures." Grace pulled the filter and grounds and started a new pot.

Grace was at the station by nine with a full cup of coffee and her brain slowly starting to catch up with the day. No one else was in her unit, and the silence while welcomed was also unnerving. Grace settled in at her chair and rolled her shoulders to get to work as much as she could without leaving the county that day.

After an hour, she gave up and called Blake. "Miller."

"Blake." Grace's lips curved slightly. "I'm half tempted to tell you to work today."

"You working?" Blake's voice rose.

"Unfortunately. I'd hoped I'd be able to drive down and meet you today instead of Monday but the sup nixed that idea."

"Why?"

Grace shrugged and leaned back in her chair, pinching the bridge of her nose. "Not a fucking clue. I think she's out to get me."

"Paige?"

"Yeah." Grace's stomach tightened with anxiety. "I don't know what's going on lately."

"Tell me about it."

Sighing, Grace closed her eyes. Where was she even supposed to begin? "It's nothing. I'll be down first thing Monday to go to that retreat center, and if you've got time, I may have a few more stops to make."

"For the baby case?" Blake's curiosity was always there.

"Yeah. There's a few families I want to check out in person instead of on the phone."

"Oh." Blake's voice rose. "This I want to be there for."

Grace chuckled low. "I'll make sure you're invited."

"You do that. Send me a list of where we're going and I'll get started on it while you drive."

"Least you get a day off."

Blake snorted, and Grace ignored it. She was about to hang up when Blake's voice caught her attention. "Halling?"

"Yeah."

"You know you can actually talk to me about non-work related things, right?"

"I know, but this is all work related."

"Is it?"

Damn Blake and her perceptiveness. "For now."

"Well, I'm here."

"Thanks, gotta run before *she* comes in." Hanging up, Grace settled her phone on her desk and stared at it. With her brain mostly functioning at that point, she picked it up again and called none other than Detective Link Abrams. He'd never said in his email if was working that weekend or not, and Grace wanted to know.

"Halling?"

The noise in the background of the call told her he definitely wasn't at the station. "Abrams, you working today?"

"The mall crowd. Got called in last minute for a sub."

Grace's stomach plummeted sharply. She clenched her jaw and warred with herself. "Oh, so you're not on mandated overtime?"

"What's this about, Halling?"

"Just curious. I'm stuck here today and thought we could go on some interviews." Grace fiddled with a pen on her desk, the rumblings in the back of her mind confirmed.

"I can join you after I'm done here, but they're really short-handed this year."

Way to lay on the guilt, except he didn't know that was what he was doing. There was no way he could know she always volunteered to be there. Dragging in a deep breath, Grace stared at her computer screen with nothing else to say.

"What's this really about, Halling?"

"Nothing, just wanted to get a jumpstart before Monday."

"You were dead tired yesterday, and you're back today?"

"Glutton for punishment, I guess." She tried to play it off as a joke, but she wasn't quite sure she accomplished that. "See you later if you can manage it."

"Yeah."

Hanging up, Grace went back to work on her case. Her profiles for each of the persons of interest were lining up nicely. She'd love to be able to run them by Morgan and see if she was doing well enough at it, but she knew Morgan was busy—and if Paige was right, she still had a grudge to hold against Morgan. If Paige was lying, which Grace suspected she was, then there was far more cause to be pissed off but not at her sister-in-law.

Grace was nose deep in tracking down a wayward cousin of Felicia's when Paige came in, a huff and a curse as she dropped her keys onto the floor while trying to wrangle her jacket off. Grace had wondered at some point in the last week if Paige was living at the station, but this pretty much confirmed she wasn't. At least not yet, though the jury was still out on that one.

Keeping her mouth shut, Grace tried to focus on her computer and her work instead of looking over her shoulder at Paige and the chaos that she brought with her. Paige cursed again when she spilled her drink. Giving up, Paige dropped the coffee mug on the corner of Grace's desk and hustled into her office. She came back with paper towels to clean up her mess before sighing and tossing them in the trash.

"What a fucking morning."

Grace couldn't contain her snort. Her morning hadn't been much better. The mall event was going to last another few hours at least, and Grace knew Link would be stuck there until the last thing if they truly were that short-handed. She only hoped Peter, Kit, and Amya were at least enjoying the day.

The screech of a chair against the floor startled Grace. She cringed and spun around to find Paige pulling a chair toward Grace's desk. Grace couldn't take her eyes off Paige until she was seated with an ankle crossed over her knee and her coffee in her hand.

"Fill me in," Paige ordered.

"On what?" Grace flicked her gaze from Paige's face to the coffee to her computer.

"On your case." Paige flicked her hand out toward the desk. "What's new with it?"

"Nothing, because I haven't been to Johnson County, and I haven't done any interviews since I came in this morning."

"Let's do up your timeline." Paige pointed at the papers. "Where are we starting?"

"Which case?"

"The missing baby, of course."

Grace rolled her eyes and pulled over the papers and sat them in front of Paige. "Here's the timeline."

"No, let's do it together."

"I already did it."

"Halling." Paige's voice had a warning tone to it.

"You have got to be fucking kidding me," Grace muttered. Dragging over a blank sheet of paper and a pen, Grace scooted her chair in. Paige moved in closer, hunched, like they used to work together before it all went to shit.

What was this even, some kind of let's be friends or let's make up or go back to the old days? Grinding her molars, Grace scribbled in the center of the sheet the date and time Felicia's body was found, which was the first and only hard fact they had for the case.

Paige nodded at it. "Where's the coroner's report?"

If Paige was going to insist they go through every damn thing and recreate a timeline she'd already done up, her day was going to stay in the shitter.

"Right here." Grace rifled through some of the papers and pulled out the simplified report. She'd kept the detailed one to her computer instead of printing it, which was very unlike her. Paige's look told her she knew as much. Grace kept paper copies of everything—except lately. She hadn't the energy to do it.

Paige read over the report swiftly. "So she died roughly three days before they found her. Write that down."

Dutifully and like a mindless drone, Grace said nothing as she scribbled above the sheet of paper the window of death for Felicia. If she kept clenching her jaw that tight, the headache that had started in the morning was going to make a swift comeback.

"She had Andrew three weeks prior to her death." Grace scribbled that date next, trying to speed along the process. She didn't want to spend more time next to Paige in this close of confines than she had to.

Two hours later, they finished rebuilding the timeline Grace had already made up with only two slight modifications from her original timeline that didn't really seem to matter in the long run. Grace's back ached from being bent over her desk. Standing, she went to the table near the door and poured herself the remnants of the coffee she'd made earlier. It was old and close to sludge, but she drank it anyway.

Standing where she was, she drew in a deep breath. Something was going to give soon, Grace knew it. The feeling in the pit of her stomach that all hell was going to break loose was so strong, she struggled to make the few steps back to her desk.

Paige stood up and stopped her. Grace cocked her head to the side. "Since we finished the timeline, am I free to head home?"

"Not yet." Paige sat on the edge of the desk.

Grace put her sludge down and crossed her arms. "When is this gig going to be up, Paige? I can't keep working these hours. I need a break."

"I told you, the FBI is going to take this case if you don't solve it as soon as possible."

Shrugging, Grace stared directly into Paige's green eyes. "Maybe that's a good thing."

"How can you say that?" Paige stood up and grabbed Grace's hand. "I've never known you to give up on a case. You're the best detective we have in here, and I don't want anyone else working this case."

"Why?"

"Why what?"

Grace sighed. "Why don't you want anyone else working this case? This type of case should have more than one person on it."

"You have Abrams."

Snorting, Grace shook her head. "He's working a murder, not a missing persons investigation. They're two radically different investigations, and you know that. How could you even think we're working the same case?"

Paige's lips parted. "I don't want anyone on this case but you. You have the passion to find him, Grace. No one else does."

"Everyone else does!" Grace's voice got louder, but she wasn't screaming yet.

"Not everyone, Grace." Paige's tone dropped, and Grace had to lean in to hear her. "You're special. You do so much work, you have so much passion not just for missing persons but for your job. I see none of that in the others."

"Stop," Grace whispered.

"What?"

"Just stop." Grace took in a deep breath. She shook her head, her eyes widening. "I can't do this anymore."

"This is your job, Detective." Paige pointed at the ground.

Grace stepped away, her heart racing. She'd never told off a superior officer before, but she wanted to. She needed to say something, put an end to this. No matter what she'd said before, Paige had clearly ignored it and not believed Grace would follow through.

"It is my job, Paige, and I love my job. But lately...I don't know. I hate it. I hate coming in to work. I hate staying at work. I hate being here."

Paige's lips parted in surprise. "You hate it?"

"Yes." Tears welled in Grace's eyes again, and she cursed herself. She was so tired of crying. She hadn't cried this much in years, and she'd about had it. "Can't you see that?"

"No." Paige's voice softened. She stepped in closer to Grace so they were only a foot apart. "Why didn't you tell me?"

"How could I?" Grace canted her hand. "You've been working me to the bone, you make me redo everything with you, you micromanage everything I do and still it's not good enough. Either you trust me as a detective or you don't, but Paige, you can't keep making me work."

Paige drew in a long, slow breath and let it out with a whistle. "Am I really that bad of a sup?"

"Some days," Grace answered honestly. "Other days you're not bad, and I'm not sure anyone else thinks you're that bad. But you can't deny that you treat me differently than everyone else. You expect more of me."

"Of course I do." Paige curled her hair behind her ear, not making eye contact with Grace. "You're special."

Groaning, Grace shook her head. "I'm not. I'm not any different than anyone else. In fact, I have way less experience than anyone else."

"But this unit is perfect for you!"

"I know it is." Grace's lips thinned. "And it's the only reason I have put up with this bullshit this long."

"Bullshit?" Paige had the audacity to look offended. "How dare you accuse me of that?"

Flabbergasted, Grace stared Paige down. Did she honestly not see it? Did she not think anything was wrong with the situation? Grace was about to tell her off and walk out, but Paige stopped her, a hand on Grace's.

Paige stepped in even closer. "I'm so sorry I've been an awful supervisor for you."

Grace's heart rapped hard, her mouth went dry. She had no idea what to say or how to say it or even know if Paige was sincere. Paige moved in another step, their bodies barely touching. Grace's mind went haywire. This could not be happening. Everything Amya was afraid of could not be happening. She had to stop it. She was about to object, when Paige lifted a hand and cupped Grace's cheek, dragging their mouths together.

Paige moaned.

Grace's stomach roiled.

When Paige's tongue touched her lips, Grace's brain caught back up with her. She put both hands on Paige's shoulders and shoved her backward until Paige stumbled a step back.

"What the fuck?" Grace shouted, not thinking about anyone hearing her. "You don't fucking touch me!"

"Grace." Paige's tone was consoling, but it was stupid. She stepped forward, and Grace moved back.

She couldn't believe Paige did that. Couldn't believe she'd actually gone through with it. There had been threats...there had been innuendos...Paige had crossed the line, but never like this. Paige moved again, and Grace countered.

"Come near me, and I will hit you."

Paige shook her head and reached out, grabbing Grace by the wrist. "Just talk—"

She didn't get a chance to finish her sentence. Grace pulled her left hand back, fist closed, and shot it forward in a precise jab right into Paige's nose. Paige stumbled backward, her hands over her face as blood poured over her lips and onto her shirt.

"What the hell, Grace?" Paige screeched.

"I told you not to fucking touch me!"

Paige launched forward, her own hand closed and swung at Grace. Grace easily dodged the blow by leaning back and twisting slightly. Paige growled. "You don't hit me and get away with it."

"You don't kiss me and get away with it." Grace grumbled, this time placing an upper jab right into Paige's stomach, precisely where she wanted to hit.

Paige doubled over for two seconds before she reared up, anger flashing in those green eyes before she ran forward. Grace dropped to the ground and shot her leg out, tripping Paige so she toppled over onto the hard floor. In two seconds, Grace was on top of her, grabbing her wrists while she straddled Paige's hips and trying to get hold of the situation.

With feet planted, Paige bucked upward and knocked Grace off her and onto the floor where she slammed the back of her head hard. Her ears rang loudly. She was so fucked if anyone walked in on them. First she was mouthy with her superior officer, and then she got into an all-out brawl with her. Wincing, Grace shifted when Paige went to hold her down and narrowly escaped being pinned.

She was up on her knees in a second, grabbing Paige's wrist and flinging it around her back to try and put her in a hold, but Paige's elbow to her gut knocked the window out of her. Grace grunted and pulled her elbow back for another blow.

"Stop!" Amya screamed.

CONFESSIONS

AMYA'S EYES widened as she saw the two of them on the floor, throwing punches. The hall behind her was quiet, no one was in the unit other than the two of them. With her heart racing, she shouted and hoped it would get their attention, but neither stopped.

Grace landed a glancing blow on Paige's chin, Paige's head knocking back from the force of it. Amya looked out in the hall again, hoping someone would be there to help her. Yes, she was a trained cop, but that was years ago, and she never liked breaking up physical altercations on her own.

"Stop it, Detective!" Raising her voice was having no affect.

Grumbling, Amya watched as Paige landed a punch to Grace's temple, saw the pain flash across her lover's face. They flipped over, Grace on top. Taking this as her moment, Amya stepped in and grabbed Grace's arm sharply, but she underestimated Grace's strength and resolve.

She couldn't stop the blow from landing on Paige's already broken nose. Amya gritted her teeth and this time used the full weight of her body as she used Grace's momentary lapse of momentum to knock her backward onto her ass. She stepped between them, facing Paige and putting Grace behind her.

Paige stared up at her, her chest heaving as she glared, baring her teeth. Amya gave her a stern look before shifting to look at

Grace, figuring the damage was done and Paige wasn't going to resume the fight now that someone else was there, particularly someone who would always be on Grace's side first.

Amya looked Grace over, finding only a small amount of blood trickling from a busted lip. She drew in a deep breath and pointed at Grace's desk. "You. Sit there."

Grace said nothing as she dragged her ass off the floor. Spinning around to Paige, Amya glared again.

"You go to your office and shut the door."

Paige covered her nose as blood continued to pour from it. "I'm going to need medical."

"And you'll damn well get it!" Amya heart wasn't slowing its race. "Remove yourself from the situation, Sergeant."

Rightfully scolded, Paige stumbled to her feet and dragged herself to her office, shutting the door. Standing fully, Amya spun on Grace. She had no idea where to even begin with this, where to start, what to even say. She had never expected to find Grace in this position. Not with Paige. Maybe a suspect, but never with another officer of the law, never with her superior officer.

"What the hell were you thinking?" Amya accused. Then she shook her head and held out her hands. "No, don't tell me. I don't want to know."

Grace's lips parted, and Amya glared, cutting her hand across the air to shut Grace up.

"You don't say a word, do you understand me?"

Nodding, Grace leaned over her desk and grabbed a tissue, blotting her lip. She grumbled but still didn't say anything as Amya glared at her. Amya had a hundred million things running through her brain at the same time.

"Are you an idiot?"

"Do you want me to answer that?" Grace fired back.

"No, because I know the answer."

Amya let out a breath, her heart finally calming. They were in a no-win situation. No matter what happened from here on out, Grace was going to be in trouble. Facing Paige's door, Amya tried to untangle the knots in her stomach.

"Tell me one thing, Grace." Turning to look at her partner, Amya waited until Grace's chocolate brown eyes locked on her. She looked an utter mess. Her hair was halfway out of its braid, her eye was already swelling and bruising, and her lip wouldn't stop bleeding.

"What? And stop staring at me like that. I'm not a fucking pity party."

Amya clenched her jaw and refrained from replying. "Do I need to call the commander in charge or do I need to call Esparza?"

Grace visibly paled. Amya had wondered if Grace had even thought of talking to him. He could easily solve this problem, or at least accurately investigate it instead of just investigating only the physical altercation. Amya had seen and heard what Paige had done over the last year and a half. She was fairly sure Grace hadn't shared everything, but this would be the one tell, the one answer that would let her know exactly what had happened.

"Grace," Amya softened her tone, pleading. "Please, tell me who to call."

It may have been coercion, but Amya wanted it to be Esparza, she wanted to be the one to make that call to Internal Affairs, hope they might look into Paige's conduct not just with Grace but with others, the ones she'd heard about in the rumor mill, the ones she'd been restricted from telling Grace about because it was a violation of her code of ethics.

Grace pulled the tissue away from her lip, and Amya could see she'd need medical too. The split went clear down her chin and would require stitches. With a pained expression, Grace muttered one word.

"Esparza."

Nodding, Amya grabbed her phone. She made the necessary phone calls, gave her statement of what she'd witnessed, and then she waited for Grace to be done with medical and giving her statement.

Amya had her arms crossed as she sat at an empty, waiting. She'd dropped Kit and Peter off at the house then insisted on coming down here to see if she could talk out their last argument. She'd never have guessed she would have walked in to find Grace in an all-out brawl. She stared at her toes while she waited, barely registering anything being said. If she wasn't in the middle of the drama, she'd be the one going from officer to officer to check in. Instead, she let Alonzo Esparza and the commander on duty do what needed to be done.

"She kissed me," Grace's voice echoed.

Amya jerked her chin, her eyes locking on Grace's defeated form. The words hadn't been loud, only for Alonzo's ears as he sat with her at Grace's desk. The words echoed in Amya's head. Paige had kissed Grace. Her worst fear had come true, yet it hadn't. Grace had done pretty much what Amya expected her to if that ever happened. She fought back.

She wanted to know the rest of the story, wanted to hear it from Grace's perspective because without the details of how it got to that point, Amya was lost except knowing Grace was in a position she should never have put herself in.

"Commander." One of Esparza's crew came out of the interview room. "We have to get her to the hospital. Can't stop the bleeding."

Grace's lips quirked upward. Amya couldn't tear her gaze from her. Esparza rubbed a hand over the back of his head and sighed. Jerking his chin toward the door, he gave silent confirmation that Paige should leave.

Grace stayed put, her eyes finally flickering up to Amya. Amya sighed and gave Grace a half-smile and a nod but kept her mouth shut. They would have time to talk later. For now, Grace was going to be surrounded by those who needed information for their initial reports. Twenty minutes after Paige left in a cruiser for the hospital, Grace was released.

Amya stood and shoved her hands in her jacket pockets as she eyed Grace. They said nothing as Grace gathered her jacket and gun and got ready to leave. All Amya could think was that at least Grace would be home for dinner that night, though she doubted she'd want to eat. As everyone left the unit, Amya stayed quiet, listening for tidbits of information she hadn't been paying attention to before.

"Hospital?" Amya said.

"Is it that bad?" Grace asked, her voice lisping because of the injury.

"It's a doozy."

"Fuck," Grace muttered. "Fine. But I don't want to see her there."

"Don't worry. I'll break up any fight you find yourself in again."

Grace narrowed her eyes. "You find this amusing, don't you?"

"Just a wee bit." Amya lifted her hand and put out her thumb and forefinger so they were almost touching.

"Can't wait until you get into a fight," Grace mumbled as she pulled her jacket on, wincing the entire time.

Concern fleeted through Amya. She gripped Grace's arm and stared at her. "Tell me the truth, how bad did she hit you?"

Grace wrinkled her nose.

Amya pointed a finger at her. "Don't lie to me."

"I think she broke a rib or two."

Rolling her eyes, Amya pulled Grace toward the door. "And you didn't say anything because...?"

Grace shrugged. "Didn't seem relevant."

"I don't believe you sometimes." With Grace firmly in her grasp, Amya escorted her out of the station and to her car. She helped Grace get in, making sure she didn't slip on the ice that the parking lot had become in the last few days. The last thing Grace needed was a fall on her butt to round out her injuries.

Once they were in the car, Amya started the engine. "I didn't think I'd walk in to find *that*."

"I didn't think *that* was ever going to be necessary."

Amya snorted. "We'll talk more at home."

Grace grimaced. "I don't want to."

"Not an option."

"Don't say that," Grace murmured, her face pointed out the side window.

"Why not?" Amya pushed.

Grace shrugged and the grimaced, no doubt regretting the move. "Because that's what she told me about working today."

"Did you tell Esparza that?"

"No."

"Grace Halling!"

"What?" Grace looked at her then.

Amya sighed. "We're going to have a serious conversation about this when we get home."

"What about the kids?"

Grace saying those words warmed her heart. Amya sighed. "Kit is staying at Annabelle's, and I'll kick Peter out of the house for a few hours. He can find some place to go."

"Isn't he working?"

Amya snorted. "He quit."

"What the fuck for?"

A sidelong glance was all Amya needed to give for Grace to know it was a conversation for a different time. Grace shifted and glared out the front of the car.

"Are we going or not?"

"Yes. X-rays and stitches."

"Don't call Crystal, okay?"

"I'll leave that blessing to you," Amya countered.

"Great. I was hoping to just avoid that one."

Amya snorted. "Good luck keeping a secret from her."

Grace barely made it into the house on her own two feet. Amya watched every move she made as she walked. She was not in her twenties anymore, and she was not a field officer anymore. It hurt like a bitch. She'd ended up with eleven stitches in her lip, inside and out, but had been amazed that her ribs were in fact not broken. Bruised, but she'd heal far faster from that and could work with bruised ribs.

Amya had insisted on getting a copy of all the reports and taking them with her to send to Esparza. Grace still wasn't sure that had been the right decision. She hated calling in Internal Affairs, but she'd had a weak moment with Amya staring at her.

She sunk onto the chair, not daring herself to be able to get off the couch without Amya if she did sit there. The dogs came over, setting their heads on each of her thighs as if they knew something was wrong. Dogs were so intuitive that way.

The running water in the bathroom surprised her. Amya had barely said two words to her on the drive home, and Grace had been left to her own devices and thoughts while she debated what to say and do next. She had to tell Amya everything that had happened—that much she knew. But where the fuck was she supposed to start?

"Come on," Amya's tone was soft and sweet. Her fingers were damp as she pulled on the zipper of Grace's jacket.

Groaning as she shifted, Grace allowed Amya to help her pull her jacket off and watched as she hung it up by the door. "I still think you look damn sexy in that."

Amya's cheeks were flushed when she turned around. "Same to you, love. But I missed out on seeing you in it today."

Grace hummed. "Yeah. Don't remind me."

Amya gave her a pitying look. "Up. You need to rest and ease your muscles otherwise you're really going to hurt tomorrow."

"Yeah, yeah." Grace gripped the arms of the chair, debating if she could get up without help or not. She wanted to, and she knew ultimately she could. The answer remained solely in how much it was going to hurt. "I'm too old for this bullshit."

Chuckling, Amya came closer. "Up you go."

Grace stood, thankfully on her own, but her head spun from the sharp pains in her chest and in her head.

"I sent Peter to get your pain meds, so he should be out of our hair for at least a little while."

Grace stilled. "You trusted an addict to get narcotics?"

Amya nodded. "In this case, yes. I'll count the pills, don't worry, but I don't think he'll do anything that stupid."

"You're giving him his addiction."

"I'm not about to leave you."

"We could have gone on the way home."

Amya clicked her tongue. "You can barely walk now, and you wanted to make another stop on the way home. Come on."

They made it down the hall to the single bathroom in the house. Amya shut the door and thankfully helped Grace pull her T-shirt and bra off because Grace wasn't sure how she was going to accomplish that one. Naked, finally, Amya had Grace hold on to her arm while Grace stepped into the hot water for the bath and slowly sat down and rested back.

"Tell me honestly because I haven't looked," Grace started. "How bad is it?"

"You look like you were in a full out brawl, Grace." Amya gathered up her clothes. "I'm going to stick these in the wash."

Sighing and closing her eyes, Grace let the heat of the water do its magic. She needed it more than she'd originally thought. When Amya returned and sat on the closed toilet seat, Grace relaxed even more.

"I'm sorry that's what you found."

"Don't be," Amya muttered. "I'm glad I did walk in on it, honestly. You two would have beaten each other to pulps."

"I was winning," Grace mumbled.

"You have ten years on Paige. Don't think you weren't also getting a good whipping in there."

"She's spry for being old."

Amya snorted. "She's in shape still."

"The ass."

Shaking her head, Amya crossed her legs. "Why didn't you tell me, Grace?"

"Tell you what?" Grace snapped her head around to look up at Amya, lost as to what she'd missed in the question.

Amya sighed. "That you didn't know what to do?"

"Oh." Grace's cheeks heated. She didn't realize it was that obvious. She was the master at ignoring problems until she couldn't anymore. But even she had to admit that she'd ignored the problem with Paige far longer than she should have. Maybe then she could have avoided Esparza. Deflated, Grace moved the water over her chest to keep the majority of her body warm.

"Grace?"

She didn't want to answer. Amya was right. She hadn't a clue what she should do to rectify the situation, and every time she had attempted something, it hadn't worked. She'd run out of ideas and buried her head in the sand as best as she could.

"What was I supposed to say?"

"I need help, Amya? I don't know what to do, Amya? Literally anything."

Grace whimpered. "I just...I'm not good at these things. You know that."

Amya sighed heavily and rubbed her forehead. "I know you're not. But I wish you'd start trusting that I'm here for you already."

"I know you're here for me. Always." Grace watched Amya carefully. "Look at me."

It seemed like forever before Amya raised her gaze.

"I love you. I trust you."

"Trust me with this stuff, please. I'm here for you, Grace."

"Okay." Grace shifted in the bath, water sloshing against the tub. "It's been getting bad lately, and I don't know how to tell her now. I mean, she threatened disciplinary action if I didn't work OT yesterday or come in today. I don't want that on my record."

"But you want hitting your superior officer on it?"

Grace scrunched her nose and covered her face with her hands. "That was a reflex."

"One that can get you into more trouble than walking out on overtime that isn't mandated."

"She said it was."

"Grace...think about it."

"I have thought about it." Grace pouted. "What would you have done?"

"I'm not answering that. We're two different people, so we would have made entirely different choices."

"Don't cop out on this one, Amya." Grace drew in a deep breath, glad to see she could without so much pain, though the drugs Peter was going to bring were going to put an even bigger dent in that. She still wanted to be awake to finish this conversation before the narcotics knocked her on her ass.

"Grace..." Amya had whine in her tone.

"Tell me. What would you have done?"

"I would have stopped it a year ago."

Grace knew Amya was right. She should have put a complete end to all this a year ago, but she wasn't sure Paige would have stopped. It hadn't gotten really bad until Paige had been put in charge of the unit. That really set everything off. "I'm so sorry."

"For what?" Amya asked. "None of this is your fault."

"Fighting is."

Amya shrugged. "I think that can be forgiven."

"I don't want to put you second." Grace's voice was so soft when she said it, she wasn't sure Amya had heard her, but she wasn't going to repeat herself. She couldn't. Saying it again would be too much.

"I know," Amya whispered. "But that doesn't mean I feel like I'm first."

"I don't know what to do." Grace broke. The tears she'd managed to keep at bay for weeks flowed down her cheeks. "I need you."

"Grace." The word broke on her lips. Amya slipped onto the floor and cupped Grace's cheek, turning her so they faced each other. "I love you."

"I love you, too." Their mouths touched in a light kiss that was one of the deepest most connecting embraces Grace had ever experienced. Amya kissed her again, and Grace winced from pain. She pulled away, a smirk on her lips. "As much as I love kissing you, Amya, it hurts right now."

"Shut up," Amya muttered and moved back in, though she was far gentler that time. They stayed together until the knock on the door interrupted them.

"Yo! I got the meds."

"I'll be right out," Amya stated. She kissed Grace again and stood up, barely opening the door as she slid out.

Grace could hear them talking through the door, but she closed her eyes and brushed the tears off her face. At least she had one thing going for her. Amya would always be there. She needed to trust that more and utilize the support she had already built in around her.

Amya came back with a pill in one hand and a glass of water in the other. She handed them over to Grace and told her to drink up. Grace complied, finishing the water since she knew she was going to need it.

"I put the rest in the safe."

"Good thinking," Grace grumbled. "I'm going to need your help to get out of this thing."

Amya let out a light laugh. "I figured. But hopefully it helped."

"It did." Grace held her hands up in a silent ask.

Amya slipped her arms under Grace's and lifted. Together they got her so she was standing, and Grace used the wall to keep herself steady until she was on the tiled floor. Amya wrapped a towel around her, but not before she eyed the growing bruises on Grace's body. She was going to be aching for days no doubt.

Once she was in her room and dressed in pajamas she rarely wore, Grace propped herself up on the bed and pulled the blankets over her legs. Amya settled her eReader next to her on the nightstand but touched the top of Grace's hand when she went to reach for it.

"Peter wants to talk to you."

"About what?" Grace looked up.

"I think he wants to make sure you're all right, but he says it's about the spring."

"Okay. Send him in." Seconds later, Peter walked in, worry all over his face. Grace patted the mattress in an invitation. "What's up, kid?"

"You okay?"

"I'll be fine. Just scuffed up. Not even the worst injury I've had."

"What happened?"

Grace sucked in a breath. She had a choice to make, either spill all or be vague. Vague seemed like the better option in the moment until she and Amya could get their stories straight. "I got in an altercation at the station."

"With a suspect?"

"You know, it doesn't really matter. What about you? What's this I'm hearing about spring?"

"I'm going back to school."

"Think that's wise?"

Peter nodded his head. "I do. I already quit my job."

"Two whole months early I hear," Grace slid the admonition in there when she could.

"I guess."

"Why did you really quit?"

"I'm going back after Christmas."

Grace's heart clenched sharply. "Why?"

"I want to get settled and find a new job out there."

"Peter..." Grace grabbed his hand. She so rarely called him by his name to his face that he looked surprised when they locked gazes. "Are you sure about this?"

"Yes."

"All right then. We'll support it."

"Thanks!" Peter moved in, his arms wrapping around Grace's shoulders in a hug.

She held back the groan of pain and hugged him back as best as she could. When he moved away, Grace sighed in relief.

"Are you going to work like that?"

"Not tomorrow." Grace grinned. "Mandated day off. I'll be back Monday."

"That's all you can take?"

"I've got a big case right now, kid. I need to focus on it. Trust me, I'm not going to be chasing any random suspects any time soon."

"You better not. And maybe, boss, you might want to start working out again."

"Ouch!" Grace pressed a hand over her heart. "Wound me while I'm down why don't you."

Peter snickered as he stood up to leave the room. "You're too easy sometimes."

Grace smiled, although it wasn't genuine. She wished that were the case. Most times she figured she was so complicated and cut off emotionally that most of the world didn't want to deal with her—Amya being the exception to that rule. Somehow.

With Peter gone, Grace grabbed her eReader and started in on one of the many books she had in her to-read pile. She'd sorely neglected this hobby as well. She made it half a chapter in before the pain medicine took control of her body and she could barely keep her eyes open. Giving up, she scooted down as best as she could in the bed and fell asleep easily for the first time in months.

MANIC MONDAY

GRACE GOT to Johnson County just before eight in the morning. Amya had insisted she rest all day Sunday, which had probably been a wise decision. It was rough getting going that morning, but as soon as she was moving, it was easier and not quite as painful, although Grace figured she'd be stiff from the hour drive.

Walking into the station where Blake's unit was, Grace tried to keep her head down. She didn't need comments or looks where it concerned her appearance. Amya had tried to put some makeup on her that morning, but Grace had refused. It was in some ways an honor for her to wear her injuries so blatantly.

Still, she probably shouldn't have gotten into a fist fight with her supervisor. But at least it had been worth it. She had no regrets. Blake sat hunched over her desk, her short dark hair styled perfectly like it usually was. Grace grinned momentarily before she remembered it hurt to do that.

"Miller!" Grace shouted.

Blake spun in her chair, her eyes wide. "What the fuck happened to you?"

"I'll explain it later."

"You get into a fight?" Blake pushed.

"In the car," Grace muttered, not wanting to spill everything that had happened in just a public place. "Come on, I want to finish out this case."

Blake grabbed her jacket and gun, checking in with her supervisor before they traipsed out to the parking lot. Blake's cruiser was chilled compared to Grace's, but Grace wanted the ability to move around so she opted to let Blake drive.

"It's about thirty minutes out," Blake commented as she pulled out of the parking lot.

"I'm going to be pissed if he's not there."

"Agreed. You going to tell me what the fuck happened to your face? You and Amya go at it?"

Grace snorted. "Paige."

"What?" Blake's eyes went wide and her grip on the steering wheel. "Paige hit you?"

"To be fair, I decked her first." Sweet satisfaction settled in Grace's belly. "She kissed me. I decked her. It degraded from there. I broke her nose."

"You didn't!"

"I did. She deserved it."

"Sounds like it." Silence fell over the cruiser, the excitement of the moment and story gone. Blake sighed. "You get a disciplinary?"

"Not yet. And I was allowed back today so long as my ribs weren't broken."

"Your ribs?"

Grace grimaced and shifted her gaze to Blake. They made eye contact. "I told you it got worse. Amya broke us up."

"Amya was there?"

Shaking her head, Grace relaxed. "No, not at first, only when we were fighting. IAB is investigating because of the harassment."

"IAB?"

Grace shrugged. "Don't ask."

"You sure you want to take it that far up, Halling?"

Sending Blake a sharp look, Grace shook her head. "No."

"All right, then."

They made it out to Deep Breathings Retreat Center in decent time. The building was simple wood with wide glass walls along the front. That'd be a bitch to clean, no doubt. Grace got out of the car, ignoring the ache in her legs and chest and arms as she moved. She was just going to have to live with that for a while.

Blake went to the front door, Grace following a step behind. She was gladly going to let Blake take the lead for this part, but as soon as they found out that Leon Gross was there, she was going to step in. The door opened, revealing a short, fit woman in her mid-fifties easily.

"Ma'am, I'm Detective Blake Miller, and this is Detective Grace Halling. We're trying to locate an individual whom we believe is staying at this retreat center."

The woman shook her head. "I'm sorry. I can't help you."

"Ma'am." Blake dropped her tone and used her voice to put the woman at ease. "This person hasn't done anything wrong, but his family and friends are very worried about him, and we want to make sure he's here and all right so he can contact them."

Her lips parted. Grace saw her resolve waver. She stepped to the side and opened the door. Blake walked in first, followed closely behind Grace. The main foyer was sparse, a couch, a few chairs, some art easels and drawing supplies as well as a grand piano. The woods were natural and well preserved.

"It's beautiful here," Grace mumbled.

"Thank you," the woman answered. "I'm Amber Kidd, by the way. I'm the owner of this facility."

Somehow they'd managed to find just the person they needed. They stopped in the center of the room, Amber looking at each of them. "Who are you looking for?"

"Leon Gross," Grace provided.

Amber nodded and stepped backward toward another door. Blake shot Grace a suspicious look, and they followed her down a hallway to a back sunroom. Leon sat on the floor on a carpet since there was no furniture in the room. His legs were crossed, his hands on his knees, and his eyes closed.

Grace's heart thumped. She knew it. She'd followed his trail here, and although it had taken her far longer than she expected, she'd found him. She shot Blake a look to confirm that this was their guy. Amber put a hand up before Grace could step ward.

"He's meditating."

"Yes, and I need to speak with him."

Amber stepped between them. "Let him finish."

"And how long will that take?"

"His meditation is done when it is done."

"I don't have time for that." Grace moved around her and walked as quietly as she could, the hush in the room nerving. She touched Leon's shoulder to get his attention, but he didn't move. "Leon."

He still didn't budge.

"Leon Gross," she said more firmly. He finally shifted, his neck straining to look up at her. Flashing her badge, Grace wrinkled her nose at the floor, really not wanting to sit down on it. "I'm Detective Grace Halling from Missing Persons. I've been looking for you."

Leon tilted his chin up toward her and waved his hand out on the floor in an invitation to sit. Grace tossed a look over her shoulder at Blake, sharing her discomfort at the idea. Giving in, Grace moved carefully to sit cross-legged on the floor next to the still silent man.

"You left without telling anyone where you were going."

Leon nodded. "I did. I'm fine, as you can see."

Grace flicked a look at Blake. "Yes, you are. Why did you leave, Mr. Gross?"

"Please, call me Leon." His lips curled up to a smile.

Grace wouldn't have recognized him if she'd seen him on the street. He looked nothing like the picture she'd been given for him. His hair was shaggy, his beard unkempt. However, his eyes looked brighter and more alive than they did in any of the photos. "Leon, what happened?"

He cocked his head to the side and stared at her. "I could ask the same about you."

"I'm clumsy."

He hummed as if he didn't believe her. "I had enough of it all. I couldn't take it. I found this place years ago, and I don't know...I called up one night and came down here that same night."

"Needed a mental break?"

"Not just a break," Leon whispered as if he was sharing a huge secret. "This is my new life."

"Meditation?" Grace raised an eyebrow at him, sneaking another look at Blake.

"Yes." He grinned. "But so much more than that. This life. Rest. Taking care of myself."

"Will you go home?" Grace asked.

"Not yet. Eventually. But I won't go back to work."

Grace looked around the room. No one else was there. She wondered how many clients the retreat center had, how exactly they were doing there, but at the same time, it didn't really matter. She got no sense anything bad was happening. Leon seemed to be there of his own free will, able to leave when he wanted if he wanted. She had a lot more follow up questions she needed to ask to close her case and write up her report, but she didn't think they were going to find anything that would cause her to think he'd been taken against his will.

Grace stayed on the floor and talked to him for another hour. By the time she needed to get up, Blake had to grasp her wrist and drag her to her feet. Grace squeezed Blake's arm with a murmur of thanks.

They left Leon there, piling back into Blake's cruiser. Grace's stomach grumbled with hunger as they pulled out onto the highway. She sheepishly glanced to Blake. "Lunch?"

"It's not even ten."

"I was up early, and the damn pain meds make me so hungry."

"Pain meds?" Blake's concern was strong.

"I bruised a few ribs."

"Should you be driving?"

"I didn't take them this morning. Scout's honor. But lingering effects."

Blake chuckled lowly. "We'll stop a few miles up the road."

"Thank God." Grace grinned from ear to ear.

"Amya doing good?"

Grace shrugged. She wasn't quite sure how to answer that question. They had talked a lot over the past weekend, but it hadn't been enough for Grace to get a good handle on Amya's feelings on the events of Saturday or the last year. Or them. Though she suspected she knew what Amya felt, she wasn't confident enough to give an answer.

"Grace?"

"She's good," Grace choked out, knowing a response was necessary.

Blake narrowed her gaze. "You know I'm a better detective than that."

"It's been rough, Blake. What else do you want me to say?" Grace groaned and rested her head on the seat. "It's been a really shitty fucking year."

"Yeah. So what now?"

"Not a damn clue. She wants me to transfer. I refuse to go to IAB, so that's not happening. I love Missing Persons. I'm good at it. These kids need me." When she looked at Blake, she saw the same love of the job reflecting at her.

"Yeah, but Halling, if it's a choice between the job and her—"

"I know what the choice is and what decision I need to make. I just don't want to have to make it."

"No one does," Blake grumbled. "But if I'd made the right choice, I wouldn't be here, now would I? Don't be an idiot and make the same mistake I did."

"You're no idiot."

"Tell that to my ex-wife." Blake's tone was so dry. Grace knew they'd touched on a sensitive topic, that it hurt starkly still.

Grace gave a wan smile. "She's an idiot."

Blake snorted. "You don't even know her."

"Don't need to." Grace clenched her jaw when her stomach gave another loud grumble.

"Right." Blake cleared her throat. "Where are we going next?"

"Food. Already discussed."

Blake snickered. "After food."

"Oh." Grace dug in her jacket for her phone and pulled it out. "I've got two people I want to interview while I'm here. An aunt and cousin to my dead mom."

"Think we can interview them at the same time?"

"Why? Got a hot date you're not telling me about?"

Blake scowled, which caused Grace to laugh. Blake pulled off the highway at one of the first fast food places in sight. Grace's stomach gave another rumble to confirm she was actually starving. Satisfied they'd were going to be filling her belly soon, Grace relaxed as best as she could.

The aunt's house was quaint. It didn't have a white picket fence, but it might as well have. Grace rolled her shoulders, her stomach completely satisfied and stared into the large bay window. An SUV sat parked in the driveway and a smaller sedan in the street. Blake was parked right behind the sedan.

"I assume you're taking lead," Blake muttered.

"Unless there's an arrest to made, then you get it." Grace gave her a broad grin. "I doubt today will end in an arrest, though. Paige threatened the FBI was going to come and take over soon, but I have my doubts of that."

"Why?"

"Logic. Which I never thought I'd use logic to prove this, but it doesn't make sense."

"What did she say?"

"Well, she insisted I work overtime Friday and come in all weekend and work on these cases, yet I wasn't allowed to come down here to do interviews, which would bump up my timeline. I wasn't allowed to really go do any interviews, and the second half of Saturday she made me redo the timeline which resulted in zero changes to the original. Why would she tell me to work overtime because the FBI was coming in and then prevent me from doing my job?"

"Because they weren't coming."

"Precisely." Grace frowned. "I'm going to have Amya check with her sister when she gets a chance, but I don't really need the confirmation."

"That's ballsy of her."

"Wouldn't be the first time. You ready to go in?"

"Yes." They walked to the front door together. Blake knocked and turned to Grace. "You could always transfer down here."

"And move?"

"Kit's graduating. Do you need to stay there?"

"Where would Amya work? We've both got to be within the county."

Blake shrugged. "Just a suggestion. We've got hospitals she could chaplain at."

"She'd hate that," Grace mumbled as the door swung open.

The woman was in her mid-fifties, maybe early sixties. Grace couldn't remember off the top of her head when her birthday was. She'd seen too many dates fly by her desk in the last few weeks. Her hair was dyed a dark brown that matched her eyes, surprisingly.

"Ma'am, are you Susan Novety?"

"Yes."

"I'm Detective Blake Miller with Missing Persons, and this is Detective Grace Halling."

Grace stepped forward and showed her badge. "I'm in charge of Andrew Erikson's case."

"Oh. Come in, come in." Susan ushered them inside, shutting the door behind them. The house was warm, far warmer than Grace had anticipated, and immediately she began to sweat under her heavy coat. Stripping it off, Grace held it over her arm as they were led to the living room and sat down. "Can I get you anything?"

Grace held her hand out. "No, thank you. We just ate."

"Oh, okay." Susan sat down, nervously. "What can I help you with?"

"I wanted to talk to you about Felicia and Jonas, and Andrew if you know anything about him."

"I never met him. I was supposed to go up and meet him, but..."

Grace nodded. "Remind me again how you're related?"

"I'm Felicia's aunt. Her mother and I are sisters."

"Right, so she spent a lot of time with you growing up?"

"A fair amount. My kids are a bit older than her, but they all got along and I think Felicia looked up to them, wanted to be like them." Susan paled. "We're going to miss her."

Grace felt for her grief, but she still had a case to solve. "How many kids do you have?"

"Three. Elizabeth is my youngest. She and Felicia were close for a while, but I don't think they've seen each other in a few years. They're closest in age. Elizabeth is...oh...eight years older than Felicia is I think."

Grace knew that. She'd done her research and backgrounds on each member of Felicia's family, immediate and extended. "Do you have any idea who might have taken Andrew?"

Susan shook her head. "No idea. It's such a tragedy, isn't it?"

"It is," Grace agreed. "When was the last time you had contact with Felicia?"

"The baby shower, I suppose. Before that it was years. Most of my contact for her was through her mother. I didn't often talk directly to her."

Grace glanced at Blake. "How about your daughter?"

"Elizabeth? I don't know. She didn't come to the shower with me, although she sent a gift up for Felicia. She was busy working before her leave."

"Leave?"

"Elizabeth had a baby about two weeks before Felicia did. A little girl. She's beautiful."

Shivers raced right up Grace's spine. Her stomach churned. There had been zero record of Elizabeth having a baby in any of her research. She shot Blake a look, one they shared that Susan didn't catch.

"Elizabeth around?"

"Yeah. She's still on leave."

Grace's heart thumped. "She was actually next on our stop, but do you think she could come here for a visit with us?"

"She should be here in the next few minutes anyway. I was going to go with her to Annie's doctor's appointment. She's got some blisters under her neck. I keep telling Elizabeth it's because the formula is getting caught up and she's not drying it off, but like she'll ever listen to me."

"Right." Grace pretended to feel for her phone in her pocket. "Oh, I've got a call. I'm going to step outside to take it. Blake?"

"I've got this," Blake answered.

Grace stood immediately and walked right out the front door.

She stepped to the side of the porch and pressed her phone to her ear, calling Blake's supervisor immediately. She spoke as rapidly as she could, explaining as much as she could. With reinforcements on the way, Grace made her next call to Link.

"Abrams."

She grinned. "Elizabeth Novety. Look her up. I'm about to interview, but she had a baby two weeks before Andrew was born according to her mother. No record of him. You might want to get your ass down here before I make your arrest."

"Damn it, Halling."

"Well, how was I supposed to know—" A car pulled up. Grace stepped back inside swiftly and hoped Elizabeth didn't see her. She also hoped the cruiser out front wasn't going to spook her. Lowering her voice, Grace muttered into her phone. "Got to go, Abrams, she's just arrived."

Grace went back into the living room and pointed her phone toward Blake. "Nothing major. Boss is going to want to talk to us when we get back, something about a report we're going to need to finish up."

"Oh, good."

Grace sat down and leaned her elbows on her knees. Before she even got the next question out, the front door opened.

They all turned to face it. In walked Elizabeth Novety, carrying a bucket seat covered with a fleece blanket. Elizabeth stopped short, her back straightening as she saw Grace and Blake staring at her.

Susan jumped up to take the baby, but Elizabeth turned her body to prevent Susan from doing it. Grace stood up, her badge on her hip clearly visible as she stared Elizabeth down. Blake followed her move, standing on the other side of the room so they could cover as many bases as possible.

"Take a seat, Elizabeth," Grace ordered.

Elizabeth looked at her mom. "What is this?"

"They're here looking for Andrew, just asking questions."

"Elizabeth," Grace started. "Sit down."

Giving in, Elizabeth moved stiffly to the chair next to her mothers and sat down, putting the carseat right in front of her.

Blake stayed standing, but Grace sat as close as possible to the baby and Elizabeth.

"Your mom was telling us about Annie. I'm sorry she's having so many issues with the blisters. My niece had those same issues. Baby powder was the cure." The lie slipped easily off Grace's lips. "How is she doing other than that?"

"She's good. Healthy. Growing. Gained two pounds since she was born."

"Good. I hear you're almost going back to work soon."

Elizabeth nodded, although it was a slight uncomfortable move. "I am. I hired a nanny to come in and watch her for me so she doesn't have to go to a daycare."

"Can't be a stay-at-home-mom?" Grace probed.

"No. I...I don't have a husband, so I've got to work."

"Ah." Every warning bell in Grace's head was going off. Elizabeth shifted uncomfortably.

"I had a complicated delivery," Elizabeth started. "So mom's been helping me a bit, but I can't miss any more work."

Grace looked at Susan. "Were you there for the delivery? I bet that was a big help. My sister said she couldn't have done it without Mom there."

"I wasn't." Susan looked pained. "But I've been there every day since she got home to help out."

"When was that? I imagine you were in the hospital for a while."

Elizabeth shifted again. She stared directly at Grace when she answered, daring Grace to find the lie. "I honestly don't remember. I've been so tired from not sleeping."

"She was in the hospital about two weeks before they released her. I picked her up there."

"Did you?" Grace turned on Susan.

"She was waiting for me right outside."

Elizabeth shot a glare toward her mom. Grace flicked her gaze to Blake, hoping the meaning was clear. She was about to ask a very direct question and she wanted Blake to be ready to act if necessary.

"Which hospital?"

"The one here," Elizabeth answered.

"Who's your doctor?"

"Why the twenty questions, Detective?" Elizabeth narrowed her gaze, her hand curling over the handle of the carseat.

Grace folded her hands together in front of her, trying to make herself seem less imposing. She wanted Elizabeth to remain calm. "I'm a curious person by nature."

"Do you think this is Andrew?"

Grace didn't reply.

"Jesus. You can look in her diaper if you want."

Grace wanted to jump on that opportunity, but she didn't think she'd get to it ever. The fact Elizabeth was pushing back wasn't the surprise or the tell. It was her thinned lips, her dilated pupils, the slight tightening of every muscle in her jaw and neck, and the fact that she shook her head no when she said it.

Still, Grace had to figure out a way to get the baby away from Elizabeth until she could be certain her theory was right or wrong. "How'd you come up with the name Annie?"

"It's my mom's middle name."

"Oh." Grace flicked a glance at Susan. "And when did you say she was born?"

"She's six weeks old."

Grace cocked her head to the side. "Wouldn't she be eight?"

"Right. Eight. That's what I meant. Like I said, I'm tired from being up all night with a newborn."

Susan stiffened, and that was Grace's cue that someone else in the room had just figured out a lie. Grace pointed at the baby. "Does she look like you or the father?"

"She, unfortunately, looks like her daddy. The bastard."

"Bad blood?"

"Awful."

Susan shifted but remained silent. Grace locked gazes with Blake again. "When's the last time you saw Felicia?"

"It's been years."

"Didn't go to her baby shower?"

"No. I was working."

That was Grace's golden ticket. She stood up and grabbed the carseat, shifting it swiftly out of the way and onto the other side of the coffee table. Blake stepped in and put a hand on Elizabeth's arm.

"Tell me, Elizabeth, how you were at work eight weeks ago when you were supposedly in the hospital after giving birth?"

Elizabeth paled. Blake grabbed her other arm and held her wrists tightly behind Elizabeth's back while she grabbed for her cuffs.

"Elizabeth Novety," Grace started. "We're detaining you under suspicion of murder and kidnapping. You have the right to remain silent…"

She finished out the Miranda rights while Blake moved her away from the carseat. Grace took the baby out and held up a hand to stop Susan from coming near.

"Sit down, Susan."

Complying, the woman sat heavily while Blake took Elizabeth out of the house and away from the baby. Officers were already outside. Grace settled the baby in her arms and looked it over. "Tell me, Susan, have you ever changed this baby's diaper?"

"No."

"Want to?"

"No." This time, instead of nerves, Susan sounded defeated.

Grace settled the infant on the couch cushion and unsnapped the outfit before pulling the diaper down slightly before lifting the onesie and checking for Andrew's birthmark on his chest. She glanced at Susan as a field officer came into the living room. "Definitely not a girl."

Susan clenched her jaw and fisted her hands. "I swear I didn't know."

Grace snorted. Susan may not have known outright, but Grace was pretty sure she damn well suspected. With the baby dressed again, Grace wrapped him tightly in a blanket and held him against her chest as she stood up. If only Paige had allowed her to come to Johnson County sooner, she could have had her case solved. Pity her boss was such an idiot.

RECOVERY

GRACE DIDN'T release the baby to anyone until medics arrived. She hovered while they checked him over, taking his vitals, doing a basic physical. Blake stood in the center of the front yard in the freezing cold while officers ran to and from her. With the baby cleared, Grace wrapped him back in his blanket and held him close to her chest as she walked toward the house.

"Halling?" Blake called.

Grace stopped near her and pulled down the blanket to reveal the baby's face. "Clean bill of health, thankfully. I'm going to wait inside where its warm."

"They took Elizabeth to the jail."

"I'll tell Link to pick her up there." Grace rolled her shoulders. "What about the mother?"

Blake raised her eyebrows. "Still need to figure out how much she knew."

"Need to figure out to what lengths Elizabeth went to in order to plan this charade." Grace patted the baby's bottom. "Social services on their way?"

"Yeah. It'll be an hour easy. They're not exactly fast here."

"Are they anywhere?"

"Some days," Blake grumbled. "If we finish up here first, we may want to bring him to the station to meet them."

"Transfer?" Grace replied.

"That's what I'm pushing for."

"Good." Grace nodded and stepped around Blake. "It's too cold out here for babies."

"Chicken shit," Blake mumbled as a tease.

Grace couldn't disagree. She'd much rather be inside. As soon as she stepped through the front door and into the much warmer house, she relaxed her grip on the baby. They still had to verify that he was Andrew Erikson, but the likelihood was strong considering all the circumstances. They'd do a quick paternity test on Jonas and go from there, but that would be after they got him back to Grace's turf.

Susan sat on the couch, staring blankly at the coffee table as officers walked around her and took evidence. Grace knew there was another crew at Elizabeth's house doing the same, and it was a good sign that Susan had given them the go ahead to search her house.

"I didn't know," Susan muttered when Grace sat down and leaned back to cradle the infant easier.

Her arm ached from his weight although it was barely anything. "I should advise you Ms. Novety that anything you say to me can and will be used against you."

Susan nodded. "I understand that. I didn't know, I promise you."

Grace kept her mouth shut and looked the woman over. She seemed defeated. In shock for sure. Her skin was pale where it hadn't been before. She had that dead look in her eyes like no emotion or event could touch her.

"I suspected something might be going on."

"Why would you say that?" Grace patted the baby's bottom again.

Susan drew in a deep breath and sighed. "Elizabeth has wanted a baby for years. She's faked being pregnant before."

Tears stole their way into Susan's eyes.

"I thought it was a one time thing, but I guess not."

"When did she tell you she was pregnant?"

"Uh...in June, I think. She would have been right around twelve weeks. It was around the same time Felicia told her mom."

Grace filed that piece of information away, holding it in her mind so she could use it later. "Did you ever go with her to any appointments?"

"No, she never said she wanted me to. She's an adult. I knew she was going through this pregnancy alone, but she said she wanted to do this on her own. She's always been very independent."

Holding back her grunt of disbelief, Grace eased the baby to sleep. "Didn't you think it was odd she was in the hospital for weeks and didn't know about it?"

"You act as though we're close." Susan eyed Grace pointedly. "I may love my daughter, Detective, but it hasn't always been easy with her. She likes attention, and when she doesn't get it, she tends to disappear until she tries again. Her baby shower wasn't as big as Felicia's—it wasn't as grand. I don't know. But she vanished for weeks and I didn't know where she was or hear from her."

"Did you try to contact her?"

"Once or twice, but like I said, it's not abnormal for her to go silent. I just took it as this was another one of those times." Susan nodded toward the baby. "I was so happy she finally got what she's wanted for years that I didn't question it."

You probably should have, Grace wanted to say, but she held her tongue. This woman was in as much turmoil as the rest of Andrew's family, if not more. Guilt, shame, despair all mixed in one. Grace should tread lightly, because she still wanted to know if Susan had anything to do with it, though she suspected not.

"I should have," Susan said, barely above a whisper.

Grace knocked her chin up in Susan's direction, pulling the baby into her chest a little more as if to protect him from some unforeseen enemy. "Excuse me?"

"I should have. I should have questioned it, pushed for more answers, done a bit more pressing on her of who the father is. I just didn't. I wanted to accept it, wanted to not tick her off again so she wouldn't talk to me and I wouldn't see Annie again. I just wanted..." Susan broke down into sobs. "I just wanted my family back."

Sucking in a breath and holding it tightly, Grace stared at her. What was she supposed to do? This was an Amya thing, not a her thing. The emotions were not something Grace dealt with well, at all. She stared with wide eyes as Susan cried, grabbing for an already used tissue and pushing it against her eyes.

"I'm so sorry." Susan's voice trailed off under muffed tears.

Grace wanted to tell her that she should be sorry. Weeks without knowing where the baby was. Her own niece was dead, murdered for nothing other than having a baby and being close enough but far enough in relation to pull this off. Clenching her jaw, Grace stared her down. "We'll be transferring Elizabeth, so she'll be in jail there."

Susan nodded. "I thought as much."

Grace stood up. "Do you have any formula?"

"She should have some in the diaper bag."

Bending down to the coffee table with the bag on top of it, Grace rummaged around while trying to hold the baby close to her. She managed to pull out a bottle of premade formula and scrunched her nose at it. The baby would no doubt need it soon, and she'd just wanted to be sure they had it before she drove the hour home with a starving infant.

Blake came in the front door and beckoned Grace over with the jerk of her head. Moving toward her partner for the day, Grace stopped and listened. "Link Abrams just got here."

"Oh." Grinning, Grace stepped out of the house and down the front steps, spying Link's tall form standing over the cruiser they'd stashed Elizabeth in. She waved at him, forgetting for a second she still had the formula in her hand and shoving it into her pocket. "Nice of you to join us."

He snorted. "Nice of you to solve my case for me."

"You know, I try to help out where I can." She winked. "I don't think the aunt knew anything."

Link straightened his shoulders. "I still want to talk to her."

"Figured you would. She's inside."

"That the baby?"

"Uh...yes." Grace dipped her head to stare at his chubby cheeks. "I'm waiting on social services to check him out and give me paperwork before I leave."

"Both being transferred?"

"Yup." Grace stepped away and toward the house. Link followed her. They spent the next hour talking with Susan and getting all their ducks in a row. Social services had finally arrived and gave Grace the go-ahead to leave.

She piled the baby into the car seat, making sure he was fastened correctly before putting him in the backseat of Blake's cruiser which they'd warmed up for the last twenty minutes. As soon as Grace was in her own cruiser after feeding him and properly warmed the car for the baby, she stretched her back and prepared for her hour long journey home.

The drive was mostly quiet, save for a few whimpers from the baby in the back. He didn't cry, but Grace had made sure to feed and change him right before she left so hopefully he'd sleep through most of it. Pulling into the parking lot at the station toward the end of shift was relieving. She hadn't even stopped by on her way out of town, not wanting to know if Paige was going to be in or not, though Grace doubted she would be.

Doreen was her contact at DCFS, and she expected the social worker would be late as usual. A text she had received while en route but didn't check until parking confirmed it. Everything seemed still and quiet compared to the raging it had been yesterday, or even weeks and months before. Grace couldn't stop thinking about the peace that settled through her.

Grace bypassed going to her unit, wanting to live in the rush of closing the case and being away from the drama she knew was impending as soon as she walked in there just a little longer. The first door to the chaplain's offices were propped open and the young, beautiful Khloe still sat at the desk. They still had a few more hours of their day before they'd go home, and Grace hoped Amya wasn't busy.

She'd failed to call to check in and see if she was, but she vaguely remembered Amya telling her it was a light load day. Grace held the car seat low so Khloe couldn't see it as she stepped inside. "Hey, Khloe."

"Hey, Grace!" Khloe's smile bloomed. "Your lip doesn't look too busted up."

Grace smirked, taking the compliment for what it was. "You should see the other person."

Khloe snorted. "I did."

"Really?" Grace raised an eyebrow.

"She stopped by here to drop a note to Amya."

"A note."

"I don't know. Amya will fill you in. Go right on in."

"Thanks." Grace gave Khloe a playing smile. "One more thing."

"What?"

Pulling her hand up, Grace set the carseat on the desktop and faced it so Khloe could see the baby.

"Oh my God, Grace!" Khloe stood, bending over the carseat to get a better look. "Is this the baby?"

"Pretty sure. Need to run some DNA first to make sure, but pretty sure."

"He's adorable."

"And stinky." Grace snorted, her lips curling upward. "Guess I'm going to have to get used to that for a little bit. Babies are not my thing, but this guy is easy so far."

Khloe laughed lightly. "Because you haven't done the overnight yet."

"Maybe."

"Grace." Amya's voice was a gentle quiet that had Grace straightening her spine and turning to look toward Amya's private office. Amya nodded her head toward the interior of her office and stepped inside.

Grace gripped the handle on the carseat tightly. Her heart thumped from Amya's quiet countenance, though she wasn't quite sure why. They'd talked themselves to death for days at that point. Surely she had nothing to worry about. Right?

When she entered, Amya shut the door with a soft click and smiled down at the baby. That sent good tingles through Grace's stomach. She put the carseat on the floor and sat heavily on the couch to unstrap him and change him.

"Where'd you find him?"

"Blake and I were at the aunt's interviewing her and the daughter showed up with a baby and a very suspicious story."

"You think she did it?"

"Pretty damn sure. She mostly fits Morgan's profile."

Amya's lips thinned. "Speaking of...I called Morgan this morning."

"Did you?"

"I was curious about something you'd said, and to answer your unasked question, since I know you're thinking it, no, the FBI was not planning on swooping in and taking over the case."

"You found that out in one phone call?" Amazed, Grace set the baby onto the couch cushion next to her and started to undo his clothes so she could change the nasty diaper. "I never think she likes me."

"Who? Morgan?"

Grace nodded, not daring to look up into Amya's eyes.

"She likes you, Grace. She just doesn't know you well, and she's very protective of me."

"So I've noticed," Grace muttered as she pulled the tab on the nasty diaper, holding her nose as best as she could. It didn't take her too long to clean the baby up and get the clean diaper taped in place.

She handed the baby over to Amya, who cradled him expertly in her arms as she slid in to sit next to Grace. "He's so cute."

"We're not having a baby," Grace muttered.

"Wasn't thinking that, Halling. But good for you for bringing that one home."

"Sorry."

"No apology needed." Amya kissed the top of the baby's head. "He's so soft."

"Amya..." Grace warned.

"What? I like babies. Can't I admire him?"

"Just no ideas in that head of yours."

"I always have ideas." Amya winked. "Khloe told you."

The air in the room stilled, thickening with tension. Grace wasn't sure where to go with it. Normally she'd be uncomfortable, but something in Amya's gaze eased her. She knew Amya would protect her, no matter what, and she had to trust that.

"I kept it because she refused to take it back."

"What'd it say?"

"Didn't open it." Amya lifted her chin in the direction of her desk.

Grace retrieved the simple envelop with her name on it. She sat back down and slapped it against her hand as she debated whether or not to open it.

"She's on paid suspension right now."

"Ah."

"Can't work with her nose anyway. You did a doozy on her."

That brought a light smile to Grace's lips, but the sweet feeling of satisfaction she expected to have didn't arise to follow. "I shouldn't have gotten into that fight."

"No, you shouldn't have. But you did."

"Brass say anything about my consequences?"

"I think they're waiting to finish out the investigation first." Amya crossed her leg and leaned into the couch, looking very comfortable while holding the baby and patting his bottom.

"I should have reported it sooner."

Amya sighed heavily. "Yes, you should have."

"I fucked up a lot."

Amya shushed her loudly. "There is a baby in this room."

"Like he can understand what I'm saying."

"They do!" Amya implored her with a glance. "They understand the feeling and emotions more than the words, but they do."

"Fine, whatever. Further proves why we shouldn't have a baby. I'll stick to teens, thank you."

They lapsed into a silence, both staring at the envelope.

"Are you going to read it?" Amya asked.

"I don't know. Should I?"

"I think you need to turn it in either way."

Sighing, Grace gave in to curiosity and slid her finger along the back of the envelope to open it. Inside were two letters, one address to Grace and the other addressed to Amya. Handing Amya hers, Grace skimmed Paige's crude handwriting.

"It's an apology," Grace stated handing the paper to Amya. They flipped pages, and Grace read the second letter, finding basically the same apology. It wasn't detailed or even remorseful about everything that had happened, yet an apology did help Grace's case even if there wasn't a whole lot of specifics in there.

Paige would never be able to deny the kiss. They had cameras everywhere at the station, and it would have been caught on those at the very least. So would the fight though, Grace throwing the first punch, and Grace going back for more when the one punch wasn't enough. Embarrassment swarmed her senses, piling in her belly until she struggled to breathe through it.

"Grace?" Amya asked, settling a hand on her thigh.

"I'm fine."

"Use my touch to center yourself."

Closing her eyes, Grace did as Amya told her without question. Her breaths were slow and steady, her heart that had been thumping calmed. She loved that Amya could do this for her. She wasn't sure how long it took, but when she opened her eyes, Amya's crystalline ones stared back at her.

"I don't know what's going to happen with Paige," Grace said. "But I know I can't stay working in that unit any longer than absolutely necessary."

Amya's brow furrowed. "You've been so adamant—"

"I know." Grace's voice dropped off, the disappointment of the decision weighing on her, although she knew it was the right one to make. Something had to give, and in this situation, it absolutely needed to be her.

"Are you going to talk to Esparza?"

Lifting a shoulder, Grace let it drop. "Do you trust me?"

"With everything I have."

"Homicide."

Amya sucked in a breath. "Are you ready for that?"

"Is anyone? I think after this case I am. Abrams was doing an unofficial interview for it. They're looking for someone to fill a spot, and if they need someone, I can easily transfer."

"Now?" Amya raised an eyebrow.

"It'll take some time. I need to ask for a transfer, remember?"

Amya pressed her lips firmly together. "Ask above."

"Planning on it already. I know Paige won't grant it."

"If she's even in charge after this."

"She will be." Grace stared at her toes. "They have no one else right now."

"That's a morbid thought."

Humming her agreement, Grace crossed her arms and rested. "We have to talk about Peter."

"That is not going to be an easy discussion."

"Do we even have a say?"

Amya shook her head. "No, unfortunately."

"Think he's ready?"

"Absolutely not." Amya bristled. "But I don't think he'll be any more ready next semester or next year. We're going to have to trust him at some point."

"I'd rather not."

Amya chuckled. "Wouldn't we all."

Curling a finger over the baby's cheek, Amya smiled down at him. It was a sweet look, one that was lacking any barriers or walls. Grace hadn't seen a look like that from Amya in far too long, and the fact it took a baby to bring it out of her puzzled Grace. They may have talked all weekend, but Grace still had a lot of making up to do and reparations to make.

Time was going to be her best friend. Which was a problem, because Grace had zero patience.

They both heard Doreen's voice. With a glance to each other, they straightened. Grace stood up and opened the door to allow Doreen inside.

"Where did you find him?"

Grace snorted. "Johnson County. You going to bring him to Jonas?"

"If he agrees."

"I think he will."

Doreen took Grace's old spot on the couch and looked the baby over. "He looks well enough."

"He was well taken care of, despite being ripped from his mother's arms as she lay dying."

Amya shot Grace a look, and Grace shrugged, not understanding where the ire was coming from. It was true, even if it was a bit crass.

"I have his carseat so he can be transported, but I'll need to keep the diaper bag for evidence."

"Tell me what's in there so we can try to keep him on the same formula if it was working."

Grace dug through the bag, writing down the diaper brand and size and the formula on a sticky note from Amya's desk. She handed it over and took the baby from Amya's arms.

"When will the paternity test come back?" Grace asked.

"We'll put a rush on it, so it should be by the end of the week. Did you..." Doreen looked them over. "Did you arrest her?"

"Not personally, but yes."

"Good." Relief washed through Doreen. "I suppose I'll find out more when you let us know."

"Yes." Grace nodded. She leaned down and dropped a kiss on the baby's cheek before sliding him into Doreen's arms.

"Thinking about fostering a baby?"

"No," Grace and Amya responded at the same time.

Doreen smirked at them. "Ah, well, I'll keep sending you teenagers."

"Great," Grace muttered. "Just what we need in the house, more hormones."

Amya gave Grace a hard look, and she shrugged. They bid Doreen farewell and suddenly the room felt empty. Amya nodded at Khloe and told her to take the rest of the day before shutting the door and effectively closing them in her office alone with no chance of interruption.

Warning bells went off in Grace's head. Amya grabbed her upper arms and pulled her in tight, their lips locking. Thrown off, Grace took a second before she eased into the kiss. She relaxed as Amya wrapped arms around her neck and held her tight, not letting go as they deepened the embrace.

Finally Amya pulled away with an extra peck against Grace's mouth. "I love you."

"Love you, too, but what was that for?"

"For not being an idiot any longer."

Chuckling, Grace shook her head. "Pretty sure I'm still an idiot."

"Stop that." Amya kissed her again.

Grace melted. She loved this side of Amya, the sweet side, the compassionate side. Nipping at Amya's lip, Grace held her tightly. "What now?"

"Don't you have a report to write up?"

Groaning, Grace closed her eyes and rested her head on

Amya's shoulder. "Do I have to?"

"Yes. I want you home at a reasonable hour tonight, thank you."

"Oh, does that mean you have something special planned?"

"Wouldn't you like to know?" Amya walked her fingers up Grace's chest to her nose before grinning. "The kids have something special planned."

"What?"

"You'll see."

"Amya," Grace whined. "You know I don't like surprises."

"You'll like this one, I promise."

"Is there an extra special Amya-only surprise after the kid surprise."

Amya narrowed her eyes. "If you behave, there might be."

"Yes!" Grace kissed Amya hard and passionately. She didn't let go for the longest time before she pulled away and walked out of the office with a much lighter step. She nearly skipped down the long hallway to her unit.

With no sign of Paige, Grace sat at her desk and finished out her reports for the day, as much as she could without everyone else's reports. She finished within two hours. She stared at the apology on her desk and glared at it. She'd bring it to Alonzo in the morning. She didn't have the energy to deal with him tonight, not when he tried to get her to transfer to his unit every damn time.

The unit was nearly empty when she shut down her computer and cleaned up her desk. The plan she had would work. It had to, but more than that, it was what was right and what she should have done months ago. With her jacket over her shoulders, Grace walked out of Missing Persons, finally feeling like she was back to where she had been when she started there. It may have been short lived, but it might always be her favorite unit to work in.

HOMICIDE

GRACE HAD debated for at least two weeks how she was going to accomplish a transfer without permission from Paige. With everything that had happened, she was wary of any interaction with Paige, who was back in the office by the end of the previous week. She'd seemed calmed, but knowing Paige that could just be everything boiling underneath the surface.

Grace had even switched desks so she could watch Paige's office and know when she was coming instead of being surprised by a hand on her shoulder or something. She shuddered at the thought. The week had been quiet, but it had only been a week since the incident. That didn't leave Grace a whole lot of hope about what the future held. For all she knew IAB had finished their report and left it in the hands of the chief, which honestly wouldn't surprise her. It was harassment, not some type of internal conspiracy like Humbard's issue.

It was close to finishing time when Grace slipped from the room and walked down the hallway. The phone in her hand was hard against her palm as she squeezed it. She'd chosen a day that Amya wouldn't be in the office on purpose. She needed to do this on her own, for them. She needed to take that step as much as she dragged her feet and didn't necessarily want to. This was for them.

Homicide was a bustle of people, which meant they must have

just caught a case. Their department was at least three times the size as Missing Persons, which didn't surprise Grace. Link Abrams leaned over his desk, shoving his gun in his holster and grabbing something else. Grace smiled when she saw him. He'd been nothing but kind to her.

"Hey Abrams," she said as she stopped near his desk.

"Halling?" He looked a little surprised when he faced her but didn't give too much away at his shock. "We don't have another case together, do we?"

She shook her head. "No, we don't."

He eyed her carefully, both eyebrows raised in question.

Grace gave in, knowing it would do any harm to let Abram know what was going on. "I thought I'd talk to your Captain."

"About...?"

Her lips thinned. "Transferring."

"Shouldn't you talk to *your* Captain?"

Grace shrugged. She should. That was how policy worked, talk to both, but typically talk to her own first. But she couldn't talk to Paige, and if Abrams didn't know that, then at least the rumors of the brawl hadn't made it too far out. That or he was just trying to be nice. She settled on nice. Thus far, everyone had known about the fight, even if it had happened on a weekend.

"Thought I'd talk to yours. You'd hinted he was interested in me transferring."

"Yeah, but..." Link's gaze shifted from her to the Captain's door. "Nevermind. Go in."

"No, tell me." Grace crossed her arms, staring up at the man who was easily a foot taller than her, if not more.

Link's jaw clenched and his posture became stiff. "He's concerned about your record."

"Which part of my record?"

"Don't know. Didn't ask."

Grace's stomach swirled in knots. "Right. Well, thanks for the heads up. I guess."

"For the record, Halling. I'd love to work with you again."

That caused a slight smile to appear. "You get a case?"

"Yeah."

"Better get to it, then."

Link raised both his hands and started to walk backward toward the door. "The dead wait for no one, don't you know?"

Chuckling, Grace shook her head and walked toward the Captain's office. She rapped her knuckles on the door and made sure to make eye contact as she waited to get his attention.

"Yes?" He glowered up at her.

She really had probably picked a bad time for this conversation, but she was there, and it had taken her weeks to get up the courage to do it, so she wasn't backing down now. "Captain, I was wondering if you had a minute."

His stern look told her he'd rather not, but he gestured to the chair in front of the desk. Grace shut the door, without being told, and sat down. Nerves swelled in her belly again, only this time they were far harder to control.

"Abram said at one point you were looking for some new detectives."

He raised his eyebrow at her.

Grace's mouth went dry, but she said what she'd come there to say. "I'd like to put my name in as an option."

"Have you spoken with Delwin?"

Cold washed through Grace's body. She answered honestly, "No."

He sighed and leaned back in his chair. "Why are you coming to me?"

She had anticipated this line of questioning but hadn't really come up with a good roundabout way to answer. She was a blunt person, and the idea of tiptoeing around what happened was not something she really wanted.

"Because I need to transfer, and I've held off long enough. While I love Missing Persons, and would love to stay there, I can't with the current environment."

The Captain cocked his head at her, and she knew he was trying to fish more information out of that line than what she'd given up.

"I have an offer to go to IAB, but I'd rather work Homicide. This last case was eye opening, and I think it'd be a good environment from what I've seen. You run a tight ship." She was satisfied that she managed to toss in a compliment into that. "I'm not good with walking circles around people, sir. I would like to transfer to homicide."

He sighed and gave her a hard stare. "I looked at your record, Halling, and while you have accolades from a lot of different supervisors, you also have had disciplinaries."

"I've calmed from my days on the street."

He gave a wry smile. "Have you?"

"Yes." Grace dared to look him in the eyes, wanting him to

know the last incident was an outlier. Yes, she had gotten into another fight, but it had been years since she'd found herself the center of one.

"I don't have any positions for you."

"Sir," Grace pleaded. "Abrams had said you did."

"And it's been filled. Did you think you were the only candidate we were looking at?"

Shaking her head, she acquiesced. "No, I didn't. I'd hoped there was still an opening."

"Sorry, Halling." He put his hands out. "But next time we have one, I'll let you know."

She grinned, fully. The honesty in his eyes was enough for her to trust he would. Until then, she was going to have to figure out what to do and how to continue to work in Missing Persons with Paige. She stared at the top of his desk, disturbed when he spoke again.

"Word of advice about Delwin."

She glanced up at him, almost forgetting that Paige and transferred from Homicide to Missing Persons nearly two years before. She cocked her head at him, waiting for him to continue.

"Keep your head down, but if she ruffles your feathers, come down and talk to me."

"Sir?"

"Delwin and I have an understanding, and if she crosses those lines, I know how to deal with her."

Unsettled, Grace nodded at him. "Thank you, sir. And sorry to take up your time."

Leaving Homicide was a let down. Grace walked through the halls, barely seeing anyone else. Now she really wished Amya had been there so they could talk after. Luckily, her work day was nearly done, and since Kit was done with school for the winter break, she could pick her up and they could go do something fun, something to take Grace's mind off this disaster. Maybe she could even grab Peter on her way.

In her cruiser, she drove home and left the car running as she dashed inside. Ignoring the dogs, she walked straight to Peter's door and knocked before opening it. He stared up at her from the bed. "Get dressed. You have two minutes."

"What?"

"Do it, kid." Shutting the door, Grace let the dogs out for a potty break, knowing it would take Peter more than two minutes. She was right. Ten minutes later, they were in the cruiser and heading toward Kit's school.

With her kids in the car, Grace smiled as she gripped the wheel. She slowly moved through the pick up line, and as soon as she was on the street, Peter looked at her. "Where the hell are we going?"

Grace grinned broadly. "Anyone want ice cream?"

About the Author

Adrian J. Smith has been publishing since 2013 but has been writing nearly her entire life. With a focus on women loving women fiction, AJ jumps genres from action-packed police procedurals to the seedier life of vampires and witches to sweet romances with a May-December twist. She loves writing and reading about women in the midst of the ordinariness of life. Two of her novels, *For by Grace* and *Memoir in the Making,* received honorable mentions with the Rainbow Awards.

AJ currently lives in Cheyenne, WY, although she moves often and has lived all over the United States. She loves to travel to different countries and places. She currently plays the roles of author, wife, and mother to two rambunctious toddlers, occasional handy-woman. Connect with her on Facebook, Twitter, or her blog.

www.ingramcontent.com/pod-product-compliance
Lightning Source LLC
Chambersburg PA
CBHW061258210726

48293CB00003B/1012